SAGE BLACKWOOD

HARPER

An Imprint of HarperCollins*Publishers*

Library of Congress Cataloging-in-Publication Data
Blackwood, Sage.
Jinx / Sage Blackwood. — 1st ed.
     p.   cm.
Summary: A young boy named Jinx encounters magic and danger as he grows up
in the deep, dark forest known as the Urwald and discovers that the world beyond—
and within—the Urwald is more complex than he could imagine.
ISBN 978-0-06-212990-1 (trade bdg.)
[1. Magic—Fiction. 2. Fantasy.] I. Title.
PZ7.B5345Ji   2013   2012005249
[Fic]—dc23   CIP
                                                                    AC

Typography by Carla Weise
12 13 14 15 16   LP/RRDH   10 9 8 7 6 5 4 3 2 1
❖
First Edition

To Jennifer Schwabach
because it's her kind of story

Contents

Jinx

In the Urwald you grow up fast or not at all. By the time
Jinx was six he had learned to live quietly and carefully,
squeezed into the spaces left by other people, even though
the hut he lived in with his stepparents actually belonged to
him. He had inherited it after his father died of werewolves
and his mother was carried off by elves.

But then a spark from a passing firebird ignited the hut,
and within a few minutes it had gone. The people in the
clearing built another to replace it, and this new hut was
not his. His stepparents, Bergthold and Cottawilda, felt
this keenly. Besides, the harvest had been bad that autumn,
and the winter would be a hungry one.

This was the sort of situation that made people in the clearing cast a calculating eye upon their surplus children.

And Jinx was definitely surplus, especially since Bergthold and Cottawilda had a new baby girl of their own. He worked as hard as he could to make up for the crime of existing, and he tried not to eat too much. He only took a single bite of his toad porridge every night before offering the rest to the baby. Nevertheless, his stepparents agreed between them that Jinx was too much trouble and expense to raise.

So late one autumn afternoon Bergthold told Jinx to put on his coat, and together they left the clearing where they lived and plunged into the Urwald. They followed the path where it twisted between great trees as big around as cottages. Then Bergthold stepped off the path.

Jinx stopped.

"What are you waiting for?" Bergthold roared. "Come on!"

"'N-never stray from the path,'" said Jinx. This was a rule every child in the Urwald was taught as soon as it could walk.

"We're straying from it now!" Bergthold grabbed Jinx by the front of his coat, cuffed both his ears, and hauled him from the path.

Jinx struggled in his stepfather's grip. Leaving the path was *wrong*. The path and the clearings of the Urwald belonged, just barely, to people. Everything else belonged to the trees. Anyone who ventured off the path was doomed.

Bergthold hit Jinx again, gave him a hard shove, and marched him into the forest.

Jinx walked, his ears burning. He made his way through the deep twilight of the Urwald, and every now and then Bergthold gave him a little shove to the left or the right around a great glowering tree, and Jinx thought that Bergthold was making sure that Jinx wouldn't be able to find the path again.

"Stop here!"

Jinx stopped instantly, not wanting to get hit again. He wondered if Bergthold was going to kill him.

"Sit down, and stay right here, and don't move until nightfall, or you'll wish you had never been born."

Jinx already wished he had never been born. But he sat down in the moss, where his stepfather pointed. He could feel the Urwald's disapproval seeping up through the ground.

"Good. And good-bye." Bergthold turned to go. Then he stopped, looking around him. He started off in one direction, then stopped, came back, and started off in another direction. Then he came back again.

He gave Jinx a rather furtive look. "Do you, er, happen to remember which way we came?"

"No," said Jinx.

"Ah," said Bergthold. He nodded, as though he was just thinking about things.

He's lost, Jinx thought. We're both lost.

"I think I know which way the path is, though," Jinx hazarded.

"Ah! Well, don't just sit there like a lump on the ground—lead on, boy!"

Jinx scrambled to his feet and started walking. He really had no idea where the path was. But at least moving, with Bergthold behind him, felt safer than sitting still, alone, under the Urwald's menacing shadows. And probably being watched by hungry creatures in the trees.

Rounding a great gnarled knot of a tree trunk, Jinx ran smack into a creature and yelped.

"Calm down, boy, I won't eat you," said the creature.

Since this was by no means a given in the Urwald, Jinx did calm down. The creature was a man, tall and thin, with twisty hair, yellow eyes, and a pointed beard. He was dressed in a long purple robe. His feet were bare and knotty, and he carried a basket—he had been harvesting mistletoe.

Jinx had never met a wizard. He had always heard they had long white beards, not short pointy brown ones. But magic poured off the man, ripples of magic as strong as the pulses of life that seeped from the trees all around them.

"Just walking in the woods with my boy, sir," said

Jinx's stepfather, too hastily and without any greeting at all.

You didn't tell people your business in the Urwald, and the wizard's nose twitched at the bad smell of the lie. "Pretty late for straying off the path," he said.

"Gotta teach the boy to find his way in the woods."

The wizard's nose twitched more. You didn't learn to find your way in these woods—you stayed out of them. "Some people abandon their children in the woods," said the wizard. "If they find it too much trouble to feed them."

"Not their own children!" said Bergthold. "Stepchildren, maybe, now I've heard of that."

The wizard looked at Bergthold through a dark cloud of disapproval. "If you marry the mother, you accept the children."

"I *didn't* marry the mother," said Bergthold, aggrieved. "She died years ago. I married the woman who was married to the man who had married the mother. The boy's got a curse on him—everyone who takes him dies."

"Actually, that seems like a fairly normal death rate for the Urwald." The wizard looked at Jinx so hard that Jinx wanted to hide. "I happen to have need of a boy. I'll take him."

"Buy him, you mean," said Bergthold.

"Curse and all?"

"He's worth more with the curse!"

"Everyone who takes him dies?"

"You could probably use that," said Bergthold. "You know, against your enemies."

The wizard sighed. "Very well. I will pay one silver penny."

"A silver penny? A measly silver penny for a boy like this?" Bergthold drew himself up. "A boy with a valuable curse? You insult me, sir!"

A dangerous glitter flickered across the wizard's face, and Jinx shot his stepfather a nervous glance. Bergthold was frightened and angry, as he usually was, but the fear was ripply with greed.

"A silver penny is a lot for a boy with a curse on him," said the wizard.

Somewhere behind them there was a crunching sound, as of a fallen stick breaking under a very large foot. Jinx peered anxiously into the terrifying gloom. His stepfather was too wrought up to notice.

"A boy like this is worth three silver pennies at least!" said Bergthold.

This was rather a surprise to Jinx, who was regularly told by both Bergthold and Cottawilda that he wasn't worth a rotten cabbage leaf.

"He's a hard worker, too! Especially if you beat him," said Bergthold. "And you hardly have to feed him at all."

"Well, I can see you haven't been," said the wizard.

"One penny's my final offer."

There were more crunching sounds, sticks snapping, and the hollow scrabble of clawed feet on the forest earth. Jinx looked this way and that but couldn't see anything moving. He looked back at the two men and wished he could trust either one of them.

"Two silver pennies then," said Bergthold.

"One silver penny," said the wizard, sounding suddenly indifferent to the whole thing. "You had best take it quickly."

"Never!"

"Come here, boy," the wizard commanded.

Several things happened at once. Jinx took a nervous step toward the wizard. From the forest behind him, heavy, ragged breathing joined the sound of clawed feet, and Jinx was overwhelmed by a smell like rotting meat. Jinx whirled around and saw trolls—they must be trolls, they were so big and tusky—crashing through the trees, bearing down on him and his stepfather. The wizard reached out and grabbed Jinx. A pale green cloud of calm surrounded the wizard all through what happened next, and it was because Jinx could see this cloud that he stood perfectly still, even though his legs wanted to run.

With a roar of triumph one of the trolls seized Bergthold around the waist and hoisted him to his shoulder. The other trolls howled with glee and danced about. A troll's claw swung right past Jinx's nose—he felt the breeze and smelled the rancid breath. Bergthold screamed and reached his arms toward Jinx, beseeching. Jinx shrank back against the wizard. The wizard didn't move. Jinx expected to feel the trolls' claws grabbing him at any second.

But the trolls didn't seem to see Jinx.

The party of trolls thumped out of the clearing. Jinx had a last sight of his stepfather, head bumping down against a troll's back, screaming and red faced—Bergthold's hat fell off and rolled away. Jinx broke away from the wizard and ran to pick it up.

Jinx stood with the hat in his hand and looked at the claw marks in the moss at his feet. Then he looked between the trees where the trolls and his stepfather had disappeared. The Urwald had swallowed up Bergthold as if he were no more huge and terrifying than a rabbit. The smell of rotting meat still hung in the air.

And then Jinx had the thought that to the forest, Bergthold was nothing, or just a very small thing. He didn't matter at all in the great green sea of life that was the Urwald.

It was as if the idea had come from the trees themselves. Well, maybe Bergthold was nothing to them. *They'd* never been hit by him.

"What's your name, boy?" said the wizard gently.

"Jinx."

"And mine is Simon," said the wizard. "So that was your stepfather, was it?"

Jinx nodded.

"Had he brought you into the woods to abandon you?"

"Yes," said Jinx. "Our house was mine, but it burned down. And there's a new baby."

Jinx didn't expect sympathy, never having had any before. But he was a little surprised by Simon's reaction—the news that Jinx was being abandoned made the wizard smile. There was a little blue glow of satisfaction with the smile.

Jinx was relieved that wizards' feelings were as easy to see as other people's. He had learned to watch people very closely, and to listen carefully. He assumed that everyone did this and that everyone could see what he saw.

"I don't expect you'll miss him very much," said the wizard.

Jinx shook his head no. He wouldn't. Bergthold was mostly a red cloud of anger that led to beatings. But now what?

"Do you come from one of the clearings?" Simon asked.

Didn't everybody? Jinx nodded.

"What's it called?"

"Called?"

"Doesn't your clearing have a name?"

"I don't know." Other clearings had names. Jinx had never heard his own clearing called anything.

"Could you find your clearing again?"

Jinx shook his head no.

"Excellent," said Simon.

He reached out a long, thin hand to Jinx. Jinx had never even seen a wizard before, and now a wizard was sticking a hand at him.

"Do you want to come with me?" said Simon.

It had started to snow. Night was drawing in, and Jinx heard stealthy rustlings like suppressed laughter in the forest all around him. The wizard had saved Jinx from the trolls. But had he also called the trolls?

"Why didn't the trolls take me?" said Jinx.

"They didn't see you."

"Was that magic?"

"Of course. Shall we go?"

Jinx knew he couldn't survive alone in the Urwald once night fell. But wizards—wizards were dangerous.

"Are you the Bonemaster?" Jinx asked. The Bonemaster was the only wizard Jinx had ever heard of by name. Everyone in Jinx's clearing was terrified of the Bonemaster, though no one had ever seen him.

"No. I am not the Bonemaster. I am just Simon Magus."

"The Bonemaster sucks out people's souls with a straw,"

said Jinx. "Do you?"

"I have some bad habits," said Simon. "But that is not one of them."

"Do you eat people?" said Jinx.

"Certainly not."

"Do you kill people?"

"Very seldom. And never small boys."

The wizard's thoughts were green and blue, and they slid around each other, shifty and secretive. But they weren't red and angry, and that was something. And the Urwald loomed, ready to swallow Jinx as easily as it had his stepfather.

"It's nearly dark. Are you coming?" Simon held out his hand again.

Jinx made his choice and took it.

The Wizard's House

And that was how Jinx came to live with a possibly evil wizard and twenty-seven cats in a huge stone house that stood alone in its own clearing, protected by invisible wards that kept monsters out but let some very strange visitors in.

Just how strange, Jinx found out that first night, after he and Simon had finished a very satisfactory dinner of bread, cheese, pickles, jam, apple cider, and pumpkin pie.

They were sitting at the kitchen table on top of the big stone stove, which filled half the kitchen and was just pleasantly warm underfoot. Onions, dried apples, and pumpkin hung from the rafters overhead. There were cats everywhere, lying on barrels and shelves—there was one curled around the water pump.

"No more pie for now, boy—you'll make yourself sick," said Simon.

"What are you going to do with me?" Jinx asked. He believed that the wizard probably didn't eat people, since his house was full of much better things to eat. But he figured Simon must be planning to use him for *something* . . . probably something evil.

"Right now? Send you to bed. Tomorrow, put you to work," said Simon.

But there was a part of Simon that seemed to hide from what he'd just said, as if it wasn't the whole truth.

"Are you going to send me to kill your enemies?" said Jinx.

"No, I think I'll spare my enemies that terrible fate."

Jinx was annoyed at being laughed at. "Anyone who takes me in dies."

"I expect they do eventually," said Simon. "But I doubt you hasten the process. You really think if I sent you to the Bonemaster, he'd drop dead?"

The Bonemaster was a formidable enemy to have. Jinx was relieved to hear he wouldn't be expected to deal with him. Still . . . "I do have a curse on me, though."

"You don't have a curse on you. Put that nonsense out of your head."

"Why aren't you afraid of the Bonemaster?" said Jinx.

"How do you know I'm not?"

"I can see it," said Jinx, surprised at this question about something so obvious. Everyone's thoughts glowed green fear whenever the Bonemaster's name was mentioned. It was the same bottle-shaped blob of terror for everyone, as if the fear of the Bonemaster had come to all of them in exactly the same way, as exactly the same thought. Which was odd, because usually different people had different-colored thoughts.

"*You* should be afraid of the Bonemaster," said Simon. "Whatever happens, don't ever go near him."

There came a banging at the door.

Simon muttered a swear word and went to open it. Jinx trailed along behind him.

Outside, the night was purple. A tornado of snow blasted past and left behind a woman standing beside a butter churn, grinning.

"Dame Glammer. Welcome," said Simon.

"Dame" was a title for a witch, just like "Magus" meant a wizard. Jinx stared. The witch stared back. Her small, sharp eyes seemed to be laughing at Jinx. Her face had a lot of nose to it. Her hair was a wild nest of gray pinned on top of her head anyhow with two long knitting needles. She unwrapped herself from several wet cloaks and piled them into Jinx's arms.

"This little chipmunk looks good enough to eat, Simon! Where'd you get him from? Is he your very own?"

A wizard and now a witch—worse and worse. Jinx glanced at the door. Outside was the Urwald, the snow, and the trolls. Inside, two magicians.

"His name's Jinx," said Simon.

"How darling! It's an awful night for traveling, Simon, even with the butter churn."

"I suppose you'd better stay, then," said Simon, with a brown puff of annoyance that didn't come into his voice. "Sit down, have some cider. Jinx, come and help me make up the spare rooms."

Jinx followed Simon up the ladder to the loft to get blankets and sheets. "Never go through that door, Jinx," said Simon, pointing to the far end of the loft. "It's a straight drop to the ground."

They made up a bed for Dame Glammer at the bottom of the north tower. Then they went up the spiral staircase, with cats weaving around between Jinx's legs trying to trip him up. Simon dropped the armload of blankets on the bed.

"I suggest you make that bed and get in it," said Simon. "Good night, Jinx."

Jinx decided not to take Simon's suggestion. He had to find out what these two magicians were up to. For all he knew, they were plotting to turn him into a toad and cook him up in a magic potion. He crept back downstairs, holding his breath for fear of being heard.

Simon and the witch were looking at a little pile of dried-up twigs on the table.

"I thought wormwood was poisonous," said Simon. Poison?

"Oh, it is," said Dame Glammer. Her black eyes flashed up at Simon eagerly. "But it makes you fly, this kind."

Simon made a doubting gesture with his lips. "People can't fly."

"All right, makes you think you're flying."

"What use is that?" said Simon.

Dame Glammer laughed, then leaned back in her chair, scattering cats, and swung her feet up onto the table. She wore a many-colored patchwork skirt that came down just over her knees and no further, so her legs in their thick woolen stockings showed to the world. Simon frowned at the feet, but the feet and Dame Glammer ignored this. She took a deep, satisfied swig of cider, and a mustache of foam stuck to her lip. She wiped it off with the back of her hand.

"You take things too seriously, Simon. Sometimes magic is just for fun, you know."

"No." Simon took a sip of cider and didn't elaborate.

"I don't think even the Bonemaster can make flying potion," said Dame Glammer.

"He can't."

The witch didn't have that green flash of fear at the Bonemaster's name—she had nothing. With a start Jinx realized that he couldn't see any clouds around her at all. He'd never met anyone with invisible feelings before. That made her even more dangerous.

"It's like history repeating itself, isn't it?" said Dame Glammer. "You've gone and found yourself a nice little chipmunk to gobble up, just like *you* were gobbled up by—"

"Nonsense—gobbled up! I'm right here in front of you." But the words came with jagged orange consternation.

"Where'd you get him from, anyway?" said Dame Glammer, nodding at the doorway where Jinx was standing.

"He came along," said Simon. "Didn't I tell you to go to bed, boy?"

"What're you going to use him for?" she asked. "If you're not going to—"

"He'll work for me. He'll keep the house clean," said Simon, with another pointed glance at Dame Glammer's feet.

"Good eating on children," said Dame Glammer. "I had a boy and a girl just this past autumn. Parents left 'em in the woods . . . well, you can imagine. I bewitched the house to make it look like gingerbread—"

So that was how they did it! Jinx had always wondered why witches didn't have a problem with animals coming to eat their gingerbread houses. And what happened when it rained.

"That's not funny," said Simon. "You're scaring the boy."

"Oh, I didn't really eat them! Just made 'em think I was going to." She cackled.

Jinx thought probably she really had.

"I'm not giving you dragon scales for that," said Simon, nodding at the wormwood. "It's not reasonable, Dame. You know I have to buy them direct from the dragon."

Dame Glammer grinned. "Why not give me the boy?"

"Absolutely not."

"Saving him for the Bonemaster?"

"Of course not. Don't be ridiculous." He nodded at the wormwood again. "Are we trading, or not?"

"What will you give me?"

"If you show me how to brew the wormwood, I may give you an ounce of cinnamon."

"Very well." She swept the twigs into a red polka-dot kerchief.

"Come into my workroom. You can show me now," said Simon.

There was a heavy oaken door in the wall opposite— Jinx supposed it must lead to the other tower. Simon went to it, then stopped and turned around.

"Everything in the south wing is off limits, Jinx. My

rooms are back here, and you are not allowed in them. Understand?"

Jinx was immediately seized with a desire to see the off-limits rooms.

"Why?" he asked.

"Because there are dangerous things in here, and because I said so. Now go to bed. And don't lie awake worrying about the gingerbread house—it's not true."

Simon went through the heavy oaken door, leaving it half open for Dame Glammer to follow. Jinx inched forward, eager to get a look at the forbidden rooms. He caught a glimpse of a cold stone hall, and dark shadows dancing in flickering torchlight. But before he could see any more, Dame Glammer darted forward and grabbed him by the chin.

"You seem like such a sweet little chipmunk. Such a shame a wizard's gone and gotten ahold of you."

Her hand squeezed his face. Jinx jerked his head away, freeing himself.

"Don't you wonder what he's going to do with you?"

"He said he wants me to work for him."

"Shall I tell you what he really wants you for?" The witch grinned, and Jinx couldn't tell if she was teasing him. Her thoughts remained frustratingly invisible.

"Tell me," he said. He was more curious than scared.

"Ask nicely."

"Please tell me," said Jinx, glaring at her.

"Little boys are more use for spells than for work," Dame Glammer said.

"I don't know any spells."

"Little boys are useful *ingredients* for spells."

Oh.

"Are you coming or not?" Simon stuck his head back out into the kitchen and frowned. "You're not scaring the boy again, are you?"

"Oh no. He's a very, very brave little chipmunk." Dame Glammer grinned, and went into Simon's rooms with her wormwood.

Jinx was very watchful after Dame Glammer's warning. But weeks went by, and Simon didn't brew Jinx into a potion, and Jinx decided she'd just been trying to scare him after all.

A lot of witches came to visit Simon. Jinx didn't like it when they looked at him and cackled. But he listened hard to their conversations, which were all about spells and magic and, now and then, the Bonemaster. They said nothing new about the Bonemaster—just that he would suck your soul out with a straw and stack your bones up crisscross. Jinx could mostly see the colored clouds around the witches' heads—Dame Glammer was the only one with invisible feelings.

Wanderers came to stay too, but they insisted on camping outdoors in Simon's clearing, although they did come in to use the bathroom. Jinx hadn't met many Wanderers before. They bought and sold stuff, mostly, and Jinx's clearing had been too poor to interest them. Jinx hung back in the shadows when they gathered around their campfire at night. He listened to their talk of other clearings, and journeys along the Path, and monsters they'd run into (and then run away from). They spoke in their own language, but Jinx found he could understand it if he listened.

Jinx worked hard. He swept and scrubbed. He milked the goats, gathered eggs, and brought in firewood. He explored the clearing and as much of Simon's house as he could. He wondered how he could get a look into the off-limits rooms.

As for his own room, he didn't like it. It was too cold and far away from everything. So he made a nest of blankets under the kitchen table, on top of the warm stone stove. Cats walked across him every night. But the kitchen smelled of cinnamon and cider, woodsmoke and cooking.

It was nearly winter, and no one had turned the garden over yet. There were old, black, dead-looking weeds poking up through the thin snow. Jinx found a hoe and went to work.

"No, no, no!"

Simon came running out of the house, his purple robes flying. "Idiot!"

He grabbed the hoe out of Jinx's hands. Jinx braced himself, but Simon didn't hit him.

"What have you done to my night-blooming bindweed?" Simon knelt down on the ground. "These are supposed to be in the ground all winter!"

"I'm sorry," Jinx said, hastily.

"Never mind sorry," Simon said through clenched teeth. "Help me dig them back in. They're very rare—I was lucky to get them to grow."

The dark purple cloud of a very bad mood surrounded Simon and blotted out the sunlight. Jinx got down and dug the plants back into the cold, damp dirt. His fingers ached with cold, and his nose ran and dripped down onto the plants, but he kept working and apologizing to Simon.

"I'm sure you meant well," said Simon. "You did rotten, but you meant well."

The thing that Jinx liked most about Simon, besides his cooking, was that he never hit Jinx at all. Not once. No matter what Jinx did and no matter how jaggedly orange or darkly purple the wizard's moods got. This was something completely new in Jinx's experience.

At the top of the north tower was a round stone room with a big, dark window in it. It always seemed to be night behind this window. A chair sat facing it.

One winter day, when the kitchen was full of Dame Glammer and she was cackling way too much, Jinx went up and sat in the chair. He saw himself reflected in the glass, a thin boy with black hair, brown eyes, and tan skin.

Suddenly the window cleared—the night was gone. Jinx saw Simon's clearing below, bright in morning sunlight. He could make out the tracks from Dame Glammer's butter churn in the snow. Beyond the clearing the Urwald rose, trees hundreds of feet high. Jinx could see just a little way into its green darkness.

Then, with a lurch, Jinx was seeing far into the forest. Tree branches zipped past him as if he were flying. He was hurtling through the trees so fast, he expected to be flattened against one at any second. Then he dove down and was rushing along the path, his eyes inches from the ground. He saw footprints, hoofprints, and clawprints frozen in the mud. A second later he was swooping upward, looking down through branches at a party of trolls running through the forest. Then the trolls were gone and he was watching a werebear climb a tree.

Now he was hovering over a clearing, looking at a girl about his own age dressed in red, who was digging in a garden, turning the soil over for winter. He would have liked to watch her for longer, but already he was zooming through the trees again, at dizzying speeds—

"Meow!"

A cat jumped on him, and Jinx was so dizzy, he fell to the floor. He was back in the tower. He got shakily to his feet and saw Simon looking down at him.

The wizard nodded at the window. "You want to be careful with that thing."

"What is it?" said Jinx.

"The Farseeing Window."

"How does it work?"

"You need a spell to control it," Simon said. "If you want to keep an eye on someone in particular, they have to be connected to the other end of the spell. Otherwise the view just slides around."

"Could it show me my clearing?" Jinx asked. He wasn't homesick exactly. Not entirely. He just thought he'd like to see how things were getting on there.

"Probably, if it wants to," said Simon. He rapped on the window, casually, as if the glass wasn't worth more money than most people saw in their lives. "It's got a mind of its own. Only shows you what it wants to. I think."

"Don't you know?" said Jinx.

Simon flickered irritation at him. "Of course I know. I just told you."

Strange Feet

Winter settled in to stay. Simon was away a lot. He went places, leaving Jinx alone with the cats, and he often came back in a foul mood. But when he was home, life was better. The wizard was terrifying, but gradually it became a homey, woolen-smelling terror, as comforting in its own way as the howling of a winter storm.

Jinx liked storms—they put Simon into a cooking mood. Simon could go on cooking for hours—pies, bread, honey cakes, soup, stewed fruits, and baked apples—and Jinx stayed nearby, fetching things and cleaning up, and feeling safe inside the warm cloud that surrounded the wizard, even if he was usually pretty cranky.

Jinx got used to the witches. Simon fed them and listened carefully to everything they had to say about magic, and then he usually disappeared into the south wing—perhaps to test what they'd told him. It was very lonely when Simon locked himself away for days at a time. Sometimes Jinx went up and gazed into the Farseeing Window, which never wanted to show him his home clearing but seemed to like showing him the little girl in the red hood.

Jinx got into the habit of talking to her. Since she couldn't hear him and didn't even know he was watching her, he had to make up her parts of the conversation.

"I wonder where he goes," he said to the girl.

But she had no more idea than Jinx did.

Try as he might, Jinx hadn't been able to see into the forbidden rooms. He had explored every other part of Simon's house, inside and out. He had even climbed onto the roof of the shed that the goats and chickens lived in, and then slid off it into the snow—at first by accident, and then several more times on purpose. But he couldn't get into the forbidden wing. Simon kept the door firmly locked at all times.

Then sometimes Simon would come into the kitchen in the middle of the night, and Jinx would awaken to see the wizard's gnarly feet. Jinx liked to crawl out from under the table and sit down and have some cider and a piece of bread and cheese in the dark with him. Neither of them said anything. They sipped and ate slowly, letting the night noises and the night chill slide around them, and now and then pushing a cat off the table.

One night in the early spring Jinx awoke to see a different pair of feet. They were pretty feet, narrow and brown with nice neat toes that, unlike Simon's, had nothing in common with tree roots.

There was a clunk of things being put on the table, and then Simon's feet appeared beside the new ones.

"You were away for too long," Simon said, quietly so as not to wake Jinx.

"Only a week." It was a lady's voice.

"It seemed longer."

Jinx didn't know much about weeks and months—he knew what they *were*, but time ran together in a blur. Winter had come and gone since he'd been in Simon's house. Longer than a week, then. And yet Jinx had never seen this lady's feet before.

"You know they don't want me coming here," said the lady.

"Uh-huh. But you do it anyway."

An icky, silver-sweet feeling ran down the edges of the table and threatened to drip on Jinx. Alarmed, he gave a loud snore to remind Simon he was there.

"What's that?"

"The boy. He sleeps under the table."

Jinx had his eyes shut tight when they both bent down to look at him. He didn't need his eyes to see people's feelings—feelings came through anyway, as a color or a sound or a shape. Sometimes even a taste.

"'The boy,'" the lady said. Suddenly the silver-sweet feeling had bristles in it. "Where did you get a boy from?"

"I got him from his family. I paid a silver penny for him."

This, Jinx realized, was not actually, strictly speaking, the truth. Simon had certainly *said* he was going to pay a penny for Jinx, but then trolls had come along and saved Simon the money.

"And what exactly do you need a boy for?" The lady's voice came from above again; they were no longer peering at Jinx. She spoke with an accent, as if the Urwish words weren't quite at home in her mouth.

"He cleans up around the place. Brings in firewood. Things like that."

"A slave," said the lady. Silver-sweet frozen, like February ice.

"He's not a slave. I'm going to pay him wages when he's older."

"So this is why you've been keeping me out of the kitchen all winter. You've been hiding a *boy*."

"I knew you'd make a ridiculous fuss," said Simon. "He's just a boy."

Jinx was still wondering how the lady could have been in the house only a week ago if she hadn't come through the kitchen. There were no other doors to the outside.

"Anyway, he's company," said Simon. "Like the cats, only less demanding."

"Children are not house pets, Simon. Why does he sleep under the table? You have plenty of rooms in this barn."

"I *gave* him a room—he won't sleep in it. He likes it under the table. I put a cat-repellent spell under there for him."

Jinx had noticed that the cats that used to climb on him and wake him up no longer did so, but hadn't known it was because Simon had cast a spell.

"Anyway, it's my business," said Simon testily. "Which I thought we agreed was completely different from your business."

The silver-sweet feeling was entirely gone now, and Jinx wasn't as pleased by its departure as he might've expected.

"If you're going to do anything evil, then it's my business," said the lady.

"*If* I'm going to do anything evil, you'll be the first to know. Jinx, get up," said Simon, not raising his voice at all.

He must've known Jinx wasn't asleep. Jinx unrolled himself from his blankets and crawled out from under the table.

A golden-brown lady in a dark red robe was sitting at the table. She smiled at Jinx. Her hair was shiny black and curly. Her eyes were like the night sky—Jinx even thought he saw a shooting star in one, before she blinked. She had a formidable nose.

"This is Jinx," said Simon. "As you can see, he's perfectly healthy. I haven't cut off any bits to use in spells. Jinx, this is Sophie. My wife."

"Your what?" said Jinx. He was still half asleep or he would have had the sense to say something more polite.

"My wife," said Simon. Jinx could feel amusement bursting in the wizard in little purple flashes—he was laughing at Jinx, but silently. He often did.

"No," said Jinx.

"No what?" said Sophie. She was still smiling. Jinx felt a soft green kindness from her and liked it.

"He means no, you're not my wife," said Simon. "Sit down, Jinx. Have some cider."

Jinx sat down and accepted the flagon of cider that Simon poured for him. He took a slice of pumpkin bread from the loaf on the table and turned it over in his hands. He had been exploring Simon's house and clearing diligently for months, and he felt he would have noticed a wife.

And wives were kind of hard to miss. Back in his clearing in the old days, he had always been scrambling to get out of their way as they surged across the clearing, arms full of wet laundry, water buckets, and firewood.

"Wives are always carrying something," Jinx explained.

"My wife carries things in her head," said Simon. "She is a well-known and important scholar."

Sophie shot Simon an annoyed look. "Where do you come from, Jinx?" she asked.

"The Clearing," said Jinx.

"And do you want to go back there?"

Jinx looked over at Simon to see what was the correct answer to this. Simon stood up and went down the steps to stir the fire. Jinx got the message—he had to answer on his own.

He thought. He was very lonely sometimes. In the Clearing—which was already becoming fuzzy in his memory—there had always been people around. In fact, you were never alone at all—especially not when you had to sleep at the foot of a straw bed with your stepparents' smelly feet in your face. Here he had his own pallet with no babies leaking on him. And enough to eat all winter long. And Simon, who seldom actually yelled and never beat him at all.

He still hadn't figured out what Simon intended to use him for—but maybe it really *was* just to work.

And then, he realized, he wasn't as afraid as he used to be. Oh, sure, Simon was scary, and witches were scary. But back in the Clearing, *everything* had been scary. Fear crept up the walls of the huts and dripped down from the ceilings, and you didn't even have to have frightening things in front of you to be afraid. Everyone was afraid all the time on general principle . . . afraid of the Urwald and monsters and winter and hunger and what might happen next and the possibility that *nothing* might happen next. It had been, now that Jinx thought about it, exhausting.

"No," he said at last. "I don't want to go back. I like it here."

Simon was still stirring the fire, but Jinx could almost hear the loud *Ha!* that he thought at his wife.

"Don't you miss your family?" asked Sophie.

"They're all dead," said Jinx.

As soon as he said it, Jinx realized his mistake. Simon had just told Sophie that he'd *bought* Jinx from his family. It was difficult to conduct business with dead people— probably even for wizards. Jinx took a bite of pumpkin bread to hide his confusion.

"I'm sorry to hear that," said Sophie gently.

Jinx nodded warily. There was a new hint of iron behind her kindness.

"Tell me, Jinx, were they all dead *before* you met my husband?"

Simon stopped stirring the fire and froze, the poker in his hand. The room went still and waiting.

Jinx smooshed the slice of pumpkin bread in his hands.

"Yes! A long time before! It was my stepparents that . . . that sold me. They weren't any relation to me." He took a bite of mashed pumpkin bread and said around it, "That's why they wanted to get rid of me."

The stillness in the room went away. Jinx had said the right thing. It hadn't been the truth, entirely. It had left out a minor matter of trolls, but it had been the right thing to say. He could see that when he watched Simon tilt a *so there!* look at Sophie, and Sophie smile an apology. The room thawed and just a little bit of silver-sweet feeling seeped back. Not enough to make you squirm, really . . . but Jinx very much wanted this midnight meeting to be over now. He wasn't sure why he had felt he had to lie to protect Simon from this sudden unexpected wife. But he was sure it had been the right thing to do.

Later, when he lay in bed listening to the kitchen fire sizzle away, it occurred to him that *Were they all dead* before *you met my husband?* was a very odd question.

Werewolves

After that Sophie was around often, though she never stayed more than a few days. There was no more of Simon disappearing into his rooms for days on end—Sophie made it very clear that she came to visit Jinx as well as Simon. Jinx liked this. Sophie was different from anybody he'd ever met—smart without being cranky or cackly, and kind, and unafraid.

She also spoke a language he'd never heard before. Simon spoke it too, and Jinx had to listen for a while before he understood it. They tended to discuss things in it that they didn't want Jinx to hear. Jinx heard them talk about a place called Samara—sometimes they argued about it. Jinx wondered where it was.

"Where's Sophie?" Jinx asked once, when she'd been around for three days and suddenly wasn't.

"She left," said Simon.

"Where did she go?"

"She went home. Her home."

"Why doesn't she live here?"

"Never you mind," said Simon.

"How does she get here? She never comes through the front door; she always comes out of your rooms."

"Well, then, that must be how she gets here, mustn't it?"

"But there's no door to the outside from your rooms." Jinx had looked all around the outside of the house.

"Perhaps she climbs in the window, then," said Simon.

"Is there a secret passage back there?"

"If I told you, it wouldn't be a secret."

"I think she must get here by magic," said Jinx.

"That seems likely, doesn't it? I think it's time you swept out the loft."

Sweeping out the loft meant Simon was tired of Jinx's questions.

Jinx was sure that magic went on in the south wing, and he knew that the rooms contained the secret of where Sophie came from. As Jinx grew less afraid of witches and wizards, he grew more and more curious. But Simon never left the forbidden door unlocked. Jinx had tried to peer through the magic cat flap, but it knew he wasn't a cat and it wouldn't open for him.

One day when Jinx was eight years old, the three of them were walking in the Urwald together. They did this a lot. The feeling Jinx had had before, that the Urwald was reaching out to grab him, to pull him in and swallow him, had changed. He felt now that the forest enveloped him, as if he and it were part of a single, enormous living thing. He wasn't afraid to stray from the path anymore—at least as long as he was with Simon and Sophie. The Truce of the Path protected you from monsters and other humans when you were on the path. But if you spent all your time being protected, you never got to find out anything new.

So the three of them left the path on their walks all the time and ventured deep into the Urwald.

"The Urwald isn't just trees. People are part of it too," Simon said.

"People used to be able to talk to the trees," said Sophie. "I've read that. They used to know the trees' language."

"Oh, we still know a little," said Simon. "Trees speak in the way their leaves rustle."

Sophie smiled at Simon, but Jinx could see that she didn't believe him. Jinx didn't either. Trees *couldn't* rustle their leaves, except in the wind.

"It's more like they sort of are," said Jinx.

"Are what?" said Sophie.

"*Are*. And then I think we have to figure out how to listen."

"Listen to the leaves?" said Sophie.

"I think you'd kind of have to listen to their roots," said Jinx. "If you wanted to hear trees talk."

"Nonsense. You can't listen to roots," said Simon.

Sophie smiled, but Jinx could tell from the shape of their thoughts that they were both laughing at him.

"Anyway, there hasn't been a Listener in a hundred years," said Simon. "If there ever was such a thing."

"You mean those people who talked to trees?" said Sophie.

"A myth," said Simon.

Jinx hung back. He wanted to see if he was right about how trees spoke. Simon and Sophie walked on, speaking to each other in that other language, which always seemed to feel as strange to Simon's mouth as Urwish felt to Sophie's. Jinx let them go. He was more interested in the forest.

The leaves did move in the wind, but trees wouldn't be able to see that, would they? They didn't have eyes.

Two tree branches rubbed together, sounding nearly like a human voice. Jinx could almost understand something, but it felt more like it was coming up through his bare feet. Jinx dug his toes into the crumbling leaves that were rotting into soil, as if he were a tree taking root.

Now he could hear the trees quite clearly. They mumbled about grubs that ate their roots. They thought about rain and summer. Dirt interested them. And sunlight, which was very hard to get in the Urwald, unless you were old and tall. And . . . pain.

The pain came from the edge of the Urwald. Jinx hadn't known there *was* an edge of the Urwald. He wondered what that was like—what lay beyond it? He buried his toes deeper into the soil. The pain was very far away. It—

There was a smell of dirty dogs. Jinx looked up. Werewolves. Three of them.

They were almost man-sized, standing on two legs. They grinned at Jinx, baring knife-sharp yellow fangs. Their claws were as sharp as their teeth. They moved toward Jinx.

He opened his mouth and said "Help." It came out very quietly.

The werewolves barked bright red flares of greed and amusement.

Jinx took a step backward. The werewolves took a step forward.

Jinx took several more steps backward. The werewolves followed, grinning.

Jinx turned and ran. He heard the werewolves running along behind him. He felt their hot breath on his neck.

One of them struck him with its claws, playfully, digging deep into his skin. Jinx ran harder. The werewolves kept up easily.

He wanted to scream for help, but he needed all his breath for running. He knew the werewolves could run faster than him, for longer than him. They were just amusing themselves until he dropped from exhaustion. Which would be soon. His lungs were sore from trying to gulp in enough air to keep running.

Then he tripped and fell.

He got up on his hands and knees and wondered why he wasn't dead. He scrambled to his feet. He heard the sound of running claws scrabbling desperately over the forest floor. He turned and looked. An enormous yellow dragon was chasing the werewolves away.

Jinx felt very lucky that the dragon had wanted werewolves for lunch instead of boys. Then something grabbed him from behind.

"You idiot!" Simon turned him around and shook him. "I told you to stay with us! How many times did I tell you to stay with us?"

Sophie grabbed Jinx away from Simon and hugged him like he was a baby, which he should have minded but didn't. "Leave him alone, Simon! He's had a terrible fright."

"So who hasn't?" said Simon. His voice was all shaky, and Jinx, even though Simon wasn't shaking him anymore, found himself still shaking. Especially his knees.

Sophie reached out an arm for Simon. "It was a wonderful dragon, dear," she said. "But why was it yellow? Oh no, the poor child is bleeding."

Jinx pulled away from her because being called a poor child was too much. "I'm all right."

Actually the werewolf scratches hurt quite a bit. Sophie tied her handkerchief around Jinx's arm.

They started home. Simon kept a firm grip on Jinx's shoulder. Jinx didn't mind much, because he kept expecting the forest to break out in werewolves at any moment.

"Those were werewolves?" said Sophie, speaking her own language. "The pictures I've seen show them looking more like wolves."

"Some are more like wolves and some are more like people," said Simon. "Magic has its uses, doesn't it?"

"I never said it didn't—"

"—not more than a thousand times, anyway—"

"—I just said it ought to be studied as theory—"

"If you just study magic as theory, you can't conjure up a dragon illusion when you need one."

"Well, it was a lovely illusion, dear—"

"Why didn't you make us invisible?" Jinx said. "Like you did that time when—" And it was only because he was speaking Sophie's language for the first time, and trying to get the words right, that he was able to stop himself in time. "That time with the trolls?"

He'd almost said *when the trolls took my stepfather.* And that was something Sophie probably wasn't supposed to know about.

"Did Simon teach you to speak Samaran?" said Sophie, surprised.

"No, of course I didn't," said Simon.

"I just figured it out from listening," said Jinx, putting his words in order carefully. Speaking it was a lot harder than listening to it. And he was still busy looking all around him for werewolves.

"How clever of you, Jinx!"

"Wouldn't have worked," said Simon. "The concealment spell just keeps things from noticing us. Those werewolves had already noticed you. I could have kept them from noticing Sophie and me. But not you."

"So that other time, you kept the trolls from noticing us," said Jinx.

Simon looked down at him hard, and Jinx looked back up, and they both knew that Jinx hadn't added *but not my stepfather.*

Sophie probably wouldn't have approved of letting trolls eat Bergthold. After all, she'd never met him.

Jinx wondered if he could learn to do magic. Simon was right: Magic was useful stuff. It could save you from trolls and werewolves.

The Forbidden Room

Nearly a whole year later, Jinx wasn't any closer to learning magic. He hadn't even found a way to get into the forbidden wing of the house. He hadn't figured out how Sophie arrived, and he hadn't seen any of the stuff that Simon must busy himself with when he locked himself behind the off-limits door—magical stuff, Jinx was sure. Whenever he hinted that Simon could at least let him in to *look*, Simon would tell him to go sweep out the loft. It was very frustrating.

Then one day Jinx was washing dishes when a cat burst out of the magical cat flap in the off-limits door, holding what looked like a glowing purple frog in its mouth. The door slammed open, and Simon came charging out. The cat went out the magic cat flap into the clearing, and Simon ran out after it.

The door to the south wing was standing wide open.

Jinx hurried to the window. Simon and the cat were running straight into the forest.

There was nothing to stop him. He slipped into the south wing and pulled the door shut behind him.

A cat came up and rubbed against his leg. Oh, the *cats* were allowed in here. Just not Jinx.

He was in a hallway about ten paces long that ended in a blank stone wall. On either side, facing each other, were two arched doorways. The one on the right led to a spiral staircase going up. Simon's bedroom, probably.

Jinx opened the other door. He stared in fascination— he'd been right. This was where Simon did his magic.

The room was big, dimly lit by a high glass window. It was a mess. If Jinx had ever let the kitchen look this bad, Simon would have been furious. There was a workbench covered with open books, bundles of herbs, what looked like a small mummy, and a spilled pool of something the color of blood.

The floor was heaped with piles of books. A spider was industriously spinning a web between two stacks. A skull sat on top of one heap, and Jinx found himself nodding a polite greeting to it.

He stared around in wonder. Above the workbench were shelves with jars, bottles, and boxes. Stacked in between them were more piles of books—mostly leather bound, some of them scaly. Jinx thought they might be bound in real dragonskin. It all looked exactly as a wizard's workroom ought to look, and Jinx could feel magic dripping all over everything.

A cat hopped up onto the workbench, walked through the red spill, and tracked red footprints across the open pages of a book.

Jinx turned the pages to hide the marks.

The pages began to smolder. Flames licked up at the edges. Jinx tried to beat them out with his hands and got burned. The book was turning pages by itself now, and they were all burning.

Jinx slammed the book shut. That put out the fire, but wisps of smoke curled up from the book, and it still looked like it had been on fire. Jinx looked for somewhere to stick it where it wouldn't be noticed.

He picked up the skull and added the book to the pile underneath it. The skull winked an eye socket at him.

He ought to leave now. He really ought to leave. Before Simon came back. But he hadn't seen everything yet. There was all that stuff on the shelves, for example.

There was a bottle shaped like a goblin's head. Jinx tried to pick it up, but it was stuck to the shelf.

He reached for a box of carved wood. The carving showed people riding on an enormous beast. Jinx tried to open the box. The lid wouldn't budge. He felt around for a catch. Nothing—it must be held shut by a spell. Drat—it was probably some really important magic. Reluctantly he put the box back on the shelf.

He heard footsteps out in the hall.

He froze. More footsteps.

"I didn't know you were here," said Simon.

His voice sounded unexpectedly friendly, and there was none of the jagged orange fury that usually surrounded Simon when he was angry. Jinx realized it wasn't him Simon was speaking to.

"The exams ended early, so I thought I'd come by," said Sophie. They were both in the hall just outside the workroom.

No more talking now—silver-sweet yuck. Jinx looked around the room desperately. They were in between Jinx and the kitchen. He couldn't get out. The room still smelled of smoke from the burning book. They were going to notice it. He couldn't see them from where he stood— they couldn't see him. Yet. But all they had to do was look around the half-open door.

As silently as he could, Jinx ducked down and got under the workbench. It wasn't much of a hiding place, but it was all the room had to offer. Simon would be furious if he found Jinx in here.

He looked at the window. Did it open? Even if it did, they'd hear him.

Out in the hall there were footsteps and—this was odd. They didn't go toward the kitchen nor toward the tower. They seemed to go toward, and then past, the point where the hallway ended in a solid stone wall. Then Jinx heard voices from the room beyond. But there *was* no room beyond. The corridor ended in a blank wall, which it seemed Simon and Sophie had just walked through.

Jinx crept toward the door of the workroom and was just about to peer around it when Simon burst out of the wall and walked down the corridor.

"—probably some in the kitchen," Simon said. He was speaking over his shoulder, his head turned away from Jinx.

Jinx jumped behind the door just in time.

"Is Jinx out there?" said Sophie. She came down the corridor too. "I must say hello to Jinx."

Now they were both in the kitchen. Jinx peered around the doorway again. How had they walked through a stone wall? Fascinated, Jinx slid out into the corridor. Listening hard for any change in the sounds from the kitchen, he ran his hands over the blank wall. It was solid stone. He felt around for an invisible doorway. There wasn't one—this was a smooth stone wall, just what it looked like. But somehow Simon and Sophie had walked through it. And Sophie had arrived at the house when Simon wasn't expecting her. This wall had to be the answer to the secret of Sophie's comings and goings.

And it might be a way Jinx could get out of the south wing without Simon seeing him.

But it felt and looked and smelled like a stone wall. Jinx almost smacked his hand against it in frustration, then realized that that would make a noise.

Jinx was trapped. He went back to the workroom and over to the window. Diamonds of thick, wavy glass were set into a lattice. He could see a latch, too high up for him to reach.

He'd have to hide under the workbench until Sophie and Simon went somewhere else. He crawled under it and sat down.

Beside him on the floor was a green-glazed jar. Jinx hadn't noticed it before in the mess. There were some sort of red markings on the outside of it. Curious, he pulled at the lid of the jar—it came off easily.

Fiery pain stabbed into Jinx's hand.

A swarm of wasps buzzed out of the jar. In an instant they were all over Jinx. Jinx leaped to his feet, hitting his head on the workbench, and swatted at the wasps with his hands. He got stung in the hand again. Then one stung him in the neck and one on the leg.

Then, suddenly, he couldn't move.

"I thought something smelled wrong in here."

Jagged orange anger. Jinx couldn't turn around to face Simon. Neither his arms nor his legs would move. His neck and hands still seemed to have some freedom, but with wasps crawling all over him, Jinx felt it was best to stay completely still.

"Didn't I tell you not to come in here? I'm sure I did." The sharp edges of Simon's anger cut his words neatly apart.

Jinx felt a wasp walking across his upper lip and decided it wouldn't be safe to say anything.

Sophie's footsteps sounded in the hall. "Simon! What have you done to that poor boy?"

Simon didn't answer. Jinx could feel them both staring at his back now, and he would have liked to be anywhere else in the world.

"Simon, you've frozen him," said Sophie.

"No, I haven't. I've told you before, it's very difficult to work spells on living human beings."

"Then why isn't he moving?"

"I've frozen his clothes."

That was it, Jinx realized. His clothes weren't *frozen*, because they weren't cold, but they were as inflexible as iron. A wasp crawled up his left cheek and waved its antennae before his eye.

"You've no right to work magic on the boy."

"Right. Or on anybody or anything," said Simon crisply. "I know."

"Simon—"

"There are dangerous things in this room. He needs to stay away from them."

Simon's tone made it clear that the most dangerous thing in the room was Simon. Jinx was trying to think up a perfectly reasonable explanation for what he was doing in Simon's workroom—something involving the cats, possibly. But he couldn't open his mouth to speak—there were wasps crawling on it.

"It's human nature to explore," said Sophie. "You can't fault him for that."

"Actually, I can. And if you want to keep sticking your nose into my business, perhaps you should come and live here."

"I don't want to live here," said Sophie. "It's too cold. And don't make fun of my nose."

A wasp crept down Jinx's neck and into the stiffened collar of his shirt.

"I did not say anything about your nose."

"You did, you said—"

"That was just an expression!"

There was a wasp on Jinx's nose now. It was the one that had been looking him in the eye—it had marched across his cheek, and now he was staring at it cross-eyed.

The one that had crawled into his shirt was stalking across his collarbone, each footstep sharp with the anticipation of another sting. The stings he'd already gotten throbbed. Earnestly Jinx willed Sophie to stop bickering with Simon and remember Jinx—he was pretty sure Simon would never unfreeze Jinx if Sophie didn't make him.

"Simon, would you please unfreeze that child," said Sophie.

There was a pause that felt something like a shrug.

"Seeing as you ask nicely," said Simon.

Jinx's clothes hung limp on him again. He stayed in exactly the same position as before. No point in upsetting the wasps.

"He's still not moving," said Sophie. She came toward him. "Jinx, are you all r— Ow! Simon, this child is covered with wasps!"

"He must have opened the wasp jar," said Simon.

"You keep wasps in a jar?"

"Not exactly," said Simon, in an it's-too-complicated-to-explain tone.

"Take these wasps off this child at once!"

There was another pause, and Jinx felt Simon giving his wife a long, slow stare, with rage boiling out of it.

"All right, *please* take the wasps off the child," said Sophie. "*Would* you please."

The wasps flew up off Jinx—even the one in his shirt

came buzzing out—and then they vanished.

"Why did you open this jar, Jinx?" Sophie asked, stooping to pick it up. "It says 'Danger.'"

"That's just human nature," Simon said.

"I didn't hear it say anything," said Jinx.

"You didn't what?" Sophie held up the jar and shook it at Jinx. "It says 'Danger' right on it in red letters." She turned to Simon. "Are you telling me this child can't read?"

Jinx was taken aback by the white-hot flame of anger she sent at Simon.

"People don't read in the Urwald," said Simon.

"You're as bad as the rest of them! Hiding knowledge! And this isn't exactly the Urwald!"

"Of course it's the Urwald," said Simon bitterly. "You think I would have been allowed to put my house anywhere else?"

"Wizards read," said Sophie. "You could read before you ever came to Samara, looking for all your magical answers. *Knowledge is power.*" She threw the three words at him like a challenge, and they hung in the air between them, hovering on an updraft of fury.

The room rippled with anger, and even though none of it was directed at Jinx now, it still made his stomach hurt. The words *knowledge is power* stood out at the front of both of their minds, and Jinx sensed that those words were prickly and too hot to touch.

"You think I'm as bad as them," said Simon at last. "And *they* think I'm worse."

"Of course I don't," said Sophie. Her voice was all shaky. "But if you don't teach the boy to read—well, that's just what they would do. They think innocence is so charming when it's on other people."

Jinx didn't know anything about this reading stuff. He wished Sophie would tell Simon to teach him *magic* instead. But there was no way she'd do that. She barely approved of Simon knowing magic.

"You owe him something. You brought him here, you took him from his people—"

"They were going to kill him," said Simon.

"They what?"

"Were going to kill him."

Sophie turned to Jinx. "Is that true, Jinx?"

Jinx still hadn't moved. He felt as if he had wasps on him. He would probably feel for weeks as if he had wasps on him. Probably forever.

"What did you do to him? He can't talk!"

"He can talk. Answer her, Jinx."

Jinx had been stunned by Simon's words. *They were going to kill him.* The people in his clearing hadn't tried to kill him! Nobody had threatened him with an ax or a knife. And it was only Bergthold who had taken him out into the woods to abandon him—it wasn't *all* the people in

Jinx's clearing. But . . . nobody had tried to stop Bergthold from doing it, had they? And, face it, it was generally understood that when people were taken into the Urwald to be abandoned, nobody ever heard anything about them again.

"Yes," said Jinx. He'd never thought about it that way before.

"Why would anyone want to kill such a sweet little child?" said Sophie.

Jinx cringed inwardly at being called a sweet little child. It was like having wasps crawling inside your skull.

"Probably because he was snooping around in people's private workrooms, messing with their stuff," said Simon.

"Then—then that was a really good thing you did," said Sophie. "Taking him in, I mean. Buying him."

"Try not to sound so surprised," said Simon.

"You saved his life."

"Even us evil wizards have our good days."

The anger in the room was drawing back now, toward the walls, and a peaceful, warm, blue feeling was coming into the room. Jinx finally moved. He felt stiff and achy from the wasp stings.

"You are going to teach him to read, aren't you?" said Sophie.

"Will you teach me magic, too?" Jinx blurted.

There was a silence that was filled with Sophie's

orange-green annoyance and a bright blue bottle-shaped blob of surprise from the wizard. It was clear he'd never thought of that before.

"Simon, you can't—"

"Don't tell me what I can't do!" Simon said. "He's *my* boy. I found him."

That sounded fairly close to yes.

A Journey in the Snow

Jinx learned to read quickly, which was fortunate because Simon was not a particularly patient teacher. He didn't get angry when Jinx had trouble understanding things—instead, he assumed that Jinx was too stupid to understand and gave up. But it didn't take long for Jinx to figure out that the letters and sounds that Simon was teaching him were actually a sort of obstacle that you had to get around in order to listen to what the book was saying. After that, reading was easy. And fascinating—Jinx read about magic and about strange lands beyond the Urwald.

The door to Simon's rooms was no longer locked, and now Jinx was allowed in—and had to sweep and dust those rooms as well. Jinx suspected that before, Simon had kept them swept and dusted by magic. Now he expected Jinx to do it, by broom and brush.

But Jinx didn't mind, because he got to watch Simon do magic—mix potions, burn dry twisty things that made purple smoke, and leaf endlessly through a red leather-bound book muttering to himself. The wizard spent a lot of time trying different spells and, it seemed to Jinx, inventing new ones. Sometimes he wouldn't remember to tell Jinx to go to bed till nearly midnight.

The stone wall that Jinx had heard Simon and Sophie walk through remained a stone wall. Jinx thought of asking Simon if he wanted Jinx to clean the rooms behind it—but he didn't dare. There was something in Simon that was like a stone wall too, and you couldn't ask the questions that led beyond it.

"Don't touch any of the things on the shelves," Simon said. "They might kill you."

Jinx knew now that most of the jars said DANGER on them, and some said it in larger, firmer letters than the wasp jar did.

A lot of the time Simon just sat on a high stool, boringly writing away in a book. Jinx sat on the floor beside the skull and read whatever books Simon would let him. Sometimes when he reached for a book, Simon would glance up briefly and say, "Not that one."

And sometimes, if Simon said that, Jinx waited till another time when the wizard wasn't paying quite so much attention.

If Simon said nothing, Jinx would take the book, open it very cautiously in case it burst into flames, and read. Some of the books were in neither Urwish nor Samaran, but in some other language. This didn't matter as long as you listened to the books, he realized. He wondered how many languages there were in the world, and how many places besides the Urwald.

When Sophie was visiting, she always asked Jinx about his reading. Sometimes she talked to him using the languages he'd only read in books. Jinx listened carefully—the words weren't pronounced quite the way he'd expected—before answering her.

"Simon, the boy's taught himself four languages," Sophie said.

"Mm," said Simon.

Some of the books they discussed were in Samaran. A lot of these were about magic, and Jinx supposed Samara must be a very magical place. But when Jinx asked Sophie questions about Samara, she frowned.

"Samara's not important, Jinx. Read about the Urwald."

"It must be important," said Jinx. "You live there, don't you?"

Sophie thought flip-floppy blue-and-silver thoughts,

like she was nervous. "Jinx, Urwalders don't belong in Samara."

"Why not?" They were speaking Samaran, and Jinx had just read a Samaran book, something about elephants, a magical beast he thought he would very much like to see.

"Because we're not wanted there," Simon snapped, not looking up from his writing. "Go sweep out the loft, Jinx."

Mostly Simon just left Jinx to read, except when he wanted to give him orders.

"Hand me Calvin," said Simon one day.

"Er, who?" said Jinx. There was no one else in the room but the skull. It grinned conspiratorially.

Simon snapped his fingers impatiently. Jinx got up and took the skull to Simon.

"Its, er, his name was Calvin?"

"It is now. Calvin's an old enemy."

"Oh," said Jinx. "Er, did you kill him by magic?"

"It is very, very difficult to take someone's life by magic."

"Oh," said Jinx.

"I don't go around killing people," said Simon, with one of those little purple laughing-at-Jinx flashes.

"Well, then what happened to him?"

Simon tossed the skull up in the air and set it spinning on one finger. "Much less than he deserved."

He didn't seem to mind the question, but he wasn't going to answer it.

"Oh," said Jinx. "The barbarians drink wine out of the skulls of their enemies."

"Really? I use Calvin for a paperweight." Simon set Calvin down on a scroll he had just unrolled. "Where do these barbarians live?"

"In the Blacksmiths' Clearing," said Jinx. "Actually, anyone who lives in another clearing is a barbarian."

This memory had just come to him. His clearing seemed a long time ago now, and he didn't really remember what it looked like. He wondered what exactly Calvin had done to annoy Simon.

"I'm not sure how people drink out of skulls," Jinx added. Calvin had too many holes in him to make a good cup.

"Like this," said Simon. He flipped Calvin over. "You just cut around the top, here, and you see you have a nice bowl. Then you add three legs to make it stand upright, and there you go."

"Oh," said Jinx, putting his hands to the top of his own head. "Right."

The magic lessons did not go well. There did not seem to be any way to *listen* to magic, at least not that Jinx could figure out. He could listen to Simon, but that didn't help much.

"*Potion* and *power* come from the same word in Old Urwish," Simon said, holding a glass phial steady over a candle flame with a metal clamp. "All magic requires two things."

He paused, waiting until Jinx said, "Power and concentration."

"Right. And some kinds of magic require much more power than others. For example, magic done on a living person would require a hundred times as much power as magic done on that rock you keep failing to levitate."

Jinx looked at the pebble on the workbench with dislike. He'd spent weeks not being able to levitate it and was beginning to suspect Simon had done something to it to make it unlevitatable.

"And some power sources are?"

"Fire," Jinx said. "And words. Chants and stuff. Um, magic drawings with chalk. And herbs and stuff and like potions."

"A potion enables a wizard or witch to pass magical power on to another person," said Simon. "If I gave you a levitation potion, you would be able to levitate that rock. Although you could do it anyway if you'd only concentrate properly."

Jinx glared at the pebble as hard as he could. Spells were much easier to do if you could keep your eyes on the object you were bespelling, according to Simon.

"Why can't I have a power source?" If he could draw on power from a chant or a chalk drawing, Jinx thought, he'd be able to raise the pebble.

"A simple spell like that shouldn't require one." Simon jiggled the phial over the flame, agitating the dark green contents. "If you can't do that, you'll certainly never be able to do the concealment spell to protect you in the forest. Which you need if you're going to keep running around off the path like you do."

"I want to learn it so I can *go* places," said Jinx.

"Well, you never will at this rate. You'll be stuck right here like a lump of lichen."

"Sophie says you should be more patient when you're teaching me."

Simon frowned. "Nonsense! I'm extremely patient. You've taken weeks to learn this simple spell, and—"

"—you keep calling me an idiot," said Jinx.

"I have certainly never called you an idiot." Simon took a tiny bird made of gold from his pocket and let a drop of the potion fall on it.

The bird glowed brightly for an instant. Simon blew on it, then picked it up and handed it to Jinx. "There."

The gold was surprisingly heavy in Jinx's hand.

"It's called an aviot," said Simon. "If you insist on going places, take it with you."

"Is it magic?"

"Obviously. Don't tell Sophie about it. She doesn't need to know."

"Sophie likes magic," said Jinx. "It's just that she doesn't like that she likes it. Because she thinks she shouldn't."

"Figured that out, have you?"

Jinx hadn't needed to figure it out. It was right in the front of Sophie's head for anyone to see.

"Magic is knowledge," said Simon. "And Sophie has great respect for knowledge."

"Knowledge is power," said Jinx.

A frozen block of surprise surrounded Simon. "Where did you get that from?"

"Get what from?"

"'Knowledge is power.'"

Jinx frowned. Where *had* he got it from? "Sophie said it one time. And it made her mad. Is the aviot like a concealment spell?"

"No. It's not as strong."

"Is it some sort of, like, talisman? For luck?"

"Something like that. Don't worry, I'll find another way to keep you safe."

There was something peculiar about the words—they were all tangled up gray in Simon's thoughts, and *keep you* seemed to mean something on its own, separate from *safe*.

"I don't want to be kept," said Jinx. He wanted to go—well, *some*where.

"It's actually *necessary* when you're little," said Simon, sounding as if he were arguing with himself about something.

"When you're grown up, you'll be able to protect yourself from things."

"I'm ten!" said Jinx.

But Simon wasn't listening. The wizard's thoughts were crawling around, hiding behind one another, and it made Jinx nervous.

Simon picked up the still-burning candle and set it down next to the immovable pebble. "Here. Use the power from the flame to levitate the rock. If you can't do that, you're hopeless."

There were still days at a time when Jinx was alone, because Simon would go off somewhere in the Urwald. Jinx was used to being by himself, and it didn't bother him as much as it used to, but he wished he could go too. He asked to be taken along, but Simon always refused.

Once, when the wizard was in an especially cloudy dark mood, he said, "If you don't stop asking me, I *will* take you."

Which was what Jinx wanted, but it sounded like a threat.

A few months later, Simon came home with a burn on his face and a purple-green cloud of despair around his head. Jinx asked what had happened.

"Nothing," Simon snapped. "Mind your own business."

But the closed-off shape of Simon's thoughts made Jinx

think it had something to do with the Bonemaster. Jinx wondered if Simon had been battling with him.

～♪～♪～♪

Whenever Simon got on his nerves, Jinx went to the Farseeing Window and talked things over with the girl in the red hood. The window showed her to him often, though only from a distance. He imagined her with yellow curly hair and sky-blue eyes (which he couldn't see from above, because of her hood). And very sympathetic.

"He *could* actually tell me how to do things," Jinx said after a particularly frustrating magic lesson. "He just barks at me and expects me to know what he's talking about. He must know how the magic is done. Why can't he just tell me?"

"It's completely unfair," said the red-caped girl, in Jinx's imagination.

"And the other day he says to me, 'Why is it witches can do magic on living people more easily than wizards can?' And I say, 'I don't know.' Then I wait for him to tell me, right? But instead he goes, 'Oh. I was hoping you would know.' And I go, 'Well, why can they?' And he says, 'I don't know.' And I say, 'How'm I supposed to know if you don't?' and he goes, 'I thought you might use your brain.' How'm I supposed to use my brain to know things that he doesn't?"

"I don't know how you put up with it," said the red-caped girl, somewhat admiringly.

"Oh, well. He's mostly not that bad," said Jinx. "He made me a good-luck charm to keep me safe in the forest."

"I think you're awfully brave to go out in the Urwald by yourself," said the girl.

"Oh. Well. I'm not scared of it. After all, it's where we live, right?"

"That's why we know to be scared of it," said the girl.

Jinx spent a lot of time in the forest with his toes in the dirt, listening to the tree roots. He was getting better at understanding them. The thoughts of the roots of trees crawled with worms and grubs, sucked at moisture, and wriggled at anthills. Still, it was company. The trees called people—and all other sorts of creatures—"the Restless." They called Jinx "the Listener." Those weren't the exact words, but they were the general idea and the closest Jinx could get to it in human-talk.

The Restless didn't interest them much, but they mentioned them now and then as annoyances, pressures on their root hairs—travelers on the paths, werewolves skulking in the moonlight, vampires pretending to be travelers, and trolls tearing their way through the Urwald, not caring if they broke someone's branches or ripped someone's bark.

These scraps of stories made Jinx nervous. But he wanted to see more of the world. And so he would wander farther and farther into the forest, always checking to make sure that he knew the way back to Simon's house, always listening for footsteps or the snuffle of anything dangerous.

One day the trees were alarmed—some Restless just off the path were cutting up fallen trees for firewood, and not the right fallen trees. They were chopping up fine old trunks that the trees had actually been planning to eat themselves. The Urwald was angry.

Jinx crunched his way through the undergrowth until he came to the path. A party of Wanderers was camped there, busily chopping up fallen trees with axes.

"Stop!" Jinx yelled.

The Wanderers looked up. "It's that wizard's kid," a boy said in his own language, and not nicely.

Jinx clambered up on the enormous dead trunk the boy was hacking at. "You can't have this one. Take that one over there. It's crushing some saplings anyway." He pointed.

"Who taught you to speak Wanderer?" said one of the women.

"You guys did," said Jinx. "But that's not important. What's important is you can't chop this tree up, or the Urwald will get mad and take some awful kind of revenge on you."

"Says who?" said the boy.

"Says the Urwald," said Jinx. "If you cut off the limbs of this tree, people will lose their limbs. The trees said so."

"Oh wonderful, he talks to trees," said the woman, but she dragged her ax over to the other dead trunk.

"Don't hurt those saplings," said Jinx as the other Wanderers followed her.

"Bosses people around like he's a bloody wizard himself," the woman muttered.

The boy hung back. "What's your name?"

"Jinx. What's yours?"

"Tolliver. How old are you?"

"Eleven," said Jinx.

"You are not. *I'm* eleven. You're little."

"I was eleven at the winter solstice." Jinx *was* littler than Tolliver. This worried him.

"How did an evil wizard catch you?" said Tolliver.

"I just met him in the forest one time. He's not evil."

"What does he use you for? Does he drink your blood?"

"Wizards don't drink blood," said Jinx. "Vampires do that."

"But he uses it in spells, right? Wizards use people's blood and livers and things in spells—everybody knows that."

"Then everybody's wrong. Simon doesn't do that. I've watched him do lots of spells, and he hasn't used even one person's liver."

"Can you do spells?"

"Yes," Jinx lied. Then, realizing Tolliver was about to ask him to do one, he added, "I'm not allowed to in front of other people, though."

"Oh yeah?" Tolliver grinned, and Jinx saw that he knew Jinx was lying. "If you can do magic, you better stay out of the kingdoms. You know what they do to magicians there? They make them dance in red-hot iron shoes."

"They do not."

"Do too. I've seen it."

"You have not." Jinx was almost sure Tolliver was lying. His thoughts were a purple cloud of laughing at Jinx. Well, as long as he was going to be laughed at anyway . . . "What *are* the kingdoms?"

"Man, you never heard of the kingdoms?"

"That's why I asked," said Jinx. None of the books he'd read had mentioned them.

"They're all around the Urwald. The biggest ones are Keyland and Bragwood. Keyland's that way"—Tolliver pointed to the east—"and Bragwood is that way." He pointed west.

"So what's that way?" said Jinx, pointing south.

"Keyland. Mostly. And a little bit of Bragwood."

"How about that way?" Jinx pointed north.

"Oh, all kinds of kingdoms," said Tolliver airily, so Jinx guessed he didn't know. "Anyway, you want to stay out of

Keyland. They'll kill any kind of magician there. They kill everybody. The king killed his brother—"

"Kings are just in stories," said Jinx.

"No they're not; shut up and listen. The king killed his brother, who was actually king, so that *he* could be king. Then the dead king's wife and baby disappeared, on account the baby would've been king, so the brother probably killed them, too. They do that kind of thing all the time, kings do. They can kill anybody they don't like."

"What did you want to be in a place like that for?" said Jinx.

"Man, that's where everything comes from. That's where we get that paper that your wizard likes so much. And that blue cloth you're wearing. When you outgrow those clothes—*if* you do—we'll sell 'em to some other clearing, and then when they wear 'em out, we'll sell 'em back in Keyland to be made into paper. Haven't you ever been anywhere?"

"Of course," said Jinx.

"Where?"

"Oh, around."

"If you never go anywhere, you'll always be stupid," said Tolliver.

"I'm not stupid!" said Jinx. But he could see Tolliver's point. Tolliver clearly knew all sorts of things that Jinx didn't, and it was probably from having been places.

"I can't do it." Jinx pushed away the book he'd been trying to levitate.

"Of course you can't if you think you can't," said Simon.

"I know I can't."

"Bah. Even worse. Don't waste my time," said Simon. "You levitated a rock, a bottle, and a spoon. What's the problem?"

"The book weighs more."

"So draw on more power."

"I don't have more power."

Simon uttered one of his favorite swear words. "Use the fire. You've always got the fire."

The fire was the only spell Jinx had managed to learn besides levitation. He could set things on fire, and then put the fire out by reabsorbing it into himself. As long as it wasn't a big fire. And whenever the fire wasn't burning, it was inside Jinx—this in itself was power, according to Simon. A very small power.

"I can't find the fire," said Jinx.

"Of course you can. It's right there." Simon pointed at Jinx. "Can't you feel it?"

"No," said Jinx, frustrated. Simon kept insisting power was something you could sense—practically *see*—and Jinx had no idea what he meant.

Jinx couldn't open and close doors with magic. He

couldn't use magic to split firewood. He couldn't levitate any living thing—he'd tried on kittens—because its life-force countermanded what little power he had. He certainly couldn't make illusions. And worst of all, he couldn't do the concealment spell that Simon had used to save himself and Jinx from the trolls.

"Can we try the concealment spell again?" said Jinx.

"For whatever good it'll do. Go ahead."

How'm I supposed to think I can do it when you know I can't? Jinx didn't say this. He went to the middle of the room, stood in the center, and tried to draw power from the fire inside him. Power and concentration. He concentrated hard on not being there.

"No good," said Simon. "You're as there as you ever were."

"I don't have enough magic."

"Magic isn't something you *have*. It's something you do. Or in your case, don't do."

"I can understand the trees, though," said Jinx, defending himself.

"Nonsense." Simon turned back to his books.

"I can too. They told me—" Jinx remembered his conversation with Tolliver. "Are there countries outside the Urwald?"

"Of course."

"With kings? Um, Bragwood and Keyland?"

"Among others, yes."

"Why aren't they in your books?"

"Oh, they're in there somewhere. They're just not very interesting places," said Simon.

"Why are so many books about the Urwald?"

"Because it's more interesting, of course," said Simon, flipping open a book. "If you're not going to do the concealment spell, go muck out the goats' shed."

Jinx remembered something else Tolliver had said. "Do you think I'm small?"

"Of course you're—" Simon stopped and looked down at Jinx in surprise, as if he hadn't seen him in a long time. "Hm. Didn't you use to be a lot smaller?"

"Yes," said Jinx. "Because I used to be six."

"How old are you now?"

"Eleven. You made pumpkin pie on my birthday," Jinx reminded him. "But am I *too* small?"

"No, no, you'll grow." Simon's thoughts were twisting around again, crawling over one another. If Jinx was worried about not growing, it seemed like Simon was just as worried about him growing.

For some weeks after that Simon took to paging furiously through stacks of books about magic. But when Jinx asked him what he was looking for, Simon just grunted or told him to go sweep out the loft.

It was ages before Simon finally agreed to take Jinx on one of his journeys.

"Where are we going?"

"If you're going to pester me with a whole lot of questions, I'll leave you home."

Jinx didn't think just asking where they were going counted as pestering, but he shut up. The next thing he'd been going to ask was *Does this have something to do with the Bonemaster?*

Simon didn't have the green-bottle-shaped fear of the Bonemaster that most people did. But his Bonemaster thoughts tended to be angry. And for some reason now they were mixed up with those worries about Jinx growing.

Anyway, Jinx was finally going somewhere. That was the important thing.

They walked all the short winter day. There were tracks in the snow on the path, stamped in by boots, claws, and cloven hooves. Once they met a man carrying an ax over his shoulder, and though he was probably just a woodcutter, you could never be sure in the Urwald. Jinx drew closer to Simon and was gratified by the look of terror the stranger cast at the wizard. They passed each other without speaking.

The winter day was never very bright, and it darkened quickly.

"Here we go," said Simon, stopping suddenly. "We'll

spend the night in this tree house."

Jinx looked up through branches laced with snow, purple in the gathering dusk. He could make out a sort of box.

"Now to figure out how to get up," said Simon.

There was a distant thumping sound from farther up the path.

"Something's coming," said Jinx.

"Mm," said Simon, ignoring him. He ran his hands over the tree trunk.

The thumping grew louder—a small thump followed by a bigger one. *Ker thump, ker thump.*

"It's something big and heavy," Jinx added.

"It looks like if I boost you up, you can probably grab that broken branch up there," said Simon. "When you get up to the tree house, you can tie this rope to a branch, and I'll climb up."

"It's getting closer," said Jinx.

"Well, hurry up then, boy, don't dawdle." Simon handed Jinx a coil of rope, then made a stirrup of his hands. "Ouch. You couldn't have brushed the snow off your boots?"

With the rope looped over his shoulder, Jinx teetered one-footed in Simon's hands and groped for the broken branch Simon had pointed out. His hands closed around the rough bark. He tried to pull himself up.

The thumping grew louder.

"Brace your feet against the trunk and walk your way up," said Simon.

Jinx did. He managed to get up and put his knee on the branch. Then, wrapping his arms around as much of the trunk as he could reach, he got his foot up—

Ker thump, ker thump.

He stood up against the trunk and scrambled onto the wooden platform of the tree house.

Ker *thump.*

"You can send that rope down anytime," Simon snapped.

Jinx tied the rope to a branch as quickly as he could— the thumping was so close now that he could hear it crunching snow on the path. He threw the free end of the rope down. It snagged on the broken branch.

THUMP.

He shook it free and saw it go slack as it dropped. Then it tightened—

THUMP, THUMP—whatever it was, it was right at the foot of the tree.

Simon's head appeared over the side of the platform. Jinx wilted with relief.

"That—that creature can't climb trees, can it?"

"Won't, more like," said Simon. "There she goes, see?"

Jinx peered through the gloaming, between two great branches, and could just make out the hopping motion of a legless barrel-shape—thrusting a long, straight stick at the ground—

"A witch, traveling by butter churn," said Simon.

"Oh," said Jinx. He was ashamed of being so frightened. "You're not afraid of witches, are you?"

"Only an idiot wouldn't be afraid of witches," said Simon.

"I never knew there were tree houses," said Jinx. He was surprised the trees would allow such a thing.

"Part of the ancient treaty."

"I never heard of an ancient treaty," said Jinx. The trees had never mentioned it.

"The trees agreed to let humans take deadwood for fuel and building. And to let us have tree houses. And we agreed that if anyone kills a tree, the trees take a human life in revenge." Simon shook his head. "I never saw the point of that."

"The trees don't *want* to take just anybody's life," said Jinx. "But they're afraid of letting there get to be too many humans."

For a long time Jinx couldn't sleep, because of the cold. And he could tell that Simon was awake too by the quiet murmur of Simon's thoughts. There was a sort of eager galloping feeling of being about to accomplish something new—something to do with magic, Jinx thought. He'd sensed this feeling of Simon's before, when the wizard was working on a new spell or trying out some magic one of the witches had told him about. But this time there was an odd pucker of guilt around the edge of the excitement.

Maybe the guilt was because Simon was thinking of Sophie and how much she disliked magic. But that didn't explain why Simon had it about *this* spell. Come to think of it, Jinx had never noticed him feeling guilty before. Not about magic, not about what Sophie didn't like, not about Calvin the skull, not about anything.

It was hard to imagine what *would* make Simon feel guilty, but it would probably have to be something pretty bad.

The Bonemaster

It was early the next afternoon that they crossed a two-log bridge over a creek and started down a smaller, snow-covered path dinted with butter-churn tracks.

Soon they came to a little thatch-covered cottage. The house was made of wood, not gingerbread, but the butter-churn tracks went right up to the door, so Jinx knew: They were visiting a witch. Simon had told him that only an idiot wouldn't be afraid of witches, and one thing Simon certainly did not consider himself was an idiot. But then, Simon had witches visiting in his house all the time.

But going to a witch's house—that was different.

They had not yet reached the door when it opened, and

Dame Glammer stepped out.

"Simon the Wizard," she said. "Come to see me through long miles of snowy woods. I wonder why."

"Greetings, Dame Glammer," said Simon with a smile.

"And the dear little chipmunk is still alive." She grinned at Jinx.

"May we come in?" said Simon.

"Of course—where are my manners." Dame Glammer stepped back. "Come in, come in. Take your boots off. Have some brew."

The house seemed small inside when you were used to Simon's, but it had a scrubbed wood floor and a fire crackling in the fireplace. They took off their boots and their coats and sat down at a proper wooden table, centuries old and unlikely to offend any living tree—much. Dame Glammer set hot mugs of something in front of them. Leaves floated in it.

Jinx cupped his hands around the mug and breathed in leaf-smelling steam. He listened to Simon and Dame Glammer talk—about the journey, about the weather, not about what they'd come for. And Jinx had no idea what that might be . . . but the little pucker of guilt that he'd noticed in Simon last night had come back. In Dame Glammer, he couldn't feel anything at all, no matter how hard he tried.

"Well, I won't rush you to tell me what you've come about, Simon," said Dame Glammer. "But I don't think it was to gaze upon my beautiful face. And you, chipmunk, can stop trying to read my mind."

"I wasn't trying to read your mind," Jinx protested. "I can't! Nobody can."

"That's right, chipmunk. Nobody can."

Confused, Jinx ducked his head down and breathed in steam. He took a cautious sip of the hot drink. It tasted of summer.

Dame Glammer got up and brought some barley cakes, which were crumbly and a bit stale and nowhere near as good as anything that there was to eat in Simon's house. They ate these and drank their brew, and Simon and Dame Glammer talked a bit about potions and magic and herbs.

"That's deep Urwald magic, that is, Simon," said Dame Glammer, nodding at Jinx. "You don't see that very often. If you want to study Urwald magic, you take a look at that boy."

"No one can read minds," said Simon. "Certainly Jinx can't."

Dame Glammer grinned. "Ask him."

"Jinx, what number am I thinking of?"

"Seven?" Jinx guessed.

"Nope." Simon turned back to Dame Glammer. "I'd have noticed it by now if he could."

"Hard to notice what you don't believe in."

"Jinx, go bring some firewood in," said Simon.

Jinx put down his empty mug and stood up. It didn't seem fair—he'd only just got here, and surely Dame Glammer was used to bringing in her own firewood.

"The firewood's in a shed just around the side of the house, chipmunk," said Dame Glammer, grinning at him.

He pulled his boots on, put on his coat, and went out. He took a couple of loud, crunching steps in the snow, forward then back, and pressed his ear to Dame Glammer's front door.

"Of course I don't," Dame Glammer was saying. "Do you think I keep something like that in my house?"

"Probably," said Simon.

"Ha. Nobody ever wanted that for any good purpose."

"I'd be willing to pay quite a bit for it."

"And it's the leaves you want?"

"The roots," said Simon. "I told you."

"Root magic's for things that ought not to see the light of day. Things that were better left undone," said Dame Glammer.

"Am I supposed to believe you never do that sort of magic yourself?" said Simon.

Dame Glammer chuckled.

"I'll pay you in gold," said Simon.

"Gold?" Dame Glammer laughed. "That useless soft metal that you can't make tools or cooking pots out of? Or am I supposed to hang it in my beautiful ears?"

"Well, not gold then. Anything you like."

"Anything?" Dame Glammer's voice was suddenly hungry.

"Within reason," Simon said quickly. "Anything you care to name right now. No unspecified favors at a later date."

"Will you give me the dear, *trusting* little chipmunk?"

"No. Not the chipmunk," said Simon. "I meant something in the way of money, or, or spices, or—"

"Magic?" said Dame Glammer. "Goodness, don't you think that chipmunk's taking an awfully long time with the wood?"

There was the sound of a chair being pushed back from the table, and Jinx turned and ran to get the firewood.

⌁ ⌁ ⌁

"You'd better stay the night," said Dame Glammer when Jinx was back inside. "Now that the deepest snow is gone, a lot of folk are out traveling the Path. I expect you might meet *anybody*."

"Might we?" said Simon. "Meaning?"

"Meaning there are some people it's better to meet by daylight."

Simon nodded slowly. "I see. Right, we'll stay, then."

⌁ ⌁ ⌁

Before they left the next morning, Jinx saw Dame Glammer slip Simon a bundle tied up tightly in a red polka-dot kerchief. Simon tucked it into an inside pocket of his robe. Jinx didn't see what Simon gave her in exchange.

They walked home by a different route. Every time they came to another path, Simon stopped and looked down it each way, as if he were expecting someone.

"Well, look at that," said Simon, at the seventh crossing.

There was another wizard coming along the path. He looked like wizards *should* look. He had a long white beard and blue eyes crackling with sparks, and he wore a blue robe and a matching pointy hat. He was smiling, which didn't quite go with the flashing pink clouds of fury that gathered around him like a rose-colored thunderstorm.

"What are you doing out of your lair, Bonemaster?" said Simon.

So this was the Bonemaster! The wizard of horrible tales and bottle-shaped fears. He looked almost kindly. The things boiling in clouds around his head said he wasn't, though. The pink clouds had knives in them. Jinx had never seen anyone whose feelings came out in cutlery before.

Jinx would have been sure he was about to die, if Simon hadn't been there.

"Not looking for *you*, certainly, Simon," said the Bonemaster. "But since we've met so pleasantly, why don't we go to your house and collect what you stole from me?"

"No," said Simon. "Not even in exchange for what you stole from me."

"Did I offer that? Anyway, I stole nothing," said the Bonemaster. "I took only what was owed."

"Step off the path and I'll give you what you're owed."

"Big talk, Simon, as usual. But you can't fight me—you haven't the power. That burn's healed nicely, I see."

The wizards were boiling rage at each other now. The Bonemaster continued to look faintly amused, but the knives in the pink cloud spun about hungrily.

The Bonemaster flicked his eyes at Jinx. "Got a boy, have you? And just big enough to be of use, I see."

Simon stepped in front of Jinx. "It's not your business."

"Well, it won't work, Simon. You haven't the power or the intelligence to make it work. Let alone the ability to finish what you start. I always said so."

They glared at each other, Simon with mounting fury and the Bonemaster with cool disapproval. Three of the knives in the pink cloud were now gently dripping blood.

"Come on, Jinx," said Simon, turning away.

"Yes, go on, Jinx," said the Bonemaster. "Don't stay to—"

"Don't you call him by name!" Simon snarled.

He grabbed Jinx by the arm and stalked off along the path. Jinx looked over his shoulder, afraid the Bonemaster was going to follow them and suck out their souls. The Bonemaster just stood there looking after them and smiling.

Simon was in a red rage. Jinx waited till it had faded

to a dull orange before asking, "Was that really the Bone-master?"

"Obviously."

"I always heard he was a really evil wizard."

"You heard right."

"He looks—"

"Don't judge people by how they look," said Simon. "And don't ever go near him, Jinx. Ever."

No fear of that—who would? Nobody could ever be fooled by the Bonemaster's smile. "He has knives in his thoughts."

"I'm sure he does."

"It's lucky for us we weren't off the path," said Jinx.

"Oh, you think he could have hurt us? You think he's a more powerful wizard than I am? Is that what you think?"

"No," said Jinx, who had been thinking exactly that.

"Anyone could have power the way *he* gets it. If they were willing to do the things *he's* willing to do. Which I am *not*."

"Oh. What—"

"And I don't owe him a thing!"

The Spell with Something Wrong about It

Simon had been behaving strangely, even for him. He didn't cook and he hardly ate. He spent days on end studying a red leather-bound book and comparing it page by page to other books, and stalking around the floor of his workroom in a circle, then retracing his steps backward, muttering under his breath.

He would not answer Jinx's questions about the Bonemaster. Jinx particularly wanted to know what the Bonemaster had meant by *just big enough to be of use*. Somehow it hadn't sounded like it had anything to do with splitting firewood or mucking out the goats' shed.

Jinx slipped into the workroom while Simon was gone,

hoping to figure out what Simon was up to. He saw Dame Glammer's knotted polka-dot kerchief up on the highest shelf. Jinx remembered Simon tucking it into his pocket as they left her house after that mysterious talk about root magic. Jinx scrambled up onto the workbench. He reached out for the bundle, but his hand was blocked a few inches away from it. He tried reaching from the top, and from behind. It was as if there was an invisible glass dome surrounding the thing. Simon had put some kind of ward spell around it.

Jinx was sure if he could have reached the kerchief and untied it, he would have found roots.

Root magic's for things that ought not to see the light of day, Dame Glammer had said.

The ward spell didn't stop the cold, dead smell that came from the bundle—or the feeling. It felt like injustice. Like wrongs it was much too late to right. It was an icy, creeping nastiness. Jinx thought about the guilt he'd seen in Simon on the way to Dame Glammer's house. He jumped down from the workbench.

He noticed a book bound in dark red leather. It was the one Simon had spent so much time consulting lately. Usually Simon didn't leave it lying around.

Jinx flipped the book open. It was in a language Jinx didn't know. There was a drawing of a bottle. Sketched inside the bottle was the vague outline of a man.

Jinx turned pages. There were illustrations showing intricate symbols—models for chalk drawings, maybe?

Simon's shadow fell across the page. Jinx looked up.

"Close that book at once," said Simon.

Jinx snapped it shut and dropped it hastily on the workbench. He expected Simon to be angry—that was the Simon he knew. But this strange new Simon was something else—worried, Jinx thought. Green clouds of something— fear, maybe? Why on earth would a wizard be afraid?

Simon snatched up the book, stuck it into his robe pocket, and left. There was still no anger around his head. Just that weird, rather frightening worry.

Days went by, and then weeks. The book was never left lying around where Jinx could find it again.

Something had changed in Simon. Jinx wasn't sure if it was because of the roots or because of the spell Simon was getting ready to do. Dame Glammer was wrong— Jinx couldn't read minds. Minds weren't like books. They shifted around all the time.

And anyway, everyone could see what was right in front of their faces, surely—the white, implacable wall of Simon's determination to get this new spell done, the pink stabs of worry that he wouldn't be able to do it or that it would go wrong. And battering against the white wall was Sophie, with her own brown-blue worry about Simon.

"You've changed," she said. "It's the Urwald. This place is getting to you."

"It's not the Urwald. I'm very busy right now."

"Why are you cleaning the workshop?" said Sophie.

"Because it needs doing," said Simon.

"But you never clean your workshop," said Sophie.

And he wasn't really doing it now, Jinx thought. Or only a little bit. Jinx was doing most of the work, of course.

"It's my workshop," said Simon. "I can clean it if I want. I don't need to explain everything I do to you."

This sounded like typical Simon-and-Sophie squabbling, and it didn't worry Jinx much. The wall around Simon, that worried him more. Usually the wall was much farther inside Simon, and it was kept up to protect him from everyone else, not from Sophie. Jinx worked a dust rag around a pile of books on the floor. The dust crawled up his nose and made him sneeze. An offended spider hurried away.

"You're doing something different," said Sophie. "It's some kind of big spell that you haven't done before, isn't it?"

"You don't want to know anything about magic, so why are you asking?" said Simon, not looking at her.

"I can't talk to you when you're like this," said Sophie, turning to go.

"Good. Don't."

A pale shudder of hurt went through the room. "You

think I'm in the way," said Sophie, her voice shaking.

"You're always in the way," Simon snapped. But his thoughts didn't go with his words at all. Jinx was confused.

"He doesn't mean it, Sophie," Jinx heard himself saying.

"You mind your own business!" said Simon.

"It is my business."

"No, Jinx, it's not," said Sophie. "Simon, if we could discuss this somewhere—"

"There's nothing to discuss."

"He doesn't mean it!" Jinx couldn't stop himself from talking. "He hates himself for saying it. I don't know why he's saying it."

Simon wheeled on Jinx. "Get out of here right now!"

"No, don't go, Jinx. I'll go," said Sophie. Her face was pale.

"Yes, do," said Simon.

She left, and it felt as if something in the room tore in two.

Jinx felt horrible. He heard Sophie's footsteps go to the end of the corridor and then keep going—she had passed through the stone wall. Jinx went on dusting the pile of books, although all the dust had transferred itself to his rag or the inside of his nose now. He liked Sophie and he was furious at Simon for being mean to her. He wished he could run after her and tell her that something strange was going on in Simon's head, that for some reason the new spell that he was working on was so important to him . . . no, that wasn't it either. It had to do with the guilt, didn't it? There was something wrong with this spell, some reason Simon didn't want Sophie to know about it.

There was a dismal green cloud around Simon that seemed to be making his eyes water.

"I said get out of here."

Jinx threw down his dust rag and got out of there.

The workroom was spotless. Everything was off the floor and workbench and up on shelves. Everything had been dusted and scrubbed. The room felt cold, mostly because of Simon. Simon didn't snap at Jinx again—he hardly said anything to him. Sophie hadn't come back, of course. Jinx didn't think she would ever come back.

Jinx and Simon set up four braziers in the corners of the room, and then Simon began chalking symbols on the floor. He kept looking at the red leather-bound book as he did this. It took days. Once Jinx accidentally stepped on a symbol that looked rather like a winged fox. Simon shot him an ice-cold gaze that made Jinx want to go put his coat on.

Finally the figures were done. Simon began brewing a potion over a brazier. Jinx sat on the high stool, which he had gotten to by stepping very carefully in between the chalked figures, and watched. A licorice smell came from the potion, and then a sweet smell like apple blossoms. Once a cat came into the room, and Simon fixed it with the same glare he'd given Jinx.

The cat shook its front paws disdainfully and turned and stalked out again, its tail held high.

Sophie's right, Jinx thought. Simon has changed. He thought of times Simon had been kind to him—making pumpkin pie because he knew Jinx liked it, and not letting the witches cackle at him too much, and occasionally checking to see whether Jinx had enough socks. And making that gold aviot charm to keep Jinx safe.

Maybe when this spell was finished, the old Simon would come back again. Jinx would do whatever he could to make that happen.

"Take this bottle and wash it as clean as you possibly can."

Jinx made his way gingerly among the chalk markings. He went out to the kitchen and put a kettle of water on the fire. Ordinarily he would have just dropped the green bottle right into it. But he was afraid of damaging it. The old Simon didn't care much if Jinx broke things, but this new Simon probably would.

When the water was hot, he scrubbed the bottle with a bottle brush, and with sand, and with soap, and then rinsed it. He rubbed it with a towel and then took it outside and held it up to the sunlight to make sure there wasn't a spot or a smear anywhere on it.

Then he took it back to the workroom and set it down in front of Simon, who said nothing.

Jinx went back to the kitchen to look for something to eat. He had finished eating everything Simon had cooked, and Simon hadn't eaten anything at all since Sophie had left.

Jinx cut up some squash, pumpkin, and onions, and plunked them into boiling water. He let it stew awhile. It tasted of nothing. He put some salt in. He added a handful of cinnamon.

He tasted it. It wasn't very good. He added some sugarplum syrup.

It tasted awful, but he ate a little.

Then he dished some up for Simon. But Simon didn't even look up when Jinx put the bowl on the workbench. Jinx pushed it toward him.

"I think we're ready to start," said Simon. "First we need to light a fire under each of those braziers in the corners."

Simon had never said "we" about a spell before. Jinx ought to have been flattered, but he wasn't. There was something wrong about this spell.

"M-maybe I'll just go into the kitchen and get out of your way."

"No, I need your help," said Simon. "Take a coal with

the tongs and go and light the braziers."

Jinx took the brass tongs and selected a glowing red coal from the dish on the workbench. As he carried it across the room, the glow and the hot smell filled his senses. There was tinder placed among the charcoal in each brazier, ready to catch. Over each one sat a pan filled with dried herbs, the potion Simon had been brewing, and a handful of twisted, evil-smelling black roots—they had to be the ones from Dame Glammer's kerchief.

As Jinx went from one fire to the next, very slowly and carefully so as not to step on the chalk figures, steam and smoke twisted into the middle of the room, forming a four-branched arch over his head. Jinx's legs began to feel heavy—it was hard to control them and not to step on the chalk. He had a sense of not really being there, of being somewhere else. He was slowly floating away from his body. He could see himself now, from above, looking small and silly. He lit the last fire. The tongs and coal fell from his hands.

Now he moved toward the center of the room—why was he doing that? Oh, Simon must have told him to. The room was rumbling with stone-heavy waves of sound that must have been Simon's voice. Jinx couldn't understand what Simon was saying, but he knew he was supposed to be in the center of the room, right here, in this jagged diagram, where the lines met—

He watched his body collapse. It lay there like a rag doll, limbs sprawling uselessly.

Simon's voice rumbled through the air again, and then the wizard jumped up—that is, it took him a century or so to do it, so it wasn't really jumping—and ran toward Jinx as slowly as if he'd been moving through solid stone.

Jinx wasn't really interested in that. He had floated to the ceiling and he wanted to float farther, but something was stopping him. It was immensely annoying. Jinx looked up, thinking it must be the ceiling that was in his way, but the stone ceiling was gone. Instead there was a great dome of black sky above him, dotted with fire-bright stars, millions of stars.

Jinx had never seen the sky like this before. You couldn't in the Urwald. There was a dim silver line, a great circle where the sky met the earth, and he felt an intense longing to go to the line and touch it. Desperately he tried to float higher. But he couldn't. Something was holding him back. Maybe his body. Maybe Simon.

Not really wanting to, he looked down again. Simon was kneeling beside the crumpled body. His hands were laid flat on Jinx's chest. The wizard trembled with concentration.

Then he straightened, holding a golden ball of light cupped in his hands.

From above, Jinx watched curiously as Simon stood up and stepped over to his workbench, cradling the ball of light.

The green bottle Jinx had scrubbed earlier—hadn't he? It was so hard to remember now—was heating over a candle flame. Simon set the ball as gently as he could on the open bottle neck. It balanced, jiggling, for a moment, and then with a *thwoop* sound the golden ball swooped into the bottle.

Quickly Simon corked the bottle, then walked back to Jinx's body.

Jinx turned around to look at the great night dome of sky again, feeling he could almost fly into it, if only Simon would let him.

Then Simon knelt down by the body on the floor and laid a gentle hand on Jinx's forehead. Horribly, Jinx felt himself being drawn downward, inexorably, back into his own body. He struggled, but it was no use. The ceiling reappeared above Jinx, stone and impenetrable—the sky was gone. Jinx began to sink. He slid into his abandoned body and knew no more.

Tied Up in a Sack

Jinx woke up. He was on the floor before the summer fireplace, covered in itchy blankets. He was too warm. He shoved the blankets aside.

Instantly Simon knelt down beside him. "Are you all right?"

And Jinx had the feeling that something was very, very wrong.

Simon put a hand on his shoulder. "Jinx? Say something, Jinx."

Jinx couldn't figure out what was wrong. But whatever it was, it was wronger than it had ever been before.

"Let me get you some water."

Jinx sat up. He stared at the beads of water on the copper dipper Simon brought him. Then he took the dipper in his hands, shakily, and drank. The water tasted of stone and copper. He drank all the water and wanted more. He would get up and get it. If he could figure out how to get up. It was as if he'd lost one of his senses.

"Jinx, say something."

Jinx looked at Simon's face and saw—nothing. Just a face. There were no colors and no clouds, no rays of light and no jagged orange anger . . . nothing but a face. Jinx had no idea what was going on behind it, no more than if it had been a cat's face.

It wasn't just that Simon's thoughts had gone opaque, like Dame Glammer's. Something inside Jinx was gone.

"No," said Jinx.

"No what?" said Simon.

But what was Simon *thinking?* Was he being sarcastic, was he angry, was he worried? Were you supposed to be able to figure that out from the way things moved, mouths and eyes and eyebrows? It was like being tied up inside a sack! Furious, Jinx threw the dipper into the fire.

Simon's eyebrows shot up. Whatever that meant. He grabbed the fire tongs and plucked the dipper out—it was blackened with soot—and set it on the hearth.

"Was that really necessary, Jinx?"

"Yes," said Jinx.

He struggled to his feet with the world shaped all wrong. He staggered. Simon put out a hand to steady him and Jinx shrugged him away.

"I can't see," said Jinx.

Simon bent down and looked in Jinx's eyes. "Of course you can see. You're looking right at me."

"I can't see."

One of his senses was gone. Maybe more. All right, he could see with his *eyes*. And he could smell, feel, and hear. He licked the back of his hand—it tasted of dirt and salt. Five senses. The sixth one was missing.

"I can't see the clouds around your head," Jinx explained, trying to fight down the rising panic. It felt like there was a blank white space in his head.

"There aren't any clouds around my head." Simon spoke very patiently, and the expression on his face was— was what? Jinx didn't know what Simon was thinking.

"I mean the colored clouds! The ones you can always see."

"I can't see colored clouds, Jinx."

"Of course you can! Everybody can."

But now Jinx was waking up and his thoughts were starting to organize themselves. *Stop trying to read my mind,* Dame Glammer had said. *Nobody can.* Was it the clouds she meant?

"I guess everybody can't," Jinx said, realizing it for the first time.

Simon's spell had taken away Jinx's ability to—not read minds, because that wasn't really what it was, but see the color and shape of what people were thinking. Simon was looking down at him with some expression on his face that meant—concern? Anger?

It didn't matter! Jinx lurched to the front door—the blank white space made it hard to walk straight. The door wouldn't open. "Let me out!"

"Not right now, Jinx. Later. Calm down. Have something to eat."

"I don't want anything to eat!" He pushed past Simon. There was another way out of the house. He climbed clumsily up the ladder to the loft. The blank white space got in his way, and when he reached the loft, he stumbled and almost fell over the edge into the kitchen. He could hear Simon hurrying up the ladder behind him. Jinx got to the door to nowhere and flung it open. Simon grabbed him.

"Jinx! No, Jinx. You don't want to do that."

Jinx struggled, trying to get out. He felt better now with the small blue sky above him and the life of the Urwald pouring in the open door. At least he could still feel *that*.

"It's a long way down, Jinx." Simon hauled him inside and the door slammed shut by itself. "Now come downstairs and eat something."

"You can't make me eat anything."

"Right. Come on, now."

Jinx half climbed, half fell down the ladder and ran to the drain by the pump and threw up.

"All right, it can take people that way sometimes." Simon pumped water into the drain and gave Jinx a damp towel.

He put a hand on Jinx's shoulder and Jinx, suddenly too tired to resist, let Simon steer him over to the stove steps to sit down.

"What did you do to me?" Jinx demanded.

"It's just a small spell."

"It wasn't a small spell, it was a huge spell!"

"You'll be all right soon."

"Not unless I can see the clouds again!"

"Jinx, you're babbling. There aren't any clouds. Maybe you should rest."

"There's something wrong with my head."

"There's nothing wrong with your head."

There was one more way out of the house. Jinx jumped up and staggered down the hall to the blank wall where Sophie had disappeared. He smacked into it. It was still a stone wall. He pushed at it, then pounded on it.

"Jinx, stop!" Simon grabbed him.

Jinx wrenched himself free. "Let me through!"

"Jinx—"

"I want to see Sophie!" He threw himself at the wall

again. "Tell me how to get through."

"You can't get through."

"You mean you won't *tell* me how." Jinx had never dared to speak to Simon that way before. He glared up at the wizard, expecting jagged orange anger, but of course there wasn't any. There was that worried-looking expression, and who knew what lay behind it?

Lies, probably.

"She's going to be really mad when she finds out what you've done to me," said Jinx.

"I haven't done anything to you. Jinx—"

"I know there's a way through here!" Jinx turned to pound on the wall again, but Simon pulled him away.

Jinx shook free and lurched into Simon's workroom. He grabbed at things on the workbench, looking for the green bottle Simon had used in the spell. He pulled books off the shelves, looking to see if it was hidden behind them.

"Stop that!" said Simon.

Jinx accidentally knocked Calvin the skull off a shelf. He tried to catch him, but the blank white spot in Jinx's head made him miss. The skull hit the workbench, rolled, and landed on his side, gazing up at Jinx crookedly.

"What did he do to *you*?" Jinx asked him.

"Jinx, sit down. Stop. Calm down. Now." Simon grabbed Jinx, picked him up, and set him on the stool. "Deep breaths."

Jinx looked up at Simon and still couldn't see any clouds. He would have liked to hurt Simon, to throw something at him, to pick up Calvin and hurl him at Simon's unreadable face, but he couldn't because Simon was dangerous. He'd never even realized before how dangerous.

Jinx took deep, ragged breaths and tried to calm down and think, difficult as it was around the blank white space. Whatever Simon had done to him, there had to be a way to undo it. And Jinx was going to have to find it.

Knowledge Is Power

Jinx spent days and nights searching the house for some clue to what Simon had done. Simon, meanwhile, was working on new spells. It seemed to Jinx that Simon was getting more powerful. Jinx was not. The only progress Jinx had made in learning magic was that now he could levitate a book, if it wasn't a big one. That was all.

It did not make up for what he had lost.

Simon had gotten scraggly-looking about the hair and eyes. He probably wasn't sleeping much. He certainly wasn't bathing much. And he spent a lot of time staring at the blank stone wall that Sophie used to appear through. That was the sort of thing that let you know what people were thinking, Jinx was learning . . . you had to go by where their eyes went and the times when they just stopped talking, and things like that.

But Jinx didn't care. Ever since he'd lost his ability to see other people's feelings, he'd become a whole lot more interested in how *he* felt. And how he felt was sick of everything. The only reason Jinx stayed in Simon's house was because he didn't see how he'd ever get his ability back if he left.

Unless he could get to Samara. He remembered something Sophie had once said—that Simon had come to Samara looking for magical answers. Jinx wondered if he might be able to find out about his missing ability there. Because Simon had taken it away with magic, and now that Jinx thought about it, maybe his ability had been a kind of magic. Deep Urwald magic, Dame Glammer had called it.

He examined the stone wall again and again. It was not an illusion. It was a wall.

Simon went out into the Urwald frequently, for days at a time. Jinx never asked to go with him. Instead he made use of the time to search Simon's workroom and the rest of the house, looking for the green bottle. He didn't find it.

Jinx read Simon's books about magic, hoping to find out what Simon had done to him. The books weren't very helpful—they tried to hide as much as they revealed. They put things in strange terms so that you would have trouble figuring out what you were supposed to do.

There was a book in Samaran called *Knowledge Is Power.*

When Jinx opened it, it burst into flames, but he just used magic to absorb them. Then he took it out to the kitchen and read it while sitting on the stove.

It wasn't a very useful book, as far as Jinx could tell. It was just a bunch of spells that went like this:

An object may be concealed in plain view. One who knows that the object is there will find it, and one who does not will not.

The book was full of stuff like that. It didn't actually tell you how to do anything, it just told you that things *might* be done. Jinx read all the way through it—if only there was a way he could figure out what it meant! Maybe it could help him get to Samara.

Jinx burrowed his toes into the forest floor. His ability to understand the trees hadn't gone into the green bottle with Simon's spell. Jinx didn't know why. In fact, since he'd lost the ability to see people's thoughts, he seemed to hear the trees' thoughts more clearly than ever. He tried asking the trees what Simon had done to his magic, but they didn't hear him. They knew he was listening. They just didn't listen back.

It was summer and the trees were talking about that—about the rain and how well things rotted when the earth was warmer. And fear. The fear was something new, moving through the Urwald.

The trees weren't afraid of ogres, trolls, or dragons. They merely found them annoying. This had to be something much, much worse. It was moving from the west to the east—toward Simon's house, as near as Jinx could figure. The trees were unspecific. They didn't even try to describe the terrible creature. They just said *fear*.

Jinx pulled his toes out of the dirt and started home.

Something moved in the woods behind him. Jinx turned around. There was something hairy, walking on all fours. A werewolf, or a werebear? It slid out from behind a tree trunk. A werewolf. Jinx turned around to run, stepped into a hole, and fell.

He got to his feet as quickly and silently as he could. When he put his right foot on the ground, pain shot through it. His right ankle bulged oddly on one side. He took a step. It hurt. He took another step. The werewolf was about fifty yards away now, sniffing interestedly at the ground. It hadn't seen him, but it would pick up his scent in a second. As Jinx watched, it did. Its ears twitched. It snuffled eagerly toward the spot where Jinx had dug his feet into the ground.

Jinx concentrated on doing a concealment spell. He concentrated harder than he'd ever done in his life.

He looked down at his completely visible feet, one starting to swell to match his ankle. He tried again. *Concentrate!*

The werewolf was pawing now at the loose dirt where Jinx had buried his toes for listening. It was no good: Jinx couldn't do the spell. He'd never been able to do it. In his head he heard Simon say, *Of course you can't if you think you can't.*

Forget about can't, then. He *had* to do it, or he'd be dinner. He concentrated harder. *I'm not here, I'm not here.* He reached for the power that Simon said was within him.

And suddenly he found it. For the first time, he actually sensed the presence of power. He didn't know where it came from, but it was there. He pulled it into the concealment spell as hard as he could.

The werewolf's ears perked up and swiveled in Jinx's direction. It sniffed the air, then came straight toward Jinx. This one was closer to wolf-shape than to human-shape, and it moved on all fours. But its forelegs looked like arms, ending in hands with long yellow talons.

The werewolf crept closer. It was just a few feet from Jinx. It came closer still. Jinx had never been nearer to death. The werewolf put its nose to the ground at Jinx's feet and sniffed. It moved around him in a circle, sniffing and sniffing. Its nose almost touched Jinx's foot.

Then it sat up on its haunches and looked all around, confused. After what seemed like hours but was probably only a few seconds, it ran off with its tail between its legs.

It took Jinx over an hour to limp home. It should have been terrifying, being in the Urwald, off the path, and unable to run. But it wasn't. Jinx had power.

"Jinx, what happened?" Simon came hurrying across the clearing, looking worried.

"I did it!" Jinx told him. "I did a concealment spell."

"Knew you could." Simon helped him into the house. "What did you have to hide from?"

"A werewolf," said Jinx. "He sniffed all around my feet and couldn't tell I was there."

"Excellent." Simon smiled and looked like the old Simon for a moment. But he wasn't the old Simon, and Jinx wasn't the old Jinx, and there was always something tight and brittle in the way they spoke to each other. "Now put your foot up on a chair, and I'll get dinner."

While Simon cooked, Jinx tried to levitate a cat. No luck. It was as if he had no more power than he'd had before. But he knew he had more. He'd felt it. He'd done a concealment spell, and it had been a really strong one.

Knowledge is power. He thought about the book. All right, so he *knew* he could levitate a cat, then. He looked at a cat and concentrated. The cat scowled disdainfully at him and did not rise.

Later, when Simon was out milking the goats (for a change) and Jinx found he could walk around without his ankle hurting, Jinx went into Simon's workroom and poked around a little on the shelves over the workbench.

He saw the small leather-bound book called *Knowledge Is Power*.

He took it off the shelf and flipped through it. Those stupid spells, if that was what they were. *An object may be concealed in plain view. One who knows that the object is there will find it, and one who does not will not.* That was like the opposite of Simon saying *you can't if you think you can't.* It was—

Suddenly Jinx realized what the spell book meant.

He listened. No sound of Simon. Jinx stepped out of the workroom and into the hallway. He listened again. Silence. Armed with the confidence he'd gained from doing a concealment spell, Jinx turned and faced the blank wall at the end of the hallway.

Jinx had run his hands over the wall many times, feeling for a door, but his hands had encountered only smooth stone. Very well.

He *knew* there was a door here.

He put his hand out. It disappeared a few inches into the stone, which suddenly wasn't really there. He touched wood. He ran his fingers over the rugged surface to where he figured—no, he *knew*—there was a latch. He touched an iron handle. He pressed down with his thumb. The latch grated and creaked as it lifted. He pulled the door toward him. He could see it now. He walked through the doorway.

He was in a room lined with shelves and shelves of books—even more books than Simon had in his workroom. This room was not dusty—it had the feel of a room that was used often.

Jinx felt drawn to the books (after all, they must all be books that Simon didn't want him to read), but there was another door, and he wanted to find what lay beyond it.

He opened the door and coughed. This room was full of dust, a thick layer covering the floor and everything else. There was a soft thing like a bed, only with a back and arms like a chair, which he guessed was for sitting on. There was a table, and a jar with long-dead flowers in it.

There was a large, heavy door in the far wall, banded with iron. Whatever it kept in or out must be important. It would probably be locked. Jinx went to it and tried to lift the latch, but it wouldn't move.

There was no keyhole. Jinx searched for bolts going into the floor or the ceiling, but couldn't find any. There seemed to be nothing special about the latch, so some kind of spell, probably. Jinx tried his levitation spell, hoping to lift the iron latch an inch, but he didn't expect it to work and it didn't.

"Oh," he said aloud.

Of course! He *knew* the door would open.

He reached out, lifted the latch, and opened the door.

Instantly he closed his eyes against bright white sunlight. A blast of hot dry air hit him in the face. There was a smell of dust, but dust much drier and more free than the dust that made its way into the corners of Simon's house. The smell of the hot air stirred a memory. Sophie had smelled of this place sometimes, when she would first arrive. Samara. Painfully Jinx tried to open his eyes, a sliver at a time. He expected every instant to feel Simon's hand fall heavy on his shoulder, hauling him back into the house before he could go any farther.

Finally he was able to open his eyes.

He was not in the Urwald at all.

He couldn't see any trees. Only houses, the glaring yellow-white sky, and the yellow sandy earth.

He looked all around him. Not a single tree anywhere. The sky was vast and empty, and there was nothing to protect him from it.

He stepped out of the house. The sand was hot and uncomfortable on his feet, so he closed the door quickly and started walking fast. He wanted to find Sophie but, even more, he wanted to explore this new place and see if it held an answer to his missing magic.

He walked between two rows of flat square houses all stuck together, yellow like the sand. He looked back the way he'd come and saw a row of doors painted different colors. The door to Simon's house was blue-violet. He'd be able to find it again.

He stepped into the shadow of a house to cool his feet.

He was in a—all right, he had read the words for these things in books: a town. He was on a street.

He turned a corner and met a man completely dressed in chickens. The chickens were hanging by their feet, flapping and squawking, tied to two poles that the man carried balanced on his shoulders. The man cast Jinx an incurious glance—probably with that much squawking going on around you, you didn't notice other people much—but Jinx noticed the glance showed none of the fear with which strangers eyed each other in the Urwald. The man passed by in a ruffle of feathers and a whiff of chicken smell.

There were more streets, more corners to turn, more square houses with brightly painted doors. Jinx thought he had turned six times now, or maybe seven. People passed by, dressed in bright colors.

They didn't look like Urwald people. Oh, they looked like them in some ways—that is, their hair and eyes were all the colors and shapes that such things come in, and their skin was every color from pale pink to dark brown. But they didn't have the faces of Urwald people; they didn't look as if they expected something to jump out and eat them at any moment.

They also didn't look like magicians.

Jinx walked on. The houses around him were higher now, and there were flat stones underfoot, gritty with sand. He'd lost count of how many times he'd turned, and he wasn't quite sure which direction Simon's house was. It was hard to sense direction when there were no trees to use as landmarks. Sometimes people stepped on his feet. People here seemed used to bouncing off each other and moving on. Jinx was not. The presence of so many people was making him nervous, and the absence of trees didn't help. The sound of voices rattled in his ears. Everyone was speaking at once, talking over each other and shouting each other down. Nothing seemed particularly magical at all.

He came out into a huge stone-paved square. Still no trees, and no noticeable magic, but there was plenty to see. Blankets and rugs were spread out on the stones, and people had heaps of things displayed for sale. Jinx saw piles of strange spiny fruits, onions, barrels of rye and precious wheat. He smelled the rare spices that Simon had in his kitchen.

A great yellow-stone building dominated the square. He'd seen a picture of something like this in a book, but he couldn't remember the word for it. There were tall columns in front supporting a—portico, that was the word—at the top of wide stone steps. A temple, that's what it was. Fascinated, Jinx made his way toward it, getting pushed and knocked around and his feet trodden on a few more times.

There was a fence of high iron spears around the temple yard. The iron gate was open, and Jinx went through. Now he could see that on the portico were carved the words

KNOWLEDGE IS POWER

The words from the book of spells! And he'd heard Sophie say those words. He wondered if he would find her here. He hoped he would find out something about his magic. A few people were passing up or down the steps, in and out of the great open double doors of the temple. They were all dressed in robes like the one Sophie sometimes wore.

He felt sure she must be here. He crossed the stone-flagged courtyard. He tried to move the way the robed people did, swiftly and purposefully, but calmly. Even without the magic that Simon had taken away from him, he could still feel the calm. He imagined if he could have seen it, it would have been lavender and thick.

The fact that he could almost see the color of the feeling gave him new hope that he would find his magic here.

He went up the steps. A woman gave him a brief curious glance but then moved on, intent on her own business. Jinx tried to look intent on his.

Tall double doors stood wide open, and Jinx passed through. Inside the temple was a vast room. There were rows of long wooden workbenches and a hundred robed people sitting at them, writing. The only sound was the scratch of pens, and now and then the *hem* of a throat being cleared, gently so as not to disturb the calm.

Nobody looked up as Jinx passed down the great hall. He peered along the rows—none of these people was Sophie. He tried to see what they were writing. Some had books in front of them and were taking notes. Others were writing away in blank books. A row of tall windows marched down the far wall of the room, but none of the scribes lifted their eyes to look out. And none of them looked at Jinx.

Jinx wondered if these were the "them" he'd heard Simon and Sophie argue about. *You think I'm as bad as them,* Simon had said. And Sophie'd said, *They think innocence is so charming when it's on other people.*

There was a doorway at the other end of the temple, leading to sunlight and an open walkway beyond—Jinx could see more robes passing to and fro out there. He headed toward it, eager to find Sophie or someone who could tell him about his magic.

"What are you doing here, little boy?"

The voice rang through the stone silence like a dropped plate. The pens stopped scratching. A hundred pairs of eyes swiveled and fixed on Jinx.

He looked up at the tall woman standing in front of him. For just a moment he thought she was Sophie, although she was too tall and had too much gray hair, and Sophie had never looked so stern and frightening.

Jinx was *not* a little boy. Nonetheless, when he said, "I'm looking for Sophie," he sounded to himself like a little boy.

"Sophie who?" Her glare was making him *feel* little, and the hundred silent watchers didn't help.

The wizards mentioned in the magic books he'd read sometimes had two names. The second name was usually the same as Simon's. Perhaps Sophie's was too.

"Sophie Magus," he said.

There was a single gasp from a hundred mouths. Only the woman standing over Jinx didn't gasp.

"If someone is called Magus, you would *hardly* expect to find them *here*," she said.

Incredibly, a few of the scholars tittered.

Jinx was getting really annoyed with these people. He wondered how Sophie could stand them, actually. Jinx liked reading as much as the next person, but he liked knowing what was happening *outside* of books too. There was a whole bright fascinating world beyond the temple doors, and they were sitting in here with their backs to it! Jinx didn't think they deserved Sophie.

He also had to admit that nothing seemed the least bit magical about them. He thought of Sophie, who objected to magic even though she liked it. And Sophie came from this place, where KNOWLEDGE IS POWER was written over the door. But *Knowledge Is Power* was a book of spells. It didn't make sense.

There came the sound of raised voices from outside—shouts, argument, and then dozens of other voices joining in, loud and angry.

"What's that?" the woman demanded.

"Some sort of fuss in the market, Preceptress." A man stood up. "I'll shut the doors."

None of them rose to look—a fuss in the market didn't concern them. It wasn't in books, Jinx thought, as he turned to look out the door. A full-scale fight was going on, a mass of punching and kicking bodies that spread outward as he watched. Even the man who had gotten up to close the doors seemed curious for a moment and paused after he had shut one door—just as what Jinx could have sworn was a familiar figure stalked out of the mob toward the temple.

The man closed the other door, shutting in the calm quiet. He returned to his seat with a shake of his head for the futility of marketplace humanity.

"Why do you think you might find somebody in the Temple of Knowledge with such a name as Magus?" asked the Preceptress.

"Maybe that's not her name," said Jinx. He thought about what he had just seen moving out of the crowd. "Er, I should go."

Suddenly the double doors were thrown open with such force that they banged against the stone walls, making a louder noise than the hall had probably heard in a century. A hundred pairs of hands covered a hundred pairs of ears.

Simon was furious. Jinx took an involuntary step backward. He heard a sudden intake of breath, which wasn't quite a gasp, from the Preceptress, and she said sharply, "Go for the guards."

Jinx heard pattering feet behind him as two or three people took advantage of her order to get out of the room. Everyone else stayed seated.

"I just want the boy," said Simon.

The Preceptress gripped Jinx's shoulder, to his intense annoyance. Her hand felt like the claw of a large bird.

"You just opened those doors with *magic*." She made it sound dirty.

"I didn't break anything. Yet. Give me the boy."

"We certainly don't intend to let you harm an innocent child."

Simon surged down the aisle. The scribes drew back and pulled the hems of their robes close about them as he passed. "He's *my* boy."

He grabbed Jinx's arm, not hard enough to hurt but quite tightly. The Preceptress's fingers dug into Jinx's shoulder, and that did hurt. Neither of them was looking at Jinx: they were both staring each other down, their foreheads wrinkled, their eyebrows lowered, their eyes boring into each other. Jinx had a feeling they might rip him in two without even remembering he was there.

Jinx didn't much like Simon coming in and claiming Jinx was *his*, but he definitely wasn't the Preceptress's. On the whole he thought he was his own.

There was a heavy thud of footsteps from the covered walkway, and half a dozen men with swords in their hands clattered into the hall and stopped. They looked from the Preceptress to Simon and didn't seem to know what to do. Then expressions of alarm appeared on their faces, and Jinx realized Simon had frozen their clothes.

"Your guards can't hurt me," said Simon. "Let go of the boy and I'll take him and leave."

"You think you'll be allowed to leave?"

"If I don't leave, many people will regret it."

Simon sounded really menacing. The Preceptress's grip on Jinx's shoulder slackened just enough that Jinx was able to shrug, duck, and wrench himself free. He and Simon started running at the same moment. The guards came to life behind them—the clothes-freezing spell worked only if you could see the people you were freezing. Jinx and Simon cascaded down the steps and across the courtyard into the marketplace, where the brawl now seemed to involve everybody.

"Let go of me," Jinx panted.

Simon said nothing but ran around the edge of the crowd, and Jinx was yanked along after him, his feet managing to hit the ground about two steps out of every three. Shouts came from the edges of the fighting crowd—

"Simon! Simon Magus! I told you I saw him!"

"Faster!" said Simon.

The pounding feet of the guards were right behind them. Out of the corner of his eye Jinx saw people from the crowd running toward him and Simon—and a lot of the crowd was ahead of them. In another moment they would be surrounded.

Then Simon fell.

Jinx was too dumbfounded to do anything at first. Simon falling was as unthinkable as a mighty tree falling. More. Simon was vanishing under a pile of guards, and Jinx stood there. Simon had let go of Jinx's arm, but Jinx didn't run away. He couldn't, and leave Simon.

"Get me out of here, Jinx!"

The guards were in a helpless heap, their clothes frozen

again, their hands struggling to control the swords that flopped in their unsupported hands. It was a waving mass of swords. Then one by one the swords dropped to the ground as the guards' wrists gave out.

"They've killed him!" someone in the crowd yelled. "The wizard's dead!"

Jinx grabbed an immobilized guard and tried to haul him off of Simon. The man glared furiously at Jinx and tried to bite him. Hands in the pile tried to grab him. Jinx recognized Simon's long, thin hand amid the bodies, grabbed it, and pulled.

There was a lot of flailing, groaning, and kicking, and finally Jinx fell backward on the stones with Simon beside him. Simon was still staring at the guards, unblinking.

"There's people all around us, Simon," Jinx said, getting to his feet.

"They'd better stay back or I'll turn them into lizards!"

Simon lifted his head slightly so that his gaze included part of the crowd, and Jinx saw that their clothes had been frozen too. But he could hear the angry mutters of the people behind them, and when he turned around, he realized that Simon was dealing with only a quarter of the people surrounding them.

Looking back toward the Temple, Jinx could see the red-robed people on the porch, watching.

"Get ready to run," Simon said in Urwish. He stood

up slowly without breaking the gaze that held some of his enemies immobilized.

Jinx had never been more ready to run in his life.

He heard a clatter of hoofbeats, and in far less time than seemed possible after the sound, armored men on horses came pouring down a road into the square. The crowd scattered ahead of them. Simon grabbed Jinx's arm and ran straight toward the onrushing army.

Straight toward the horsemen? That was crazy! Jinx tried not to follow. He tried to drag his feet, but Simon kept pulling him onward, and Jinx didn't dare fall down for fear of the horses trampling him to death. Then the horses were around him and Simon. There was no smell of horseflesh and nothing touched them.

"Illusion," Jinx said aloud.

"Shut up and run," Simon panted.

They ran, and after a minute or two they heard running footsteps behind them. Simon's illusion of the horsemen hadn't lasted, or the crowd had realized it was an illusion. They turned down one street, and then another.

Jinx didn't recognize anything familiar about the street, but Simon ran up to a blue-violet door and opened it. Then they were inside, back in the dusty, unused sitting room, and Simon slammed the door shut and fell against it, and they both stood gasping for breath.

Matters of Life and Death

Jinx recovered his breath first. "What was—"

"*You idiot!*" Simon was still leaning against the door. "How did you—how did you—" He was too out of breath to continue.

"I'm not an idiot," said Jinx. "That was the place Sophie comes from. Samara. Where *was* it?"

He knew it was through the door. But now they were back in Simon's house, which was in the Urwald, which Samara most definitely was not.

"Go. Into the house." Simon spoke through clenched teeth.

"Can I look at these books?"

Simon didn't answer, and Jinx decided not to press the point.

He came to the blank wall, reached out for the door, and opened it.

"How did you do that?" Simon demanded behind him. His tight-sounding voice scared Jinx.

"I know it's there," said Jinx.

Simon didn't answer, and Jinx walked fast to the kitchen, wanting to get away. Simon hardly ever got really angry at Jinx, not like this. Usually he was just cranky.

Out in the kitchen, Jinx was headed straight for the front door when Simon said, "Jinx, come here."

Something in his voice didn't sound right. Jinx stopped and turned around. Simon was sitting on the stove steps.

"Take a look at this and tell me how bad it is," Simon said.

Jinx had a sudden cold wave of dread, as if he'd just swallowed ice. There was a steady line of dark-red drips along the floor from the passageway to the step where Simon sat. Jinx went over to Simon, who was trying to point to a spot on his back just below his shoulder. Reluctantly, fearing what he would see, Jinx looked. There was a spreading stain on the back of Simon's purple robe.

"I—can't tell. You'll have to take it off," said Jinx. His voice sounded as loud and strange as it had inside the

Temple of Knowledge. Reality seemed to have been sucked out of the room.

"Pull this sleeve for me."

Jinx pulled on the sleeve, helping Simon out of the top of his robe. The shirt he wore underneath it was drenched with blood.

"I—I guess I should cut your shirt off," said Jinx.

"Press that sleeve against the wound first. See if you can stop the bleeding."

Jinx wadded up a sleeve of the purple robe and pressed it against where he thought the blood was coming from, right under Simon's left shoulder blade. Jinx had seen pictures of the insides of people in one of Simon's books. Did wizards have hearts in the same place as normal people?

"Press harder," said Simon.

Jinx did. Blood was soaking through onto his hand. He wanted to go back to the beginning of today and start over and have it all go differently.

"You said those guards couldn't hurt you."

"Lied," said Simon succinctly.

"Simon!"

Jinx was enormously glad to hear that voice.

Sophie burst into the kitchen, a wave of fury. "What on earth were you thinking of, coming to Samara! Are you insane?"

Her fists were clenched. She looked ready to hit

somebody, and Jinx wasn't about to tell her that Simon had gone to Samara looking for him.

"Stirring up the Temple, stirring up the populace—it's lucky no one was killed!"

Sophie's raging seemed to draw reality down into the room again. Jinx was relieved to have it back. Simon's face was getting paler, and the look he was giving his wife was a funny one. Jinx had no idea what he was thinking.

"I—I think Simon might've gotten killed," Jinx said.

"What?"

"He's—" Jinx nodded at his hand, which was still pressed as hard as he could against the seeping blood.

Sophie pushed aside the bloody sleeve, Jinx's hand, and Jinx with the same motion. "Get some dittany, Jinx. And boil some water."

Jinx ran to the workroom to find the herb. Then he pumped water into a kettle, swung it over the fire, and used the bellows to puff the fire to life. After that he ran for other things Sophie wanted—a white sheet, and more herbs, and then a needle and thread, which he was supposed to boil. Then he spread a blanket on the floor and helped Sophie help Simon to lie facedown on it.

Sophie ripped the bloody shirt down the back. The blood had stopped pouring and was only welling up slowly now, from a jagged purple cut. Jinx felt sick.

"Bring me more candles," said Sophie. "And get these

cats out of here."

Jinx found all the candles he could and set them burning around Simon, stuck into bottles and candlesticks. It looked too much like a funeral, especially since Simon's eyes were closed and he'd stopped talking. Sophie was doing something with wet cloths and dittany, but Jinx couldn't stand to look. He gathered up armloads of cats and dumped them in both wings of the house, closing the doors on them and locking the cat flaps.

"What should I do now?" Jinx asked.

"Go away," said Sophie, not looking up.

It had to be very bad for Sophie to speak to Jinx like that. He went, wanting to help but not knowing how.

He went through the door into Simon's part of the house. He looked at the wall that was really a door into Samara. Then he went into the workroom. The *Knowledge Is Power* book was lying open on the workbench. Jinx must have left it there. That was how Simon had known to follow him. Jinx slammed the book shut and stuck it among the other books on the shelf, shoving it as far back as he could. He wished he'd never seen it.

Except that he was glad he'd been to Samara. Even though he hadn't found his magic there, the world was much bigger now than it had been. He wanted to go back, to explore it some more. He walked back to the hidden door. There was a bloodstain on the floor, half covered by the stone wall. Jinx reached through the stone and touched the door.

He went back into the workroom and started putting away the things he'd disturbed while he was fetching herbs for Sophie.

The door to the kitchen creaked; there were footsteps in the hall. "Jinx?"

Sophie came into the room.

"Oh, there you are," she said.

Her hands were covered with dried blood. She looked exhausted. Jinx waited for her to tell him.

"What happened, Jinx?"

"Is he dead?"

"No," said Sophie. She went over to Simon's stool and sat down. "No. If he has a heart, they missed it."

"So he's going to be all right?"

"I don't know. There are"—she paused and shook her head—"a lot of things that can happen. If only we could take him back to Samara. There are physicians there—"

"Can't we bring them here?"

"No," said Sophie. Her voice shook, and Jinx had a horrible feeling that she was going to cry, which he wanted to see even less than he had wanted to see all that blood.

"I'll get you something to drink," said Jinx, getting out of there.

When he came back with a mug of cider and a wet towel for her hands, she had gotten control of herself. Jinx was relieved. She wiped her hands clean and drank the cider. After that she looked a little better.

"What happened today?" Sophie asked again.

"Oh. Er, what did Simon say happened?"

"He didn't say anything, Jinx. He's unconscious."

"We—well, we went to the Temple and then the guards chased us, and he fell down and got stabbed, and then we ran back here."

"Why on earth would Simon take you to Samara?"

"Well, he didn't. I sort of went. Where is Samara?" he asked, to change the subject.

"You answer my questions, and I may answer yours. How did you get to Samara?"

Jinx was reminded that he had once been able to actually see the iron behind Sophie's niceness. "I found the door. Knowledge is power."

"I see. Simon didn't tell you how to get there?"

"No, I found the book that tells how."

"And what did you do in Samara? Where did you go?"

Jinx told her. He remembered the noise and chatter. He would've liked to talk to some of those people in the streets. They were all so unlike Urwald people, so much quicker and less frightened.

"And Simon came straight to the University? He didn't go anywhere else?"

"No," said Jinx. Actually, he realized, he didn't know.

"What is Knowledge Is Power? Is it a kind of magic?"

"KnIP is Samaran magic."

Kanip? Oh . . . Knowledge Is Power. "But they don't do it at that temple place, do they?" It hadn't felt magical at all.

"No, of course not. Magic is no longer permitted in Samara."

"Is that why those guards chased Simon?" Jinx asked. Sophie nodded.

"But why is it not permitted?"

"Because of the things people use magic for, of course. Wizards control people. They care more about power than about people. To them, people are just a way to get more power." Sophie said this with considerable vigor, and Jinx could tell she really believed it.

"We study magic in theory at the University," she said. "Magic among many other things. But to actually *do* it—that's against the law. The penalty is death."

"But you do it when you come through the door into the Urwald," Jinx said.

"I certainly don't. I simply come through the door. It's not my fault that the door happens to be magic."

"You have to use magic to work it," said Jinx.

"The KnIP spell was done when the door was created," said Sophie. "Now it's just a door."

Jinx was sure she was wrong about this. But the tired

look on Sophie's face stopped him from arguing.

"There are still magicians in Samara," Sophie added. "People who do KnIP. But they're criminals. Every now and then the government catches one and makes an example of him. Or her."

Jinx would have liked to ask what they did to the magicians, but he looked at Sophie and decided that wouldn't be a good idea.

"Magic corrupts people," said Sophie. "Look what it's done to Simon."

"Wasn't he always sort of like that, though?" said Jinx.

Sophie looked surprised. "Like what?"

Jinx couldn't think how to answer this. "So you're one of those people at that temple place? One of the scholars?"

"Yes. I'm a professor of Urwald Studies." She smiled. "I'd studied Urwish for years, but until Simon came along, I'd never met anyone who actually spoke it."

She got to her feet. "I'd better go check on him."

"But you're not like them," said Jinx.

Sophie looked surprised. "Not like who?"

"Those scholars, all sitting inside and studying their books and not really wanting to *know* anything." He picked up the candle and followed her out.

"They're not all like that. They do want to know things, it's just that it's . . ." She turned and looked at the wall that hid Samara. The candle made a yellow circle of light on it. "I don't want you to go back there, Jinx. Promise me."

"It's just that it's what?" said Jinx. "What were you going to say?"

"It's hard to learn anything when you already know everything." Sophie smiled. "That's the problem with the scholars. Some of them."

"Oh," said Jinx. He turned to go into the kitchen, but Sophie caught his arm. "You didn't promise."

Jinx wanted to ask why he had to promise. But she was looking at him so hard that he found all he could say was "Yeah."

"Say it, please," said Sophie, with iron.

"I promise," said Jinx. And then, seeing that this still wasn't good enough, "That I won't go back into Samara."

It was like a door slamming shut on the wide world. He followed her into the kitchen, feeling trapped.

Simon was still alive. Seeing him unconscious on top of the cold stove gave Jinx a funny feeling in his stomach, as if the world had been turned upside down. What if Simon died?

"I'll sit up with him," said Sophie. "You'd better go to bed."

Jinx thought he ought to offer to sit up instead. But what if Simon started bleeding again? Or stopped breathing? Jinx wouldn't know what to do. So he went up to his room, the one he never slept in, and sat down on the bed. A puff of dust rose from it. The stone walls reminded him of a tomb. Simon would die someday, even if it wasn't today. Everybody dies. That's the most unfair thing in the world. *Jinx* would die someday. The thought made him stand up and leave the room.

He climbed up the winding stone steps to the Farseeing Window. The sky was getting light already. The view from the window sailed through a tangle of tree branches. Jinx saw a wolf skulking along the ground beneath.

The thing was, he didn't hate Simon. He couldn't even really stay angry at him. He'd meant to, but Simon was . . . well, always there. It was hard to stay angry at someone who was always there. The truth was, he was actually sort of fond of Simon.

Jinx imagined life without Simon. Would he be allowed to stay in Simon's house? But he wouldn't want to stay here, alone with the cats. And he didn't think Sophie would come here to stay with him. Would she take Jinx back to Samara? Jinx wanted to see more of Samara, he really did. He was angry at Sophie for making him promise he wouldn't try to go back. But to live there, with the hot sun and no proper trees? And, face it, no magic?

The scene in the Farseeing Window shifted to a party of trolls, running along a wide path. The Troll-way—Jinx had heard Wanderers mention it. It led up into the Glass

Mountains. Jinx had never seen mountains. There was a lot in the Urwald that he'd never seen. Well, if he couldn't go back to Samara, at least he could see more of the world.

And maybe somewhere out there, there was a way to find out what Simon had done to him, what he'd taken away from him. What Dame Glammer had called mind-reading and deep Urwald magic.

Somehow there must be a way to get it back. And if anyone besides Simon would know it, Jinx realized, it would probably be Dame Glammer. After all, Dame Glammer had sold Simon the roots.

The scene moved again. Now it showed a girl walking along the Path. Jinx leaned forward. It was his girl, the one in the red cape and hood. She had a basket over her arm and a pack on her back. She was starting out on a journey. Jinx could tell from the way she walked that she was more excited than she was scared—that she couldn't wait to discover the things that lay ahead of her.

"I wish I could be walking in the Urwald with nothing to hold me back," said Jinx.

"You can if you want to," said the girl, in his head.

And he realized she was right.

A Quarrel

Simon was alive, awake, and querulous. Jinx had scrubbed all the blood off the floor. He tried to stay out of the kitchen because Simon was making it seem a lot smaller these days. He went out into the Urwald, dug his toes into the ground, and listened.

The thing the trees were afraid of was much closer than it had been. Jinx tried thinking a question—What is it? Is it the Bonemaster? But the trees didn't answer.

He went inside. Sophie was sitting on the stove, not too close to Simon. They were surrounded by books. One book was open to a drawing of what your insides looked like after a sword was stuck into them.

"I ought to go back to Samara," she said.

"Please don't," said Simon.

Jinx hoped she wouldn't. He was planning to leave, not stay here taking care of Simon.

"They'll notice I'm missing, and how will that look?"

"What do you care how it looks?" said Simon.

Jinx looked at them looking at each other. Before the bottle spell, he would have known exactly how they felt. Now he didn't, and it looked like they didn't either.

"Let me put these books away," said Sophie. She gathered them up and went down the hall and through the wall into the hidden part of the house.

Jinx went over to the stove. Simon was lying just about at Jinx's eye level.

"You should tell her you're sorry," said Jinx.

"Thank you for your so helpful advice," said Simon. "I've told her six times. You should tell *me* you're sorry."

"For what?" Jinx had put up with too much to listen to this. In fact, he had had enough—enough of being told what to do and called an idiot and of having his magic taken away and *everything*. "I didn't ask you to come after me! I wasn't in any trouble till you came along."

"Oh, you could have found your way back to my house, could you?"

"Probably! And who said I wanted to come back? I don't have to live here! I don't have to hang around here doing all your work for you and getting spells put on me."

"I'm teaching you magic, which most people would give their eyeteeth to learn."

"You took *away* my magic! And that was a lot worse than taking my eyeteeth, whatever they are. You took it away and didn't even ask me!" Jinx flung away from the stove and began walking around in rapid circles. His insides were itchy with anger and he couldn't stay still.

"Hush! I didn't take your magic. And don't tell Sophie that."

"Don't worry!" Jinx yelled. "That's why you sent her away, because you knew she wouldn't like it, and if I tell her now, then she'll leave again and I'll have to take care of you."

"Tell her what?" Sophie came into the kitchen.

Jinx stared at her, trying to think what to say.

"Tell the truth, it saves time," said Sophie.

"The boy is mad because I don't pay him," Simon said. "So I'll pay him."

"That's not why I'm mad! That's not what I want!" Jinx looked around for something to kick and decided on the stone wall of the stove. He hurt his foot and didn't care. He started walking in circles again.

"What *do* you want then?" said Sophie. "You ought to pay him, Simon. I always said so. You can't go buying people for a penny—"

"He didn't buy me for a penny!" said Jinx. "He never gave anyone a penny for me. He *offered* Bergthold a penny and then he summoned trolls to come and get him."

Sophie gave Simon a sharp frowning look. "So you did kill him."

"I didn't summon the trolls. The stepfather summoned them."

"He couldn't have!" said Jinx. "He didn't know any magic!"

"Greedy, violent people attract trolls as naturally as blood attracts wolves. They smelled your stepfather, I assume."

Jinx had never heard of that before. He wondered if it was true. You couldn't trust Simon was the thing. Jinx went on walking in furious circles.

"Anyway, he'd taken you into the woods to abandon you, so let's not shed too many tears," said Simon.

"I wasn't shedding tears! I just thought you should tell Sophie the truth."

"Jinx, stop it. You're making me dizzy," said Sophie.

Jinx stopped pacing and stood with his arms folded, glaring at Simon.

"You've been under a lot of strain, Jinx," said Sophie.

"*He's* been under a lot of strain?" said Simon.

"Well I hope you don't think *you* have!" said Sophie. "Because all you've had to do is lie there—"

"Trying not to die from being stabbed by the people you insist on working for even though they've sentenced me to death!" Simon heaved himself up into a sitting position and rocked unsteadily.

"It's not my fault you broke our laws, is it? And I do have a job, you know!"

They were yelling. Their voices rang off the stone walls—the cats had all fled.

"I would have put you before any job, if it had been me!" Simon shouted. "Especially a job working for people who had sentenced you to death. But apparently not everyone thinks that way."

"The court sentenced you. It had nothing to do with the Temple of Knowledge."

"The Temple of Knowledge owns the courts and everything else in Samara. Bought and paid for, everything and everybody. Including you, it seems."

"I don't have to stay here and listen to this!" Sophie turned angrily toward the hallway that led to Samara.

"Yes, you do!" said Jinx, grabbing her arm. "Simon, stop making her mad!"

"I didn't make her mad, you made her mad."

"Jinx, let go of me."

"You have to stay and take care of him."

"I'm not sure he's worth taking care of."

"He was really sorry about the stuff he said to you

that time," said Jinx. "He stares at the wall all the time, all right? He didn't want you to leave."

"Jinx, I don't think you know what you're talking about," said Sophie.

"I do. I saw it in his head, all right? I could tell what he was thinking."

"Oh, Jinx. Don't be ridiculous."

"I'm not being ridiculous! You don't believe me either! He took my magic away and he never believed I had it and neither do you!"

Sophie frowned. "What do you mean, he took away your magic?"

"Jinx, shut up. I didn't take anything."

"No, I want to hear this," said Sophie.

"He doesn't know what he's talking about! Don't listen to him!"

"I do too know what I'm talking about!" Jinx was yelling now. "You got those roots from Dame Glammer on purpose so you could do the spell on me! And she said it couldn't be for any good purpose! And you drew all those symbols on the floor and did the spell on me, and I floated up to the ceiling, and then you took away my magic and put it in a bottle, and that's why you sent Sophie away, because you knew she wouldn't let you, and now you're lying about it."

In the ringing silence that followed this, Jinx realized

that once you've said things, it's impossible to unsay them.

Sophie turned to Simon. "You what?"

"It wasn't what it sounds like."

"That's it. I'm leaving," said Sophie.

"Are you even going to listen to my side of it?" Simon demanded.

"No, I've done quite enough of that in my life already."

"You can't leave!" Jinx said. "I don't know how to take care of him, and he'll die."

"Well, then he won't be able to do spells on innocent little children and murder their stepfathers," said Sophie.

"I'm not an innocent little child," said Jinx. "And my stepfather actually kind of beat and starved me a whole lot."

"But that's not as bad as doing *magic*," said Simon.

"You can't go, Sophie, you can't let him die, if you do you'll be just as bad as he is," said Jinx.

"Oh thanks," said Simon.

"You haven't reformed at all, have you, Simon?" said Sophie. "You did deathforce magic on the boy."

"I never do deathforce magic!" said Simon. "If you knew anything at all about magic, which you refuse to—"

"What's deathforce magic?" said Jinx.

"—you'd know deathforce magic when you saw it. And anyway, I did it to keep him safe," said Simon.

"To hear you tell it, you've never done anything for a

bad reason," said Sophie.

"What's deathforce magic?" Jinx repeated, with a feeling of rising panic.

"It's magic that uses a human life," said Sophie, glaring at Simon.

"Well, I'm not dead!" said Jinx. "So he can't have done deathforce magic on me."

"The boy's even taking your side," said Sophie. "I suppose that's because of a mind-control spell."

"There's no such thing," said Simon. "He's taking my side because I'm right."

"I'm not taking his side!" said Jinx. "He took my magic. I told you. And I want it back. And I'm going out into the Urwald and find it!"

"You can't go into the Urwald," said Sophie.

"He can if he wants," said Simon. "So go, then, boy."

"Simon! You can't let him. It's too dangerous."

"*Life* is dangerous," said Simon. "Young people need to see the world."

"There are all sorts of monsters out there," said Sophie. "He could be killed."

"He knows how to conceal himself very effectively." Simon lay back down. "And he knows the forest; he's not afraid of it, not like most people are. He has some crazy idea that the trees talk to him."

"I can't believe you'd let him go!"

"I have to, don't I? He's not my slave," said Simon. "If he doesn't appreciate what he's got, let him leave."

"Maybe he wants to go back to his people," said Sophie.

"I don't want to go back to them," said Jinx. "I want to get my magic back."

"Where is his clearing?" said Sophie.

"I don't know," said Simon. "By the time I found him, he was already lost."

"You must have made inquiries," said Sophie. "I know you—you always find things out."

"It's called Gooseberry Clearing," Simon admitted. "West of here, a day's journey. It's not very big, and they had a bad bout of winter plague and werewolves a couple years ago."

"What! You just left them to die?"

"Why not? They'd left Jinx to die," said Simon. "Besides, they're not my responsibility."

"No, nothing is, is it?"

"Anyway, they didn't all die," said Simon. He was watching Sophie's face carefully. "I sent some rye and potatoes after they started starving."

"You're an extremely strange person," said Sophie.

"Are you going to give my magic back, then?" said Jinx.

"I don't have your magic," said Simon. "Haven't I explained this to you before? Magic is something you do, not something you have."

"Then I'm leaving," said Jinx.

"So good riddance," said Simon.

"Simon!" said Sophie. "You don't mean that."

"What, now I can't say things I don't mean?"

Jinx refused to let them distract each other from him. "It was deep Urwald magic," he said. "Dame Glammer said so. And I'm going to go into the Urwald and find it."

Simon looked startled. "Don't go near Dame Glammer. You can go where you want, but stay away from her."

Jinx didn't bother to answer that. Dame Glammer could tell him what had happened to his magic.

"And stay away from the Bonemaster, too," said Simon.

But Jinx had no intention of going anywhere near the Bonemaster. Why would he? He was going to Dame Glammer.

The Truce of the Path

The next day, which was drizzly, Jinx set out into the world to seek his fortune.

He had a knife at his belt and a pack with a blanket and some food in it. He'd been hugged by Sophie and glowered at by Simon. Well, let him glower. Simon wasn't about to die, and Jinx was relieved about that, but he was pretty disgusted with the wizard on the whole. The feeling seemed to be mutual.

Tucked into a hidden pocket inside his tunic Jinx had the gold bird talisman Simon had made him—Simon had insisted he take it—and five silver pennies. In his outside pocket he had four farthings that he'd made by chopping up another penny. It was tricky splitting the pennies in exactly the right place. But Jinx was pretty good with an ax—he'd been chopping firewood for years.

"I *told* you I was going to pay him," Simon had said, ostentatiously counting out the six pennies in front of Sophie. "Six pennies for six years. Good enough?"

Since Sophie didn't say anything, Jinx figured it must be good enough.

He followed the path. It joined another path. Jinx stopped. To the west lay the thing the trees were so afraid of. Jinx didn't much want to run into it. But Dame Glammer's house was that way too. Jinx turned to the right and headed west.

Jinx had been in the forest a lot, and he had left the path, and he had learned not to be afraid of the dark unknown. When he had had Simon's house to run back to. Now he didn't. There was an exhilarating thrill to being on a journey of his own, but it was scary, too.

He reminded himself that he could do a very strong concealment spell. Or at least had done one, once.

The trees hung heavy overhead, and Jinx imagined things lurking in the branches—werewolves. Could werewolves climb trees? The human part of them probably could. And there might be elves, vampires—

Resolutely he thought of the Truce of the Path. Nothing could attack him as long as he stayed on the path.

He tried to recapture the elusive joy of freedom.

Bam! Something hit him hard on the back, and he was lying flat on the path, his face pressed down so that he tasted dirt. He struggled against the hand pressed into the back of his skull, then stopped when he felt cold steel biting into his neck.

"Let me go!" he said.

"Your money or your life!"

"Okay, you can have my money," said Jinx, with some difficulty because the robber was kneeling on Jinx's back, and Jinx's mouth was full of gritty dirt from the path. "Let me up so I can get it."

"Where is it?" said the robber suspiciously.

"In my pocket, on my belt."

The robber seized Jinx's belt and pulled the pocket around to the back. Jinx felt him unbutton the pocket and reach inside.

"Is this all you've got?"

"Yes! And I worked a year for it. Let me up!"

The weight was off Jinx's back. Jinx stood up, turned around, and faced a boy about a head taller than he was. Jinx hadn't even been robbed by a full-grown robber!

"Haven't you ever heard of the Truce of the Path?" Jinx demanded.

"No," said the boy, tucking Jinx's money into his own belt pocket and buttoning it. He sheathed his knife.

Jinx punched him in the stomach.

The robber doubled over in pain. Jinx grabbed the robber's head, but the robber stood up, catching Jinx with his shoulder, and threw him. The ground came up and hit Jinx so hard, it felt as if it had passed right through him. He lay flat on his back and wondered if he would ever be able to breathe again. The robber plainly knew more about fighting than Jinx did. Jinx decided to stay where he was.

The robber clutched his stomach and uttered a foul word.

"Same to you," said Jinx, getting his breath back at last. "At least I didn't break the Truce of the Path."

Well, actually he had, but the robber had broken it first.

"What is this Truce of the Path of which you speak?" the robber asked.

He had a clipped, formal manner of speech that reminded Jinx of Sophie. But he didn't seem to have as much trouble with the sounds of Urwish as Sophie did.

"You're not from the Urwald, are you?" said Jinx, sitting up painfully.

"No, thank the gods. But my king owns it."

"Nobody owns the Urwald," said Jinx. He got to his feet. He brushed off his coat and his breeches. He noticed that the robber was well dressed—at least by Urwald standards. You could afford to be if you were a robber, probably. The robber had a whole penny of the six Simon had given Jinx. A whole year of cleaning Simon's house, splitting firewood, mucking out the goats, and putting up with Simon's moods. It made Jinx angry.

"The Truce of the Path," he told the robber, "is that you can't harm anyone while they're on the path. Every thinking creature in the Urwald obeys it. Even monsters obey it. If a werebear jumped out of the woods right now, it wouldn't hurt us. Everybody honors the truce. Only you"—he jabbed the robber angrily in the chest—"don't."

The robber took a step backward. "I didn't know about it."

"Then you're an idiot."

The robber looked hurt. "That wasn't very nice."

"Neither is jumping on people's backs and stealing from them! Idiot." Jinx turned and walked away.

A moment later he heard footsteps trotting behind him, and he spun around to face the robber again.

"My name is Reven," said the robber, extending a hand.

Jinx stared at the hand and then at the robber. He had light brown hair and a thin face, and Jinx thought that the robber would not grow up to be the kind of thick, hairy man that survived best in the Urwald.

"And whom do I have the honor of addressing?" the robber asked, putting his hand down again.

"Jinx."

"Do you mind if I walk with you for a while?" said Reven.

Jinx looked at him in disbelief. Quite aside from the fact that Reven had just robbed him, Jinx still had five pennies sewn inside his clothes and Simon's gold talisman. And he had more important things, like his blanket and his knife (he'd never thought of using the knife when he fought Reven), which he didn't want to have stolen.

"I suppose I can't stop you," said Jinx, and turned around and walked on, with the robber beside him.

Three Spells Too Many

The path had wound and split a couple of times, and Jinx wasn't sure if he was still headed toward Dame Glammer's house. It was getting dark.

"We should stop soon and make camp for the night," Reven said.

So you can steal the rest of my money? Jinx just stopped himself from saying this—no point in admitting he had more money.

"I usually camp just off the path and cut a few pine boughs for a shelter," Reven said.

"You *what?*" Jinx had to stop and stare at this latest declaration of idiocy.

Reven repeated himself. "I make quite good shelters. Want me to show you how?"

"No. You don't ever, ever cut anything off a living tree." Jinx sounded to himself like Simon, scolding. "Never."

"Why? Are they holy or something?"

"No. They'll take revenge. You kill a tree, the trees kill a person. You cut off limbs—so do they. Or anyway, they make sure limbs get lost."

"That's crazy. I've been in the Urwald"—Reven paused to count—"ten nights, and I haven't lost any limbs yet."

"*You* haven't. But somebody has. Or will."

Reven shook his head. "Superstition. Why do you keep staring up into the trees?"

"I'm looking for a tree house," said Jinx. But he didn't see any, and that meant he was going to have to camp out. He hoped it wouldn't start raining again.

"I stayed a couple of nights in clearings," said Reven. He wrinkled up his nose in disgust. "They expect you to pay money to eat their rotten, wormy food and sleep in the straw in their smelly houses. And to be surrounded by ignorant, suspicious, inbred—"

"We are not!" Jinx snapped. "Take that back."

"No offense intended." Reven sounded surprised. "I can see you're not one of them."

"I am too one of them," said Jinx. "There aren't any tree houses. We're going to have to stop here."

He found a stick and lit the end of it. The magic was much easier outdoors than it had been in Simon's house. "Here. Go gather some firewood—*dead* wood—but don't go too far, and don't you dare touch a living tree!"

Reven just stared at Jinx, looking suddenly frightened. "How did you do that?"

"Do what?"

"Make that fire. Are you some kind of magician or something?"

"Yes."

They heard a scream. A girl's voice, panicky and cut off suddenly.

"A damsel in distress!" Reven grabbed the torch out of Jinx's hand and took off running down the path.

Jinx looked at the vanishing light, sighed, and ran after him. When he caught up to him this is what he saw.

The darkness was a seething mass of wolves. There was no sign of the girl who had screamed, but Reven was in the midst of the wolves, surrounded. He was waving his torch at them and yelling "Back, beasts! Aroint thee!" Something large and gray with wings—several somethings—formed a flapping mass attacking a huge creature that Jinx couldn't see clearly. The air was full of howls and barks and grunts, and smelled of blood and filthy fur.

"Jinx! To me!" cried Reven.

Jinx looked around frantically for something else to

make into a torch. He saw a dead branch sticking out of a tree and, thinking an apology as loudly as he could, broke it off and set the end on fire. Then he swung the blazing, crackling torch at the wolves, trying to get to Reven, who he couldn't help thinking didn't really deserve Jinx's help.

The wolves pressed close but stayed out of the way of the flames, and Jinx made his way to Reven. They stood back to back, surrounded by wolves.

"Okay, I'm to you. Now what?" Jinx tried to sound as sarcastic as Simon would have in the circumstances.

"Perhaps if we moved forward, swinging our torches—"

"They would move backward, and then when we were far enough apart, they'd move in between, and I wouldn't be 'to you' anymore."

"Er. Right. Well, you can set things on fire by magic?"

"Obviously."

"Then can you set the wolves on fire?"

"No!" said Jinx. "I mean, yeah, I could, but that would be really cruel."

Reven made an exasperated noise. "Well, if you don't, they're going to be really cruel to us, I swan."

Jinx considered the idea briefly. He imagined the wolves running away from the fire, but they wouldn't be able to get away no matter how hard they ran. He imagined the smell of burning fur and flesh and—no. And they would set the trees on fire. And the Urwald would not forgive that.

"Can't do it. Think of something else."

"Excuse me, I have an idea."

It was a girl's voice. Jinx looked all around.

"Up here." The voice came from one of the trees. "I had some furies in my basket, and as soon as they're done attacking that werebear over there, they *might* drive the wolves away."

"Er," said Jinx. It didn't sound like much of a plan. He looked at the wolves all around him, their eyes glowing in the torchlight. The torch in his hand crackled and spat sparks. These torches were not going to last forever.

"Fear not, fair maiden! We shall save you," said Reven.

"Shut up. She's talking about saving *us*," said Jinx. He called up to the girl. "Can you tell the furies to chase the wolves away, then?"

"Nope. Furies won't listen to anyone. Hang on."

There was a sound of climbing overhead. The wolves growled.

"Ow! My torch has gone out. Have you got another?" said Reven.

"I'll just run and get one, shall I?" said Jinx. There was not an inch-wide opening in the ring of wolves. "Here, let me relight that one."

"There's nothing to relight. It burned down to my fingers and I—oof!"

Something heavy landed on them from above. Jinx fell

to his knees and dropped his torch, which went out. Then the air was alive with wolves and great wings flapping, and there were howls and groans and screams and screeches and more smells of blood and terror. Jinx stayed huddled on the ground with his head down and his eyes closed.

"I think it's over," said the girl, right beside him.

Jinx opened his eyes. He couldn't see much, but in the moonlight he could make out the forms of Reven and the girl. And no wolves.

"They're gone," said the girl. "I *thought* that would work. The furies were charged to protect me, so if I was in danger from the wolves along with you—well, I thought it might work," she finished proudly.

Jinx felt around for his torch, found it, and lit it again.

He looked at the girl in surprise. Her cape and hood glowed red in the torchlight—this was the same girl he'd seen in the Farseeing Window. But up close, she didn't look quite like he'd imagined her. Her hair was not noticeably golden—it was the color called dirty blond. Or maybe it was just dirty. Certainly it was lacking in the curl department, and her eyes were brown instead of blue.

"My mother gave me the furies. She said to open them only in an emergency. Well, they're gone now. My name is Elfwyn."

Reven took her hand and bowed over it. "And I am Reven, your faithful servant, fair maiden."

Elfwyn beamed at Reven.

"He's a robber," said Jinx.

"And this is my stout companion, Jinx," said Reven.

"I'm one of the people he's robbed," said Jinx. "We'd better build a fire before those wolves come back."

They gathered deadwood and built a large blaze in the middle of the path. Jinx took off his boots and socks, stepped just off the path, and dug his toes into the humus.

"What are you doing?" said Elfwyn.

Jinx said nothing for a minute, concentrating. He had never tried to tell the trees anything before, and he wasn't exactly sure how to do it.

"You should put your socks on, at least. You'll catch your death," Elfwyn said.

"I'm trying to tell the trees we don't mean any harm building a fire and that we'll put it out when we leave," said Jinx. "And your babbling doesn't help."

Elfwyn shut up, and Jinx focused on trying to think like a tree, feel the world like a tree, and talk like a tree. He felt the hum of the nearby roots murmuring to each other. His eyes flew open in surprise.

The fear, the terror that the trees had—whatever it was they were afraid of—it was no longer approaching from the west. It had arrived.

Where? Jinx thought frantically at the trees. What?

He didn't know if the trees heard him or not, but

it was all they could talk about. Fear, terror, death. A horrible creature—it was here.

"You can come and eat, even though you're not very nice," said Elfwyn.

Jinx was very hungry. He moved toward them. Then he stopped and looked up into the trees. No good—he couldn't see anything in the dark.

We're safe as long as we stay on the path, he thought.

"Aren't you going to eat?" Reven held a loaf of bread up, offering it to Jinx.

"Yes," said Jinx.

He tore a piece off the loaf and chewed, still looking all around him.

"Don't you want any stewed apples?"

Elfwyn had cooked them in a little pot that she'd had in her pack. She spooned some onto Jinx's bread.

"Thank you," said Jinx, lest Elfwyn accuse him of not being nice again. He was, too, nice. *She* was the one who was nowhere near as sweet and respectful as he'd imagined her. "The trees are afraid of something," he said. "There's some kind of monster out there."

"How do you know?" said Elfwyn.

He explained about the trees talking through their roots.

"You can understand trees?" said Elfwyn.

"He's some kind of magician," said Reven.

"Like a wizard?" Elfwyn at least looked a little bit impressed.

"I'm just learning," said Jinx modestly. "But the trees have been talking about something huge and dangerous moving in from the west for over a week. And now they say it's here."

Elfwyn and Reven looked all around.

"I was attacked by a werebear," said Elfwyn. "He was huge and dangerous. And then there were those wolves."

"You think the trees would be afraid of those?" said Jinx.

"No," said Elfwyn.

"I've been walking west to east," said Reven. "I haven't seen anything. Well, a couple of werewolves. And I think I saw an elf through the trees."

"This feels like something worse than that," said Jinx. It was hard to put into Urwish what the trees had said. But some of the trees were seven feet thick and hundreds of feet tall. Anything that would frighten them had to be pretty horrible.

Something struck him as odd, though. "How did you get attacked by a werebear? What about the Truce of the Path?"

"He tricked me into leaving it," said Elfwyn. "He told me to climb a tree to get away from the wolves. He said he was a woodcutter named Urson. He followed me for days, and he wouldn't leave me alone, and he kept trying to get me to leave the path." She looked around. "What happened to him, I wonder?"

She picked up a stick, lit the end in the fire, and started toward the place where Jinx had seen the furies attacking something.

"Don't leave the path!" Jinx barked.

She turned around. "Do you always talk to people that way?"

She stepped off the path. Jinx muttered one of Simon's favorite swear words—hadn't he just told her there was something nasty out there?—and followed her. Reven came with them.

"This is where the werebear was," said Elfwyn. "I guess he ran off."

Jinx was looking all around in the darkness for the trees' fear, but he spared a glance at the scrabbled, bloody ground. There was a big ax lying there. Jinx picked it up. As soon as he had it in his hands he felt better. The ax might not be a match for the thing the trees were afraid of, but it was better than nothing.

"Let's get back on the path," he said.

"Maybe we should take turns keeping watch all night," said Reven. "That's what they do in tales."

"Yeah," said Jinx. "I'll go first."

The other two rolled up in their blankets and settled

down to sleep. Jinx sat by the fire with the ax in front of him. The fire burned and crackled. The smell of woodsmoke reminded him sharply of home, which he'd left only a few hours ago, but it seemed longer. Right now, if he were home, he might be in Simon's workshop, both of them ignoring the time and the cycle of day and night—no, he'd forgotten all about Simon's injury.

Still, the thing was, Jinx could've been safe at home now, not sitting in the dark watching for a creature so awful the trees were afraid of it.

Not that he was afraid, he told himself.

His new companions were both wrapped up in blankets like cocoons, apparently asleep. Reven's pack was under his head. Jinx wondered if his four farthings were in it. Carefully and quietly, he slid his fingers toward it.

Without opening his eyes, Reven snaked a hand out of his blanket-cocoon and grabbed Jinx's wrist. Then he let go. Jinx got the message.

Jinx threw a few sticks on the fire, then opened his eyes and saw that they had already burned down. This was no good; he was falling asleep. It was time to wake Elfwyn.

She got up muzzily, and he wrapped up in his blanket and lay down. The ground was hard and cold, and the breeze on his face and the rustle of dead leaves across the forest floor (and maybe other things, like scurrying feet) kept him awake. Even when he was three-quarters asleep he was still listening for the thing the trees were afraid of.

He became aware of a distant *thump, clunk, thump, clunk.* He sat bolt upright. "That's a witch!"

"I know that," said Elfwyn. "Calm down. Go back to sleep."

"But there's a witch coming!"

"I'm sure she won't bother us."

"Don't you know anything at *all* about witches?"

"Yes, I do, actually. My mother was training to be a witch, before she decided to get married instead."

"Oh," said Jinx. He stood up and unwrapped himself from his blanket. "Well, I still think we should hide."

"You mean leave the path?" said Elfwyn.

"I can do a concealment spell," said Jinx.

Reven had woken up. "I'd like to meet a wicked witch."

The thumping grew louder. Jinx wasn't going to conceal himself if the others weren't afraid. He looked at the ax on the ground. He'd feel safer with the ax, but he'd be more threatening. He decided to leave it where it lay.

The black shadow of a witch in her butter churn came hopping into view. Elfwyn stepped forward into the middle of the path. Jinx stayed near the ax in case he had to grab it in a hurry. Reven kept well behind both of them.

The churn came to a stop in front of Elfwyn.

The witch was a young one, Jinx saw in the firelight, not so warty nor so hairy as Dame Glammer. The grin she gave Elfwyn was very Dame Glammer-like, though.

"What's this, then?" said the young witch, looking down at Elfwyn. "Not afraid of witches?"

"No. I'm not afraid of witches," said Elfwyn.

"Not, eh? Then you're not the smartest girl in the Urwald, are you?"

"No, I'm not," said Elfwyn, looking petulant.

"Not? And whose not-the-smartest girl are you, then?"

"Berga of Butterwood Clearing's."

"Oh, a witch's brat!"

"She's not a witch. She gave it up."

"And where are you going?"

"To see my grandmother."

The witch appeared delighted at this. "Are you! And won't she be pleased to see you! Dame Glammer hasn't had a child to eat in months."

"Dame Glammer is your grandmother?" said Jinx, surprised.

"Yes. I'm too old to be scared by stories like that," Elfwyn told the witch.

"More fool you. And what about your boyfriends? Are they going to see Dame Glammer too?"

"They haven't told me where they're going."

"Well, if you want to find Dame Glammer, go that way three days." The witch pointed ahead of her, to the west.

"Thank you," said Elfwyn.

"If I were you, I wouldn't be camping so close to the Troll-way," said the witch. "No matter how many boyfriends I had to protect me."

She grinned at Jinx and Reven. Jinx glared at her. Her grin turned into a cackle of laughter.

"I never saw three such helpless little ducks trying to make their way through the Urwald! I certainly haven't the heart to cast a spell on you. Smells like you've had three too many cast on you already. And you're going to Dame Glammer's house, hah! Like mice climbing into the cat's basket."

"She's my *grandmother*," said Elfwyn.

"Well, you can't pick your relatives. And how did you get that nasty curse slipped to you, dearie?"

"It was done by an evil fairy at my christening," said Elfwyn.

The witch chuckled gleefully. "An evil fairy? Really? An evil fairy?"

"Yes," said Elfwyn.

For some reason the witch seemed to find this hilarious. She laughed so hard that the butter churn nearly capsized. Then she pushed her stick into the ground, and the churn hopped off down the path.

Unexpected Meetings

J inx wanted to ask Elfwyn what her curse was. But he could see it irritated her to talk about it, and he was afraid of being accused of not being nice. Real girls were clearly a lot more touchy than imaginary ones.

"Did you have a spell cast on you?" he asked Reven, instead.

"There's nothing to be afraid of from witches," said Reven, ignoring the question. "They're all talk."

"Simon says that anyone who isn't afraid of witches is a fool," said Jinx. He guessed Reven didn't want to talk about the spell he was under. Well, Jinx knew what the third spell was—the one Simon had done on him.

"Witches do eat children, I think," said Elfwyn. "But only the really wicked ones, and you hardly ever meet that kind. And, you know—very small children."

"You think it's not so bad if the children aren't big?" said Jinx.

"Well, no, of course not, but—"

"You're going to Dame Glammer's house?"

"Yes," said Elfwyn.

"I'm going there too," said Jinx.

"Is she your grandmother too?" asked Elfwyn.

"No, but—" Jinx decided he didn't want to explain about his lost magic. "She's a friend of Simon's."

"Who's Simon?" Reven asked as they settled down around the fire and Jinx stirred it to life. None of them felt like going to sleep again.

"The wizard I work for."

"I'd really like to meet a wizard," said Reven. He opened his mouth as if to say more, then stopped, looking confused. "I could—he could—" he stopped again. "I mean, I just think it would be amazing to see a real wizard."

"If you stick around the Urwald, I'm sure one will turn up," said Jinx. He turned to Elfwyn. "I kind of mostly know the way to your grandmother's house."

"Oh, good," said Elfwyn. "The directions my mother gave me weren't very exact."

Jinx was glad she was going his way. He liked Elfwyn,

even though she was harder to talk to than she'd been in his imagination. And it was good to have company.

"I'll accompany you too, fair lady," said Reven. "I would fain meet your grandmother."

"You would what?" said Elfwyn.

"He means he'd like to," said Jinx. Some of the books in Simon's house used old-fashioned words like that.

"But where were you going?" said Elfwyn.

Reven didn't say anything for a moment. "I was crossing the Urwald," he said at last, carefully. "But I should be glad to make a detour to meet your grandmother."

How long does it take to cross the Urwald? Jinx wondered.

⌁ ⌁ ⌁

They headed westward along the path the next morning. Jinx thought it was odd of Reven to turn around and head back the way he'd come, just to meet Dame Glammer. In fact, there were a lot of odd things about Reven. It would have been all right with Jinx if Reven had gone on crossing the Urwald from west to east and left him and Elfwyn alone.

They crossed more paths, and of course there were no signs telling you which way to go.

"Are you sure this is the right way?" said Elfwyn after several turns.

"Yes," said Jinx. "We're going west."

"We're headed back to my country," said Reven.

"What's your country?" said Jinx.

"Bragwood. It's this way."

"Were you on your way to Keyland, then?" said Elfwyn.

Jinx remembered Tolliver the Wanderer telling him that Bragwood lay to the west and Keyland to the east.

Reven ignored the question completely. "I have to leave Bragwood, and I haven't done it yet."

"Yes, you have," said Jinx. "You said you'd been in the Urwald for ten days already."

"The Urwald belongs to Bragwood," said Reven.

"It does not!"

"King Rufus claims it."

"King Bluetooth of Keyland claims the Urwald," said Elfwyn. "He lives ten days east of Butterwood Clearing."

"The Urwald doesn't belong to any king!" said Jinx. "It belongs to—to itself."

"Well, I agree," said Elfwyn, "but that doesn't change the fact that King Bluetooth says it's part of Keyland." She turned to Reven. "Why did you leave Bragwood?"

"I was banished," said Reven proudly.

"What for?" Elfwyn pressed.

"The king said I was anathema."

"He doesn't like athemas?"

"Anathema means, like, accursed," said Jinx. "Probably

it was for robbing people."

"No, it wasn't," said Reven.

"What did you get banished for?" Elfwyn asked.

"For being too friendly with the king's daughter." Reven said this with his eyes looking sideways, and Jinx had the impression that it was a lie. "But I'm sure *your* king is pleased with you, fair lady," he added.

"I don't *have* a king," said Elfwyn. "I'm an Urwalder."

"Pardon me, but you said King Bluetooth—"

"I just know who he is, that's all. But he's evil. Everyone knows that. He killed his brother, who was the real king, and his brother's wife and their little baby, too."

"Ah. Yes. I heard about that," said Reven.

"Of course the brother was pretty evil too. *His* wife died right after the baby was born, and nobody knew what of, and then he married another wife."

Jinx had heard this story before, from Tolliver the Wanderer. He wasn't very interested in it, except to notice that kings' personal lives were as messy as Urwalders'. He hefted the ax on his shoulder. The path split two ways here. One branch went a little too far south and the other a little too far north. He chose the one that went south.

"Anyway, I don't care about kings," said Elfwyn. "I'm from Butterwood Clearing. It's the best clearing. We're famous for our butter and our cows and—oh, and we've just been invaded by barbarians."

"That's terrible!" said Reven.

"No, it sort of worked out all right. Some of them seem like pretty nice barbarians. My mother is marrying one of them."

"Oh," said Reven.

"Only she thought they might not like me, because of—well, because. And so she told me to go live with my grandmother. Are you sure this is the right path, Jinx?"

"Of course I'm sure," said Jinx.

"It's a much wider path than any I've seen so far," said Reven. "Do you think it's the Troll-way? I was told to stay off of that."

"It's not the Troll-way," said Jinx. "The Troll-way goes up into the Glass Mountains. This path isn't going up at all."

"Maybe it climbs gradually," said Elfwyn.

"There are claw marks here in the mud," said Reven.

"There are claw marks everywhere in the Urwald," said Jinx.

"Do you think we'll see real trolls?" Reven sounded eager.

"This isn't the Troll-way!" Jinx was getting really annoyed with them, especially because this path did seem too wide to be the one that he'd gone on with Simon to Dame Glammer's house.

Elfwyn put a hand on his shoulder. "Jinx, I really think we should go back and look for a different path."

"Fine!" They had probably come a mile on this path already. But if she wanted to turn around and waste all that effort, fine. Jinx spun around and marched back the way he'd come, and the others followed.

Without saying anything about it, they all started to walk a lot faster.

"I hear something coming," said Reven.

He got down and put his ear to the ground, which Jinx thought was pretty stupid considering they were now trying to move as quickly as possible.

"Something running," said Reven. He pulled the knife from his belt.

Elfwyn set her basket down on the path and pulled a big knife from it.

"I'll do a concealment spell," said Jinx. "Come here."

Feeling rather self-conscious, he took hold of Reven's and Elfwyn's arms. He concentrated hard on not being there. He felt power coming up through his feet and filling him. We're not here, he thought.

They could all hear the running clawed feet now. There was a smell of rotten meat; then the troll burst into sight around a bend in the path. Jinx's legs were telling him to run. But this time he *knew* he'd done the concealment spell right. Then it all went wrong.

Reven pulled away from Jinx's grip and stepped into the troll's path.

"Reven, stop!" Jinx said. "Get back here!"

Reven raised his knife. The troll grinned a huge, broken-tusked grin and swiped at Reven with its clawed hand. Jinx ran forward and swung his ax. Then there was troll everywhere, thick hairy arms and grabbing clawed hands, an ugly roaring face—Jinx never forgot a face. He forced his eyes to stay open even though he wanted to hide his head, and he swung his ax again and again. He heard howls and screams and had no time to wonder whose they were or what was happening. Something sharp raked across his face. He swung his ax, it met resistance, he pulled it free again. He swung again, hard, as though trying to split a thick oaken log.

Then he was lying sprawled on the ground. A shadowy form blotted out the sun. Jinx swung his fist at it.

"Stop it!" said Elfwyn. "I'm just trying to look at that cut on your face."

Jinx sat up. Reven was sitting beside him, his arm bandaged in a red-and-white checked napkin. The troll was gone. There was blood on the path. And something large and inert. Jinx's stomach did a flip flop. It was the troll's arm. Jinx put his hand to his face and it came away bloody. The things that had just happened began to sort themselves out in his head. Jinx never forgot a face, even one that appeared on the wrong sort of body.

"Wow, a troll!" said Reven. "That was my first troll."

"That troll was my stepfather," said Jinx.

He saw Reven and Elfwyn exchange a glance.

"I think you hit your head pretty hard when you fell," said Elfwyn. "Maybe you should lie back down."

"Bergthold. My stepfather. I cut off my stepfather's arm."

"You were amazing," said Reven a little too heartily, as if he were talking to someone not quite right in the head. "The way you swung the ax—where did you learn to do that?"

"Firewood," said Jinx. "If you hadn't stepped out of my concealment spell, I wouldn't have had to swing anything. I mean it, that troll was my stepdad."

"Er—do you mean that your mother married a troll?" said Elfwyn.

"Of course not! My mother's dead. And he didn't use to be a troll, he— Why are we still sitting here? Let's get off the Troll-way!"

"Oh, *now* it's the Troll-way?" said Elfwyn.

This sarcasm was better than her treating him like he was insane, so Jinx didn't mind it. They walked rapidly, almost running, Reven carrying the bloody ax. Jinx didn't want to bring it—the sight of it made him sick—but Reven insisted. He said he wanted Jinx to teach him ax fighting.

When they were off the Troll-way and had come to a small stream, Jinx agreed to stop and wash the gouge on his face. Elfwyn said it would probably leave a scar.

Jinx told about how his stepfather had been carried off by trolls.

"Simon says that violent, greedy people draw trolls to themselves," he explained.

"So what does that make us, then?" said Reven.

"Simon says, Simon says," said Elfwyn. "Does it ever occur to you that Simon might be lying? I think that wizard of yours turned your stepfather into a troll himself."

"He can't," said Jinx. "It isn't that easy to do magic on people, Simon sa—well, it isn't easy."

"Did he say he couldn't *do* it, or just that it wasn't easy?" said Elfwyn.

"He said it's a hundred times harder than regular magic. But easier for witches." Jinx frowned. Of course Simon could do magic on people. He'd done it on Jinx. But it had taken a lot of preparation, and extra power drawn from fire and chalk figures, and those sinister-smelling roots of Dame Glammer's.

"Anyway, Bergthold wasn't a troll the last time I saw him," Jinx said. "He was a man, and he was being carried away by trolls. And then I think he turned into one."

"People can turn into trolls?" said Reven.

"I don't know. I never heard of them doing it before."

"I never heard of it either," said Elfwyn, frowning. "I thought trolls came from—you know, starting out as baby trolls."

"Maybe if you act like a troll, you turn into one," said Reven. "I'm not saying your stepfather acted like a troll—"

"He did."

"Oh, well. There you go then." Reven seemed to feel that this explained it. "I mean, stuff is just magic in the Urwald, right?"

Now Elfwyn and Jinx exchanged a glance. They were Urwalders, and they knew magic was complicated.

~ ~ ~

The fact was that they were lost.

It had been three days since Jinx had cut off his stepfather's arm, and the feeling of sick revulsion sometimes left him for whole minutes at a time.

Jinx had stopped saying "It's this way" each time they came to a new path and had to decide which way to go. The others were still letting Jinx choose. But he could see them exchanging glances that said that they knew he was lost.

Well, so what? So were they.

It began to rain.

They slogged on, their feet cold in their soggy boots, and their sodden clothes clinging and weighing them down.

"Maybe you should leave the ax," Jinx said, not for the first time.

"No, we need this! You were killer with this thing," said Reven. He seemed to have the ability to stay cheerful no matter how tired, cold, wet, and miserable things got. It was annoying.

"He doesn't want to talk about it, Reven," said Elfwyn.

"Why not?" said Reven, splashing through a puddle. "The way he cut that troll's arm off was—"

"You said that already." Jinx tried to shut out the memory. He wondered if Bergthold had survived.

"Remember what you said to me before about those tree limbs I cut to make shelters? You said the forest would take limbs off people. Wouldn't it be funny if that were true?"

"It is true, and it's not funny," said Jinx.

"Trolls aren't people," said Elfwyn.

"Actually, I think maybe they are," said Jinx. "I mean, that one was my stepfather. And they obey the Truce of the Path—"

"That one didn't," Reven said.

"That wasn't the Path, that was the Troll-way."

"There's something over there," said Elfwyn. "A clearing, maybe."

The smell of smoke came through the rain, and there was a small path branching off. They went down it. They all wanted to get out of the rain.

The clearing was small, gray, and drizzly. Wisps of steam spiraled upward from fresh-turned earth, which was rapidly becoming mud. Shovels, abandoned when the rain began, stuck up here and there.

The houses were triangles of twigs and thatch, black with soaked-in rain. Jinx splashed up to a door and knocked. Reven and Elfwyn stayed behind him.

"Who's there?" came through the door.

"A party of wet travelers seeking shelter," said Jinx.

"Hoity-toity!" The door swung inward. "'Seeking shelter'? Here we just look for dry. Come in."

Jinx ducked, even though the doorway wasn't too low. Something about the little hut just made him feel too big for it. He heard Elfwyn and Reven come into the house behind him.

"You can put the ax down; we don't none of us need chopping up," said the woman.

Jinx stared at her. He never forgot a face.

"You can sit down if you want," said the woman. "'Stead of standing around crowding up the place."

Besides the woman there was a girl about three years old, and a man sprawled on a bed in a corner.

Jinx and Elfwyn sat down beside the fire, cross-legged so as to take up less room. Rain was falling down the chimney and hissing in the flames, and the wind blew down it and filled the room with puffs of eye-stinging smoke.

Reven held his hands out to the little girl and smiled. "Hello, princess."

She ran and hid behind her mother, then peered out at Reven suspiciously.

Jinx looked from the woman to the man on the bed, and decided to be blunt. "You don't recognize me, do you?"

"Should I? I never had any truck with any rich people." She leaned past him to stir the cauldron hanging over the flames.

"You're my stepmother," said Jinx.

She dropped the ladle into the pot. "Fudge!" She brushed her hair out of her face and glared at him.

He looked steadily back at her.

"Now how am I going to get that out of there?" She reached for the fire tongs.

Jinx wasn't sure why he did what he did next—maybe because he didn't want to eat soup that had had the ash-covered fire tongs stuck in it, but more likely because he wanted to force his stepmother to react to him in some way. She didn't look the least bit interested in what he'd just told her.

So he stood up, looked into the bubbling, steaming pot until he could see the ladle swimming among chopped squash and cabbage leaves, and levitated it. He'd gotten better at levitating things, and he'd noticed magic was easier when he wasn't inside Simon's stone house. The ladle rose easily through the water. It hung in the air a few inches above the pot. Everyone stared at it. Jinx pulled his sleeve down over his hand, grabbed the thing, and handed it to his stepmother.

She took it, squawked, and dropped it on the floor.

"Sorry. It's hot," said Jinx. He really hadn't meant to burn her. Honestly. Probably.

He wasn't sure how he felt about her.

He looked at her and her family. Their clothes were patched and colorless, the dye probably washed out years ago by other wearers who might be dead by now. He realized he was among people who would never wear new clothes in their lives.

"I guess you got married again," he said.

He heard an intake of breath and a tsk from Elfwyn, and guessed he was in danger of being not-nice again. He tried to control himself and think nice thoughts. After all, the woman—Cottawilda—had let them in out of the rain.

"Are you a wizard, or an elf, or what?" said Cottawilda, backing up to the bed and sitting down next to the man. She turned to Elfwyn, maybe as one woman to another, and asked, "What is he?"

"He's a wizard's servant," said Elfwyn.

Cottawilda and her husband recoiled in horror.

"You shouldn't have told them that," Jinx muttered.

Elfwyn shot him an apologetic look.

"What! The Bonemaster?" said Cottawilda.

"No, the evil wizard Simon," said Elfwyn.

"Can't you keep anything to yourself?" Jinx snapped,

not caring if she thought he was nice or not. What a blabbermouth!

"No," said Elfwyn.

"I'm your stepson," he told Cottawilda. "Jinx. Remember?"

He was conscious of dominating the tiny house and being at the center of an audience. Reven was sitting against the wall and had somehow coaxed the child into his lap.

"You don't look nothing like him. He was a tiny brat."

"Yeah, well, it was a while ago. I've grown." The woman didn't seem to feel guilty or anything. "You don't remember? You abandoned me, you left me to die in the Urwald."

"I would never do anything like that." Cottawilda shook her head firmly. "I'd've sold you."

"You *did* do it!" Jinx struggled not to raise his voice. He saw the little girl bury her face against Reven, in fear of Jinx. "Bergthold took me out in the woods to abandon me."

"Oh, Bergthold." Her face twisted with disgust. "He was a mean old thing."

"Why'd you marry him then?"

She shrugged and looked at the man. "He was next in line."

That was how people got married in the clearings; they married whoever was next in line.

"Anyway, trolls got him and the boy both. People went

looking, and they found the tracks."

"They got him," said Jinx, his anger deflating as he remembered Bergthold-the-troll's arm. "They didn't get me."

"And you've done right well for yourself. Nice clothes, fancy talk, and an evil wizard to look after you. If you *are* a servant and not some rich man's son. So what are you complaining about?"

Jinx didn't know what to say. Standing in the squalid, cabbage-smelling hut with the rain beginning to leak through the thatch in one corner, it was hard to complain because he'd been forced to leave it and go live with Simon. Cottawilda and Bergthold hadn't known Simon would come along—trolls or werewolves were a much more likely outcome—but Jinx found he didn't feel like arguing the point. And he certainly wasn't going to point out that Simon had taken his magic.

The thing was, had his magic been too high a price to pay? Yes, it had. And yet Jinx was very glad he didn't live like this.

The man on the bed cleared his throat. "I don't need no wizards around my family. I think you should leave."

"We'll leave when it stops raining," said Reven easily. "We haven't come to harm anyone. We're just travelers in need of shelter, which we'll pay for."

Jinx watched the expression on Cottawilda's and her husband's faces change. Jinx was getting better at understanding faces.

"We'll feed you all for a farthing," said Cottawilda.

"And let us stay the night," said Elfwyn.

There were nervous looks from Cottawilda and her husband at this. Jinx didn't really want to stay the night, but the rain looked like the kind that stays around for a while, and he didn't want to sleep outside in it.

He jerked a thumb at Reven. "He's paying."

The next morning Jinx walked around the clearing, which was bright with sunlight and raindrops. People gathered in clumps to stare at him. Word of the flying ladle had gotten around. He saw people he recognized, some of whom he had never thought of once in the years he'd been gone. There must be people missing, because of the werewolves and the winter plague that Simon had mentioned, but Jinx couldn't tell who they were.

Nobody seemed to recognize him. He spoke to a few people who should have. They didn't remember him. Most of them shied away from Jinx and his companions, though, suspicious of strangers and of anything that came out of the Urwald.

He had hoped—well, maybe *hoped* was too strong a word, but somewhere in the back of his mind had been the idea that since he had first had the magic of seeing people's thoughts in Gooseberry Clearing, maybe it would come back to him here. It did not.

"Everything must seem smaller to you, eh?" said Reven, walking beside him. "I've heard that happens when you go back to where you were little."

"Yeah," said Jinx. Actually, everything seemed dingier, poorer, drabber, sadder. He wanted to get away from the place.

A girl a little older than Jinx was standing beside a hut, watching them.

Reven smiled at the girl and she stared back blankly.

"Inga," Jinx remembered. "You're Inga, right?"

"How do you know my name, wizard boy?" the girl asked, suspicious.

"You—" Jinx stopped. Inga used to hit him, and had once held his face down in the mud in a pigsty. Jinx decided not to mention this in front of his new friends. "I remember you from when I was little."

"Do you know the way to Dame Glammer's house?" asked Elfwyn.

"Dame Glammer . . . you mean a witch?" said Inga.

"Yes." Elfwyn seemed to sense that it wouldn't be a good idea to say the witch was her grandmother. "We're on our way there, but we got lost."

"You shouldn't go to a witch's house," said Inga. "You should stay home in your own clearing. It's dangerous to go places."

"Even if you stick to the path," Jinx said.

He was being sarcastic. It made him sad that Inga nodded in agreement. He couldn't believe that he'd once let himself be held facedown in a pigsty by a girl who was afraid to leave Gooseberry Clearing.

Anyway, she wouldn't be able to do it to him now—she was taller than him, but he bet he was stronger.

Except maybe he wouldn't have been strong if he'd been stuck here, subsisting on toad porridge and cabbage soup. And he wouldn't even be able to read! It was unthinkable. If he'd stayed here, he wouldn't be himself.

Anyway, they hadn't wanted him. They'd made him leave the path.

And I never even thanked them, Jinx thought.

Curses

When they left Gooseberry Clearing behind, Jinx felt as if a troll-sized weight had been lifted from him. He was disappointed he hadn't learned anything about his lost magic there. But he was relieved that everyone had forgotten him. He wasn't *from* there anymore. He was from Simon's house.

Whatever Simon's faults, at least he wasn't drab and drizzly.

They'd been walking all day, cheerful and not thinking much at all about the thing the trees were afraid of (which Reven had named the Terror).

"Is that really where you were born, Jinx?" said Elfwyn.

"Yup."

"Well, it's certainly . . ." Elfwyn trailed off, then tried again. "Certainly very . . ."

"Wretched," said Jinx.

"I don't blame you for going and being apprenticed to an evil wizard," said Reven.

"He's not evil," said Jinx. After all, Simon was the Bonemaster's enemy, so surely that meant he must be good. Of course, he'd done a horrible spell on Jinx. But maybe Simon didn't really understand how horrible it had been. He was kind, mostly, wasn't he? Taken all in all? "Anyway, I didn't have a choice. My stepparents kicked me out because they had a new baby."

"Ermengarde?" said Reven.

"No—who's Ermengarde?"

"The child in the hut," said Reven.

Jinx thought. "How old is Ermengarde?"

"Three," said Reven.

"Couldn't be her, then. She's not old enough."

"I wonder what happened to your stepsister, then," said Reven.

"She must have died," said Elfwyn. "Or else they abandoned her in the forest too."

Jinx had the feeling he should've asked. But he had just never thought about the baby stepsister—Gertrude, that was her name. "I think this is the path."

This time he really did recognize the path to Dame Glammer's house. As they turned onto it, Jinx had a funny feeling that someone was watching him.

"I'm supposed to stop at the bridge and call her," said Elfwyn.

"Maybe we should wait till morning," said Reven. It was getting dark.

"Wait where?" said Elfwyn. "Why should we spend another night on the path when my grandmother's house is right nearby?"

She lifted her hands to her mouth and called, "GRANNND-MAA!"

They heard the thump of a butter churn moving along the path.

"Well, here they are." Dame Glammer's eyes glowed orange in the twilight, and her grin reached into her voice. "Just like Dame Esper told me. Three little chickabiddies, coming to see an old witch in her cabin."

"Hello, Grandma," said Elfwyn.

The half of Dame Glammer that wasn't in the butter churn leaned over to examine Elfwyn. She took Elfwyn's chin in her wrinkled hand and peered into her eyes.

"So, who is this who calls me Grandma?"

"Elfwyn. Berga's daughter."

"Ah. Berga's daughter." Dame Glammer grinned as if she might eat Elfwyn. "I haven't seen you since you were two years old."

"I knew it!" said Elfwyn. "She told me I'd never met you, but I remembered."

Dame Glammer's expression was unfathomable. "Remembered? What do you remember?"

"I remember you coming along in the butter churn," said Elfwyn. "And we picked strawberries."

"Ah," said Dame Glammer. "And your mother lied to you, did she?"

"Well, I wouldn't say—"

"I would. Told you you'd never met me when you had, eh? I call that lying. Come along, chickabiddies."

Dame Glammer thumped off down the path. Elfwyn, Reven, and Jinx followed. A few minutes later they heard cursing ahead of them. They hurried along the path to Dame Glammer's cottage.

The witch was writhing on the ground, trying to get free of the overturned butter churn. Reven rushed forward to help her. In the end it needed all three of them to pull her free.

"Thank you, chickabiddies. I'll have to see about getting a new butter churn made. That one's getting a bit snug. Come inside. You're just in time for dinner."

This seemed to alarm Reven considerably. And even when they got inside and it became clear that they weren't on the menu, as Dame Glammer began setting out bowls of soup and bread and honey, he kept glancing nervously at the stone oven set into the chimney.

"Oh, you're a little big for that oven, chickabiddy," Dame Glammer told him, grinning. "I'd never fit you in there, nor you me."

She cackled, and Jinx, who had outgrown being afraid of her ages ago, was suddenly afraid of her again.

"And what brings you here in the company of Simon's little chipmunk and this other nervous boy, granddaughter?" Dame Glammer asked as they sat down to eat.

Elfwyn told her grandmother how she had been attacked by a werebear and some wolves and had met Jinx and Reven.

"And why did your mother let you leave your clearing in the first place?"

Elfwyn told how barbarians had taken over Butterwood Clearing, and the directions her mother had given her for going to her grandmother's house. She answered each question very precisely.

"And your mother is getting married again? What happened to the last one?"

"Yes. Werewolves," said Elfwyn with a wince. Jinx wondered if "the last one" had been Elfwyn's father or her stepfather.

"Well, I don't mean to speak badly of your mother, chickabiddy, but she always was a fool. There's no need to keep *marrying* people. I'm glad to see you're more sensible than her. Even if you do have a curse on you."

Jinx remembered the witch on the path mentioning Elfwyn's curse. He wondered what it was. Elfwyn looked embarrassed and concentrated on eating her soup. Dame Glammer turned her attention to Jinx.

"So. Still trust Simon the Wizard, do you, little chipmunk?"

"I'd rather you didn't call me chipmunk."

"Would you, chipmunk? It just goes to show we don't always get what we want in this world."

Jinx felt as embarrassed as Elfwyn looked, and he was not going to look at Reven, who he was sure was laughing at him. Jinx was just realizing that every time he'd seen Dame Glammer before, Simon had been there.

"And you're not trying to read my mind anymore." There was a tinge of pity in Dame Glammer's voice.

And it made Jinx angry. She had no business feeling sorry for him. Not when the whole thing was her fault.

"Perhaps I shouldn't have given him the roots," she went on.

"You didn't give them to him, you sold them to him," said Jinx. He heard a "tut" from Elfwyn and realized he was being not-nice again. He shut his mouth. He didn't want to anger Dame Glammer. He'd never noticed that far-back gleam in her eyes before. She looked dangerous.

"And you." She turned her attention to Reven. "Who are you and where do you come from?"

"I'm Reven, fair—er, Dame. And I come from King Rufus's court."

"King Rufus." She frowned. "A little backwater kingdom to the west? King who likes to put witches into barrels stuck about with nails and roll them down a hill until they're dead?"

Reven went pale, and Jinx also felt a bit sick and put his spoon down in his soup.

"Not just witches," said Reven, looking at the table. "He did it to my stepmother, too."

"Oh yes, witches and wicked stepmothers," said Dame Glammer, nodding.

"My stepmother was not wicked!"

The change in Reven was startling. He wasn't ingratiating, or charming, or fascinated, or slightly nervous—he was furious. His eyebrows drew down like angry swords, and you could believe that his eyes could cut you down where you stood. Jinx inched his chair away from him.

Dame Glammer was not alarmed. "Why did he do it?"

Reven opened his mouth to speak, but no sound came out.

"I see. And your father—what's your father's name?"

Again Reven opened his mouth and no sound came out.

"And Reven—is that your real name?"

The same thing again. He opened his mouth and nothing came out. Jinx and Elfwyn looked from Dame

Glammer to Reven and back again.

"That's a terrible spell, dear," said Dame Glammer, shaking her head. "I expect a wizard could take it off you, but I can't do a thing with it myself."

Reven's anger had vanished. He flushed bright red and looked as if he would have liked to jump up and run out of the cabin, if only he hadn't been too well brought up.

Dame Glammer turned back to Elfwyn. "Well, chickabiddy, what do you think of your old grandma?"

"I think you like to make people uncomfortable and remind them of hurtful things, and it's not very nice," said Elfwyn.

Dame Glammer cackled. "What a delightfully honest child you are."

"Why can't you take Reven's curse off him?" said Jinx. "Simon says curses are easier for witches than for wizards."

"Does he? And do you still trust what Simon says, dear?"

"Could the evil wizard Simon take my curse off me, good Dame?" said Reven.

"He's not evil," said Jinx.

"Oh, isn't he?" Dame Glammer sipped soup, smacked her lips, and then said to Reven, "I think he could not. Simon is not a very powerful wizard."

Her eyes glittered at Jinx as she said this, to see how he would take it. Jinx didn't believe her.

"And it would take a very powerful wizard. The Bonemaster, perhaps," said Dame Glammer.

Reven looked interested.

"The Bonemaster is evil!" said Jinx.

"Simon says?" said Dame Glammer sweetly.

"I've met the Bonemaster! He—he has knives in his thoughts," said Jinx.

"Be that as it may," said the witch, "he's the one who can take that nasty curse off our boy here. If anybody can."

Jinx looked to Elfwyn for help. But Elfwyn was staring down at her soup.

"The Bonemaster would kill him!" said Jinx.

"Oh, I think not," said Dame Glammer. "He wouldn't harm our boy. No, I really think not." She grinned. "Any more than Simon would harm you."

Jinx hadn't wanted to discuss this in front of the others, but—"I want to know how to undo that."

"Undo what, chipmunk?"

"The spell. The—" He thought about what Sophie had said. "The deathforce magic Simon did on me."

"Oh, deathforce magic is the *Bonemaster's* specialty, chipmunk. Not our dear wizard Simon's."

"Then what did he do to me?" Jinx demanded. "You said I could do deep Urwald magic! And now I can't, because of that spell with those rotten evil roots."

"Oh, yes. Deep Urwald magic." Dame Glammer's eyes

glittered dangerously. "Born of fear, that kind of magic is. You need fear to stay alive in the Urwald. And so you learned to watch everything, didn't you? Even the insides of people's heads. So you knew how to tiptoe around things, and when to hide, and when to run."

"That doesn't make any sense," said Elfwyn, looking up from her soup.

"I'm not afraid of anything," said Jinx.

"Aren't you, chipmunk?" She pointed her spoon at him. "Only a fool isn't afraid in the Urwald. And you're twelve years old and still alive." She tapped the spoon on his nose. "I expect you're no fool."

"But I can still do—other stuff," said Jinx, wiping soup off his nose with his sleeve.

"What other stuff is that, chipmunk?"

"Like hearing the trees and stuff," said Jinx. "Isn't that deep Urwald magic? Why didn't I lose that?"

"That's the half of you that's underground, isn't it, chipmunk? I expect if someone did a spell on the human bits, your roots wouldn't notice."

"Humans don't have roots," said Elfwyn.

"Everyone has roots," said Dame Glammer.

"I'm not a tree," said Jinx. He was quite sure he was completely human. He did not, for example, have leaves.

"There's more of you underground than you think, chipmunk."

"How come I can still do *magic* magic? Like, spells?"

"Can you?" Dame Glammer grinned. "Show me."

Jinx tried to levitate the spoon out of his soup. It was nowhere near as easy as the ladle in Gooseberry Clearing. The spoon gave a feeble wriggle but didn't rise.

"Hope you're not relying on that magic to keep you alive in the Urwald, chipmunk." Dame Glammer grinned. "If it's deathforce magic Simon did on you, then I reckon you have to ask the expert."

"You said it wasn't deathforce magic," said Elfwyn.

"No, she didn't," said Jinx, who was used to this sort of magicianly double-talk. "You mean I have to ask the Bonemaster, don't you?"

"You should stay away from the Bonemaster," said Dame Glammer. "Didn't Simon tell you that?"

"Yes," said Jinx. "He did."

"I expect the Bonemaster could tell you a few things about Simon."

Late that night, after Jinx and Reven had gone to bed in the loft, Jinx woke to hear Elfwyn and Dame Glammer talking at the kitchen table.

"How did you get that nasty spell put on you, chickabiddy?" Dame Glammer murmured. "Was it a christening type of situation? Bad fairy?"

"Yes," said Elfwyn. "The thirteenth fairy."

"Your mother is such a fool."

"I wish you wouldn't call my mother a fool, please, Grandma."

"You think I *like* calling her a fool? She's my own daughter, after all. But she trained as a witch, she should know better—christenings? Fairies? Bah."

"Do you think a wizard could take it off of me, like you told Reven?"

Jinx inched to the edge of the loft so that he could peer down and see Dame Glammer's expression. In the dying firelight the wrinkles in her face cast deep shadows, which made her look more evil than she had earlier.

"Why on earth would you want it taken off you?"

"Because it's horrible!" said Elfwyn.

"Oh, you just haven't learned to use it properly, dearie. No, I think you should stay away from the Bonemaster." She flicked her eyes toward the loft. "Wizards are best left to boys. Girls belong with witches."

"I'd really like to get rid of it," said Elfwyn. "It's an awful nuisance."

"Perhaps something could be arranged," said Dame Glammer. "I'm not saying it couldn't. But don't you think you might like to *be* a witch, dearie?"

"I don't know," said Elfwyn. "I just want to get rid of my curse."

"You could have a real talent for witchery. I expect you

do. Your mother did, but no, she had to go off and get married. Well, we won't talk about it tonight, chickabiddy." She looked directly at Jinx. "The walls have ears."

The next morning after breakfast, Jinx showed Reven how to use an ax. He wanted to do it here, where there was deadwood to practice on, because Reven had shown a disconcerting tendency to take swings at living trees as they walked, though fortunately he had never connected.

Reven was not very good with an ax.

"I'm used to a sword," he explained. "I'm quite capable with a sword. Would you like me to teach you?"

"No," said Jinx. "Thanks." He didn't have a sword; neither did Reven. "What's the spell you have on you?"

"Who says I have a spell on me?" Reven took a mighty swing at a log and missed.

"Dame Glammer did. And that other witch, Dame Esper, I guess. But you can't say what it is, can you?"

"You have a spell on you too."

"Yeah."

"And Elfwyn has one too," Reven added.

Jinx was grateful for the change of subject. They could talk about Elfwyn; she wasn't there.

"Wonder what hers is," said Reven.

Jinx shrugged. "She sort of tells people what she thinks of them a lot."

Reven tilted his head to one side as if weighing this, then shook his head. "That's not much of a curse."

Jinx had to agree that it wasn't. "Only for the people that are being told. Not for her. And she blabbed about my business to those people in Gooseberry Clearing."

"Well, that's just girls," said Reven.

Jinx didn't know if this was true, but Reven probably knew a lot more about girls than Jinx did.

"So what is deathforce magic?" Reven asked.

"It's, um, magic that requires a life."

"You mean like a human sacrifice?"

"I guess," said Jinx.

"And Simon did that to you? He, what, killed somebody?"

"Of course not," said Jinx.

"Well, then how—"

"I don't *know* how!" said Jinx. "It's just what Dame Glammer says. I don't have to believe her." And Sophie, he thought. Sophie'd said it too.

Reven raised the ax and let it fall slowly on a log, managing to hit it this time and making a little dent. "Is that why you left? Because of the spell?"

"Sort of. I just got mad," said Jinx. It had mostly been about the spell. But partly he'd wanted to go out and see the world.

"Oh. I know about getting mad," said Reven feelingly.

"But you got banished, right?"

"Well, yes, but I was pretty mad, too."

Jinx wanted to ask if King Rufus had really killed Reven's stepmother, but he didn't. He was trying hard not to be not-nice, even though Elfwyn wasn't there to disapprove. And probably it *was* true. It wasn't the sort of thing people joked about, was it?

"What about going and finding this Bonemaster, then?" said Reven.

"He's evil."

"Well, yes, but do you think we could get him to—do what the good Dame mentioned?"

"What, take your curse off you? He'd want something in return," said Jinx.

"What?"

"I don't know. They say he drinks people's souls through a straw."

"Oh. Well. Hm. Is it true?"

"Probably. Everyone's afraid of him. He lives in a house made of bones."

"How can a house be made of bones?"

"How should I know? But his is. He sucks the marrow out of his enemies' bones and then stacks them up crisscross."

"Well, we could at least go and ask him, couldn't we? There's no harm in asking."

"Did you hear what I just said? The Urwald's not a game, you know. Horrible things happen here. Anyway, Simon told me to stay away from him."

"The same Simon that put the deathforce spell on you."

"Well, yeah, but . . . Simon's never actually hurt me."

"The spell didn't hurt?" Reven threw the ax up in the air. Jinx jumped out of the way as it came spinning down, and Reven caught it neatly by the handle.

"How did you do that?" said Jinx.

Reven shrugged. "Catching things is easy. You just have to be where they are when they land. You know where the Bonemaster lives?"

"Not exactly," said Jinx. "But I know Simon's gone and fought him and nearly got burned up." He remembered Simon coming home with a burn on his face and Bonemaster-shaped thoughts.

"You think that witch would tell us how to find his house?" said Reven.

"Oh yes," said Jinx. "She likes to make trouble for people."

"She said the Bonemaster might be able to tell you how to get rid of the curse Simon put on you."

"Maybe he can," said Jinx. "But why would he?"

"Well, is he a friend of the wizard Simon?"

"No," said Jinx, remembering the Bonemaster's and

Simon's meeting on the path. "More like a deadly enemy."

"Then mayhap he would take the spell off you for precisely that reason. I think we should go there and ask him. Agreed?"

"No!" said Jinx. "He's—look, have you even been listening to me? I could see his thoughts. They were all these pink evil clouds with bloody knives flicking around inside them."

This did not help. Reven looked at Jinx like he was crazy.

"Can you see my thoughts?" said Reven very gently.

"No. That's the magic Simon took away."

"So don't you think the Bonemaster could give it back?"

Jinx hesitated. The Bonemaster probably was much more powerful than Simon.

Dame Glammer had said so; Simon had practically said so himself. What was it he'd said? *Anyone could have power if they were willing to do the things* he's *willing to do.*

"Maybe he could," Jinx said. "But it would be really, really dangerous just going to ask him. He'd suck out our souls and our blood and stack up our bones."

"You're afraid?"

Jinx looked at Reven's rather superior smile and was annoyed. Who was it who had bested Bergthold-the-troll, anyway?

"Of course *not!*"

"*Good!*" Reven slapped him on the back. "Faint heart never won fair lady!"

"Dead heart never won fair lady either," said Jinx.

***

"I don't think you should go," said Elfwyn.

Jinx was putting his pack together, tying his blanket in place. "Yeah, I don't either, but—"

He looked at Reven, who was over by the woodpile practicing. He'd gotten to where he could split a log if he could hit it.

"You're going just to protect him? That's sweet," said Elfwyn.

Sweet. Yuck. Still, it was better than not-nice.

"I have to go," said Jinx. "So I can find out what's wrong with me."

"But the Bonemaster's evil."

"I know that," said Jinx. "But he can tell me what Simon's done to me. I mean, he'd know if anybody would, right? He's the expert."

"But the Bonemaster sucks people's souls out with a straw."

"Yeah, I know."

"He sucks the marrow from people's bones and stacks them crisscross."

"I know."

"He pries people's eyeballs out and strings them to make necklaces."

"He what?"

"You ought to stay away from him," said Elfwyn.

"We're not going the whole way," he said. "Just close enough to—you know, look and see, sort of."

"Look and see what?" said Elfwyn.

"Whether we can talk to him. Make some kind of deal. You know, like, I don't know, send in a letter or something."

The door creaked open behind Jinx. "Simon wouldn't want you going, chipmunk."

"We're not going the whole way," Jinx repeated.

Dame Glammer's eyes glowed orange at him and he felt nervous. He went over to get Reven and tell him it was time to go. They said good-bye to Elfwyn and Dame Glammer and went down the path and across the two-logged bridge.

The Canyon of Bones

They went north, following Dame Glammer's directions. Jinx hadn't exactly forgotten about the Terror. But Dame Glammer had been quite enough of a terror herself to keep his mind occupied, thank you. Now he thought about it again.

"I need to listen to the trees," said Jinx. "I want to know where the Terror is."

"I thought we left it behind, way back there." Reven gestured vaguely to the east.

"Yes, but it can move, same as us."

Jinx took off his boots and his socks and stepped off the path. He burrowed into the ground with his toes. He listened. He expected the Terror would have moved even farther to the east.

The trees set him straight. The Terror was right here.

Jinx's eyes flew open. Reven was standing with the ax handle balanced on his foot, stroking the edge of the blade with his thumb.

He smiled at Jinx. "What's the matter?"

Jinx didn't know what to say. He dusted his feet off and put his socks on. He put on his boots and tied double knots.

"The Terror's right here," he said at last.

"Oh. Then we'd better get moving, hadn't we?"

Yes, except that wherever we move to, the Terror will be there with us. "How about if I carry the ax for a while?"

"Sure, if you want." Reven handed it over. His face was completely open and friendly.

They walked on. Jinx remembered how he'd sensed the trees' fear days before he'd left Simon's house. Days before he'd gone to Samara, even. Probably right around the time Reven had entered the Urwald.

Jinx wished like anything that he still had his magic now. If only he could see the color and shape of Reven's thoughts, he could guess what kind of danger Reven was— or his curse was.

"Do you think your curse could make you hurt someone else?" Jinx asked at last.

"Is that something the trees told you?"

"No." If only he knew what Reven was thinking!

"You think this Terror thing has something to do with—with my little problem, don't you?"

He can't even say "my curse." Jinx moved a little away from Reven and, cautiously, nodded.

"Well, I can tell you it doesn't," said Reven.

Well, he might as well say it. At least he was the one holding the ax. "The trees are afraid of you."

"Yes, but why are *you*?"

"I'm not!" said Jinx.

Reven looked at the ax on Jinx's shoulder and raised an eyebrow. "Well, the trees needn't worry. I'll do just as you say."

They walked all day, going north, following Dame Glammer's directions. Jinx was busy watching Reven and keeping a tight grip on the ax.

Reven talked. He told Jinx stories about life in King Rufus's court, and about the king's daughter, who was very beautiful, and Reven's stepmother, who was very wise. He watched Jinx watching him, but he stayed cheerful.

Jinx was finding it hard to believe that Reven was the Terror. Reven was friendly, and he spoke well, and he knew how to say the right thing to people and put them at ease. It was probably because he'd been brought up at a royal court and he knew how to act around people. Jinx had been brought up in a wizard's house and had only recently learned that he wasn't even nice. The truth was, he envied Reven.

"At least I'm not a thief," he said, not even realizing he had spoken aloud.

"Only because you haven't been driven to it," said Reven cheerfully. "Yet. What are those tracks?"

"Bear," said Jinx.

"Werebear or real bear?"

"Could be either one," said Jinx.

"I never heard of werebears before," said Reven. "Only werewolves. Are there other kinds of weres?"

"Werechipmunks," said Jinx.

Reven laughed.

"I can't help it that she calls me chipmunk!" said Jinx.

"Oh, I wasn't laughing at that," said Reven. "Anyway, you're too dangerous to be a chipmunk. Maybe you're a werechipmunk."

"There's a tree house," said Jinx. "We should stop."

"But it's hardly even dark yet."

"It'll get dark fast. And there's a bear around."

This tree house had a rope ladder hanging down from it. Jinx climbed up first. Reven passed the ax up to him. While Reven was climbing up, Jinx hid the ax on the flat roof, out of Reven's sight.

They sat on the ledge and watched the forest going to sleep. There were rustlings of animals in the undergrowth, and birds made twittering settling-in noises. Jinx had no intention of sleeping. He wondered if he should wait for Reven to fall asleep and then sneak off.

"You can never see the sun rise or set in the forest, can you?" said Reven.

"Of course you can—it's setting right now," said Jinx.

"I mean see it disappear over the edge of the world."

"It does that?"

"You don't have a horizon here," said Reven. "I never realized it before."

"The line where earth and sky meet? I've seen that!" When he'd drifted away from his body, the night that Simon did the spell on him. "I'd like to go there and touch the sky."

Reven laughed. "You can't. When you got there, the horizon would be somewhere else, just as far away."

Jinx didn't like Reven laughing at him. He turned away.

"There's something moving down there," said Reven. "Your bear, probably."

"It sounds like a person," said Jinx. He strained his eyes in the gathering dark. "I see something sort of red."

Elfwyn was walking along the path.

"Elfwyn!" Reven called.

Elfwyn looked every way but up.

"Up here," said Jinx.

"I'll come down and hold the ladder for you," said Reven.

"No, I will," said Jinx, pushing past Reven.

When he got down, he took Elfwyn's arm and hurried her away from the tree house, out of Reven's hearing.

"What are you doing?" she said.

"Shh!" In a whisper, Jinx explained that the Terror was following them.

"And you think it's Reven?"

"Well, it's either him or me, and I know it's not me."

"*How* do you know it's not you?"

"Because I've been listening to the trees for years and they've never been afraid of me before!"

"Maybe they changed their mind. I'm not afraid of Reven. I think he's nice."

Elfwyn shrugged away from him and started toward the tree house, which was just off the path. Jinx followed her.

It was dark now. He heard rustling nearby and a sound of heavy footsteps.

"We're right here, Reven," he said. But there was no answer.

Jinx wasn't sure where the tree house was. Over to the left, maybe? And then . . . Jinx had no idea where he was.

"Elfwyn!" he called.

"Right here." She was behind him.

He took her hand and they stumbled onward. There

were more footsteps, nearby. Jinx heard a snuffling noise.

"Reven!" Elfwyn called.

"What are you two doing down there?"

Reven's voice came from about a hundred yards behind them. Jinx and Elfwyn started toward the sound.

Ahead of them, branches crackled under someone's feet.

"You can stay where you are, Reven," said Elfwyn. "We're almost there."

"I *am* staying where I am." Reven's voice, surprised, came from above.

It wasn't Reven whose footsteps they heard.

"Hold still," Jinx whispered. "Concealment spell."

He knew now that he could do it. The power came up easily through his feet, and he understood for the first time that he was drawing on the lifeforce of the Urwald itself. He and Elfwyn stood rooted in place.

"Jinx? Fair lady?" Reven's voice sounded puzzled.

He doesn't realize that there's something else besides us down here, Jinx thought.

The footsteps moved past them, toward Reven. There was heavy breathing and a grungy, unwashed smell.

"Where are you?" Reven called.

"Reven, be quiet!" Elfwyn yelled back.

That broke the concealment spell. Jinx reached for the knife at his belt. He heard the sound of claws digging at a tree trunk nearby. The thing was going after Reven.

The tree house was off the path, and so the Truce did not apply.

"Reven, the ax is on the tree house roof!" Jinx yelled.

It didn't matter if Reven was the Terror; Jinx couldn't let him be eaten. Jinx ran forward in the dark, trying to think. He didn't know any magic that would do any good.

"Aroint thee, foul dastard!" cried Reven.

There was the *thwok* of an ax hitting wood. Then grunts, flesh hitting flesh, sounds of struggle.

"Reven!" Elfwyn called.

The sound of blows and grunts came from above—a squawk of pain.

Elfwyn turned to Jinx. "Light a fire!"

There was the loud thud of something falling. Then more fighting, down on the ground. Reven's voice, yelling.

Elfwyn thrust a stick into Jinx's hands. "Light that so we can see!"

He lit it. They could see a crouched, horned figure raising a claw to strike at Reven, pinned underneath it. Jinx did the only thing he could think of. He used magic to set the creature on fire.

It roared. Reven screamed. Instantly Jinx pulled the fire out of existence. He hadn't meant to burn Reven.

The creature got to its hind legs and turned to face Jinx. It was completely covered in singed, curly fur—but then there were the horns and a mouthful of tusks. It took a step toward Jinx and Elfwyn.

There was a nasty sound of an ax hitting something soft. The creature screamed. Jinx and Elfwyn jumped out of the way as it fell. Behind it, Reven stood holding the ax.

"Set it on fire now!" said Reven.

"No, don't!" said Elfwyn.

The thing swiped out a paw and grabbed her ankle. Elfwyn yelled as it pulled her to the ground. Reven fell on the creature, swinging his ax. Jinx grabbed Elfwyn and hauled her away. He concentrated on looking to make sure her leg wasn't hurt so that he could ignore the chopping sounds in the dark. Elfwyn got to her feet, shakily.

"Reven, stop," she said. "Please. I'm sure it's dead."

She moved forward with the torch to have a look.

"It's a werebear, isn't it," she said. "I wonder if it's Urson."

"Why does it have horns, then?" said Reven. "Do bears have horns?"

"No—maybe it's an ogre. Jinx, come see."

"No," said Jinx. He felt sick. "I think we should leave."

"But it's safe now," said Reven. "The tree house—"

"You can stay in it if you want," said Jinx. "But we're leaving."

"I'm not leaving unless Reven does."

"Very well," said Reven. "Let me get our things." He

looked at the bloody ax, smiled, then handed it to Jinx. "I think I'm getting the feel of this thing."

They walked along the path in the dark. Jinx made the torch glow brightly enough that they could see the edges of the path, and he hoped the light would keep wolves and bears away.

"Why did you follow us?" said Jinx.

"To talk you two out of going to the Bonemaster's house," said Elfwyn.

"It's not easy to talk me out of things, fair lady," said Reven.

Jinx thought of the chopping sounds and how they had gone on long after the werebear—or whatever it had been—was already dead. No, Reven might be friendly and unfailingly cheerful, but it wouldn't be easy to talk him out of anything.

"I just think—" Elfwyn paused. "You saw how my grandmother is. She likes to . . . amuse herself with people. I think she's sending you off to the Bonemaster to see what he does to you. Which personally I don't think is very amusing."

"She's not sending me," said Reven. "I'm going."

"I just want to find out what he can tell me about my magic," said Jinx.

"He might not be able to tell you anything. You can't

trust my grandmother. And Simon told you to stay away from him."

"That's because Simon knows the Bonemaster can tell me what he's done to me."

"If you believe my grandmother!" said Elfwyn. "He'll suck out your soul with a straw and make a necklace of your eyeballs. There were two men from Butterwood Clearing who went to his house to sell him butter, and they never came back. He sneaks into clearings at night and steals babies from their cradles."

"And his thoughts are full of bloody knives," said Reven.

"They're what?" said Elfwyn.

"Jinx can see people's thoughts."

"You can?" said Elfwyn.

"No," said Jinx. Reven was just as bad as Elfwyn, blabbing about whatever you told him.

Uncomfortably, Jinx remembered some of the things he'd blabbed to Sophie during his fight with Simon.

"I used to be able to."

He told Elfwyn about being able to see the color of people's thoughts.

She stopped walking. "You mean you really could read people's minds? No wonder he took it away from you! He probably saved your life."

Jinx shook his head—she didn't understand. "No, he didn't. It was horrible. It was like being killed."

"If you could read people's minds, they would *want* to kill you. You were a menace to society. Trust me, I know about this sort of thing." Elfwyn seemed to think for a moment. "Although I suppose you would have been very hard to kill."

"It wasn't reading people's minds. It was like what was going on inside their heads would make a sort of cloud around them, and it would have a sort of color."

They started walking again. A wind had come up, and the flames of the torch blew sideways. Branches creaked overhead.

"How'd he take the power away from you?" Elfwyn asked.

"He did a spell and put it in a bottle."

"Perhaps you could take it out of the bottle," said Reven.

"He hid it somewhere. And even if I found it, what would I do? Uncork it and drink?"

"Well, can't you just learn the magic again? I mean it's your magic, right?" said Elfwyn.

"Maybe," said Jinx. "It's not like something you learn, though. It's more like a sense."

He thought about the power that he'd newly discovered, that he could draw from the Urwald. No wonder he hadn't been able to do much magic in Simon's house—thick stone walls had blocked him off from the Urwald. But out here, he could sense its enormous presence. He felt he could levitate a house—he could make a fire as big as the sky.

But he also felt that he couldn't. Because it was the Urwald's power. And he wasn't sure the Urwald would like him levitating a house, and he *knew* it wasn't interested in big fires.

"Does your grandmother not expect you to return, my lady?" Reven asked.

"No. I told her I was going back to Butterwood Clearing," said Elfwyn.

"I thought you were going to live with her," said Jinx.

"Well, yes. That was the idea. But I didn't tell her that. I sort of don't entirely like her very much."

There was a sudden loud *crack* overhead. Elfwyn and Jinx lunged forward, but Reven didn't know to run. An enormous tree branch crashed down on the path.

"Reven?" Elfwyn called.

They ran back. Jinx made the torchlight brighter. A branch lay in the path. Standing just in front of it was Reven.

"Forsooth, you told me not to cut limbs off trees," said Reven. "And here they are throwing them at me."

"It's awfully windy," said Elfwyn. "Maybe we should go back to the tree house."

"We've come too far," said Jinx. "And we probably couldn't find it in the dark anyway."

They hurried on. The wind was picking up. The torch blew out, and Jinx didn't want to waste time lighting it again. The trees groaned and lashed their branches overhead.

When the next tree branch cracked overhead, Reven ran. He was faster than Jinx and Elfwyn. Ahead along the path Jinx heard another branch break, and Reven yelled, "Ow!"

"Are you all right, Reven? Jinx, light a fire!"

A big dead branch filled the path. Jinx relit the torch. Reven was sitting beside the branch holding his arm.

Elfwyn knelt down beside him. "Where did it hit you?"

"My arm. 'Tis nothing, my lady."

"It might be broken," said Elfwyn.

A fierce gust of wind tore through the trees, which swayed and rasped horribly.

Reven got to his feet, wincing. "We'd better keep moving."

Before the Urwald decides to drop a whole tree on you, Jinx thought. He grabbed Reven's good arm.

Reven's face flickered amusement in the torchlight. "I can walk unassisted, good Jinx."

"The Urwald," said Jinx, "doesn't want to kill me."

He felt quite sure of this. He was the Listener, and the Urwald didn't want him dead. Why it wanted Reven dead he didn't know—but none of those three branches had come near him or Elfwyn.

"It's windy, that's all," said Reven.

The torch blew out again.

Jinx couldn't remember ever being out in such wind before. Branches fell all around—no, only behind them, Jinx realized. And on the path. And the wind howled and blew at their backs, urging them along the path.

"When we get to that canyon the good Dame mentioned," said Reven, "there won't be any more of these terrible trees."

"You're not going into the Canyon of Bones, are you?" said Elfwyn.

"We have to, to reach the Bonemaster's house," said Reven. "And to escape this storm."

"Maybe the wind will die down before we get there," said Jinx.

But somehow he didn't think it would.

The wind did not let up. They walked all night. In the early afternoon they reached a place where the path turned sharply to the right and zigzagged.

"Switchbacks," said Reven. "We're coming down into the canyon."

Elfwyn cast a nervous glance back at the forest, as if she were going to suggest stopping. A furious smack of wind tore through the trees and pushed them onward, forcing them down the switchbacks.

They came out at the top of a steep bank. They heard

rushing water below.

They climbed down, using the exposed roots of a tree for a ladder. As Jinx grabbed the tree roots in his hands, he heard the Urwald mumbling that the enemy was trapped.

The river had cut its way deep into solid bedrock, and Jinx couldn't see the bottom through the rushing water. In front of them the water crested into a wave, and water zipped over the crest faster than Jinx could run.

"We can't cross that," said Reven. "The current would grind our bones to powder."

There were no trees around them now, and they couldn't feel the wind down here. Jinx looked up and saw that the trees were barely stirring in the wind now.

"We could go back," said Elfwyn. "It looks like the wind's died down."

"It will die back up again if we do," said Jinx.

Elfwyn nodded.

"Dame Glammer said that we go up the canyon from here," said Reven.

"Only if we want to find the Bonemaster," said Elfwyn.

Jinx was undecided. He wanted to go close enough to talk to the Bonemaster, yes. But down here in the canyon, away from any trees, he felt exposed and helpless. It didn't seem like such a good idea.

But Reven started walking, and Jinx and Elfwyn went with him.

They walked along the flat rock lip a few inches above the foaming river. To their right, hemlocks hooked down from the cliff with half their roots reaching out into the air like hands imploring Jinx and his companions not to go any farther.

Jinx took hold of a root, but the tree spoke only of trying to get a living from the solid rock. It wasn't concerned about the Bonemaster or about Jinx's problems.

The chasm walls grew higher on either side of them, steep and sheer. Jinx had never walked so far without trees around him, not even in Samara. The feeling was strange and cold, and he kept looking up to make sure the Urwald was still there, just visible at the cliff tops on both sides.

"It's so beautiful," said Elfwyn.

"What is?" said Jinx.

"This place." She gestured around at the river, the rocks, the multicolored cliff face. Jinx didn't think it was beautiful.

He couldn't feel the Urwald's lifeforce anymore, and he knew he wouldn't be able to draw on it.

They stopped after a while to rest and eat, and Reven went to get some driftwood for a fire. He brought it back and set it down in a rattling heap, with a funny expression on his face.

"Those are bones," said Elfwyn.

Jinx picked one up. It was smooth and cold in his

hand. A leg bone, maybe—of what? He thought a fire into it. It was much harder to do magic down here away from the trees, even though the fire was inside him. When the bone was aflame, he set it down amid the other bones in the heap.

"Jinx, put that out," said Elfwyn. "It's not right."

Jinx sucked the flame away with a thought. "They might be animal bones." But he could see her point.

"We don't really need a fire," said Reven.

While the other two unpacked the food, Jinx wandered over to look at the rest of the bones. They had all been washed up in a heap, jumbled together. He didn't see any skulls. With skulls you could tell right away that they weren't human—unless they were, of course.

He heard footsteps on pebbles behind him. He spun around. It was only Reven.

"They're not human," said Reven. He sounded uncertain too.

Jinx poked around in the pile, looking for a hoof or a fang or something to tell him these weren't human bones.

"I think we should turn back," he said.

Elfwyn came up beside them. "So do I."

"Well, at least we'll go look," said Reven. "Or I will."

Elfwyn and Jinx looked at each other. They weren't turning back if Reven wasn't.

None of them felt much like eating. They put the food

away in their packs and walked on.

"There, that's the fork up ahead, where the good dame said we'd find him," said Reven.

It was a high gray bluff, a tall stone island splitting the canyon into a Y. The river came rushing down from the left-hand side of the Y. From the right-hand side it came too, but much more quietly. On the top of the island was a castle.

"I guess that's the Bonemaster's house," said Elfwyn.

"Yup," said Jinx. "I always heard it was made of bones, though."

"Maybe you misheard," said Reven. "Bone, stone."

Jinx had a cold feeling in his stomach. He wished Reven or Elfwyn would suggest turning back.

"See, there's a bridge sort of thing," said Elfwyn. "I guess that's how you get up."

Jinx looked where she pointed, up the right-hand fork. It looked more like a rope ladder than a bridge. It started on their side of the stream and climbed upward toward the top of the island. It sagged.

"It doesn't look like such a bad climb," said Reven.

"I think it looks horrible," said Elfwyn. "What if you fell off onto the rocks below?"

They walked up the right-hand fork of the Y and drew closer to the bridge. There were two long ropes strung on either side of the bridge, as railings, with short ropes every few feet to affix them to the bridge. The deck of the bridge was supported on two more ropes and was made of—

"Those aren't bones, are they?" said Elfwyn.

"It could be an illusion," said Jinx. "In fact, it probably is. This is the Urwald. Wood is a lot easier to get than bones."

"Hmm. Perhaps for you, my boy. It depends where you look."

The voice came from behind Jinx.

He turned around and looked up at the Bonemaster.

Bonesocket

The Bonemaster smiled. It was a warm smile, and his blue eyes were kind.

"Well, well. Look at this. Visitors—I do love to have visitors. Please come upstairs."

"We—we'd rather not," said Elfwyn. "Thank you."

"And who are you, young lady?"

"Elfwyn of Butterwood Clearing," said Elfwyn, looking miserable.

"And your friends—ah!" The Bonemaster beamed at Jinx. "I recognize you. Simon's boy. Now wait, it'll come to me—Jinx! Well, that settles it, you *must* come upstairs."

Jinx looked at Elfwyn and Reven in despair. Clearly

Elfwyn hadn't been fooled by the Bonemaster's warm greeting. Jinx might have been if he didn't have the memory of those bloody daggers. Reven looked fascinated.

"Perhaps you didn't hear me," said the Bonemaster, the knife blades creeping into his voice. "I said you must come upstairs."

He gripped Jinx and Reven each by a shoulder and dragged them toward the bridge. Jinx tried to struggle free, but the grip became much tighter and more painful. Reven wasn't struggling at all. Huh. Why *had* Reven insisted on coming here, knowing they'd follow?

"You'd best go ahead of us, young lady," said the Bonemaster. "Otherwise you might try to run away. And that could make something very nasty happen to your friends."

"Run away, Elfwyn!" said Jinx.

"You want to die so soon, Jinx?" said the Bonemaster. "Start climbing, Elfwyn."

Elfwyn stepped forward, gripped the two rope railings in both hands, and took her first step onto the bones.

"Careful—they're a little slippery underfoot," she said, and began to climb.

The Bonemaster gave Jinx a hard shove, so that he stumbled forward onto the bridge, shaking it and making Elfwyn rock and slide and nearly fall off. She said nothing, though, and kept climbing. Jinx followed.

If the bones were an illusion, they were a very good

one. You could see through the wide cracks if you looked down, to the river and the ground swaying sickly below. Jinx swallowed and looked resolutely upward, at the stone castle. He clutched the ropes so tightly, he could feel little hempen splinters working their way into his hands. He wondered if the bones would break under his feet.

Behind him, he heard Reven and the Bonemaster begin to climb. The bridge rocked more and more. Could it actually hold the weight of four people?

Jinx leaned too hard on one of the rope railings and felt a horrible pitching sensation as he swooped out over empty space. Reven grabbed him and pulled him back.

"Easy, Jinx," said Reven. "Hold on to the bones, not the ropes."

"Do be careful," said the Bonemaster. "It would make such an unsightly mess if you fell."

Jinx did as Reven suggested and held on to the bones, climbing the bridge like a ladder. He wasn't afraid of heights, really—well, he never had been before.

At last he saw Elfwyn, just ahead of him, reach the top. Then he did. He crawled off the bridge onto what should have been solid stone. But the ground rocked like a cradle. Jinx stayed on his hands and knees. He couldn't have stood up if he'd wanted to, because he wasn't sure which direction was up.

"Oh dear. Not got a head for heights, I see, Jinx. I

fear you may not enjoy your stay in my little abode, then."

"Jinx, what's the matter?" Elfwyn's voice seemed to echo from far away.

"It's just vertigo," said Reven.

Just vertigo? It felt worse than anything since the day Simon had taken his magic.

"You ready to get up? Take your time," said Reven.

Jinx let Reven help him and was very relieved that standing didn't make him throw up. The ground had stopped rocking, and he could see Reven and Elfwyn looking at him with concern. The Bonemaster must be behind him. So was that dreadful bridge.

The castle loomed. It was made of the same gray stone as the cliff-flanked island itself. Behind it pink-blue ladders of light stretched across the sky—more sunset than Jinx had ever seen. He could see nothing growing except lichen.

By itself, the castle's great wooden door creaked open.

"Welcome to Bonesocket," said the Bonemaster. "Won't you step inside?"

The Bonemaster led them into a great stone hall with a ceiling arching thirty feet over their heads. A fire crackled in the middle of the room, and a table was laid for four.

The Bonemaster stepped to the head of the table. "Won't you please be seated."

They sat. Jinx was nonplussed. They'd just been taken

prisoner, none too gently. He hadn't expected dinner. The food smelled real. There was roast turkey, and browned potatoes, and candied squash.

"Is the food real or illusion?" Elfwyn whispered.

"Can't tell," Jinx whispered back. He wondered if it was safe to eat. Now that he was over his nausea, he was really hungry.

"You must try the candied squash, Elfwyn. It's my specialty," the Bonemaster said, passing her the dish.

Elfwyn took the dish as though it were going to explode and looked at it with alarm.

"Now, I have everyone's names except yours, young man." The Bonemaster looked at Reven.

Reven stood up and bowed. "Reven. Your servant, good Bonemaster."

"What charming manners. Please sit down. Try the turkey."

He insisted they put some of everything on their plates. Reven didn't seem suspicious about the food at all. Jinx watched as the Bonemaster speared a piece of turkey on his knife and ate it. Reven, who had been politely waiting for the Bonemaster to start, spooned up some squash.

"'Tis most excellent fare, sir," said Reven.

Reven didn't drop dead from eating it, so Jinx figured it was safe.

The food didn't taste like an illusion. It tasted real. Jinx had missed Simon's cooking, but he had to admit that the Bonemaster's was better. The turkey was a little strange because he hadn't eaten meat in years, but he got used to it.

"Do try the wine. It's a particularly fine vintage," said the Bonemaster.

Jinx looked down at the cup beside his plate, which was half full of dark wine. The cup was grayish white, but the rim was of beaten gold. It had three legs. Jinx picked it up and looked underneath. It was rounded on the bottom, with crazed squizzly lines crisscrossing it. Jinx put the cup down without drinking. He looked around the table. The other three cups were the same.

Reven picked up his cup and took a sip. "A fine vintage indeed, sir."

When they were done eating, the Bonemaster led them over to the fire. He waved a hand to move the chairs from the table to the fireside.

"Now then." The Bonemaster looked at each of them with his knife-sharp eyes. "I am certainly looking forward to hearing what has brought me such delightful visitors."

Jinx looked at Elfwyn. They both looked at Reven.

"Jinx? Perhaps you will explain," said the Bonemaster.

The eyes stabbed at him. Jinx tried to look away, but he couldn't. He looked into the Bonemaster's deep blue eyes and the Bonemaster looked into his. The eyes held Jinx in place as if he'd been run through with a sword. It had been stupid to come here thinking he could ask the Bonemaster for help.

"Tell me, Jinx, how did you escape from Simon?"

"I didn't escape from Simon," said Jinx. "I just left."

"Really? You just left? You expect me to believe that Simon permitted you to simply walk away?"

The eyes were giving Jinx a headache. "I don't care what you believe."

"Ah. I see you have Simon's manners." The Bonemaster looked away at last. Jinx closed his eyes and rubbed them.

"Now, will you tell us what brings you here, Reven?"

Reven said nothing.

"Hm. You're so much more polite than our friend Jinx. Won't you speak when spoken to? What brings you here?"

Reven looked agonized.

"Ah. Interesting." The Bonemaster turned to Elfwyn. "And what brings *you* here, Elfwyn?"

"I followed the boys to try to make them turn back."

"Ha. Interesting. And why did you want them to turn back?"

"Because I thought you would harm them."

"Did you. Clever girl. And what made them want to come here in the first place?"

"Jinx wanted to find out what Simon's done to him. And Reven thought you could take his curse off him."

"Ah. And what is this curse that's on him?"

"I don't know."

"Interesting. Very interesting." The Bonemaster smiled. "But you have suspicions, perhaps."

Elfwyn didn't say anything.

"Ah. It has to be a question, does it?"

"Yes," said Elfwyn miserably.

"What do you suspect the curse on Reven is?"

"That he can't tell what the curse is."

"That much is obvious," said the Bonemaster with a flicker of irritation. He turned back to Reven. "Can you say who you are?"

Reven said nothing.

"Excellent! Who put you under this spell?"

No answer.

"Oh, an expert, I see!" The Bonemaster rubbed his hands together. "A challenge. Where do you come from?"

"King Rufus's court, in Bragwood," said Reven.

"Ah, you can answer that. We'll assume it's not really where you come from, then. Where are you going?"

No answer.

"Where is he going, Elfwyn?"

"I don't know," said Elfwyn.

"Lovely," said the Bonemaster. "Three wretchedly nasty spells. Young Reven can't say who he is, you are bound to answer any question truthfully, and Jinx here has lost his life."

"What?" said Reven.

"I haven't lost my life!" said Jinx.

"He's still alive, for one thing," said Elfwyn.

"Oh, he's *alive*," said the Bonemaster. "But he hasn't got his life."

Jinx thought of the ball of light Simon had put into the green glass bottle while Jinx floated through the ceiling and saw the starry horizon.

"Would you care for some fruit?" The Bonemaster snapped his fingers, and a bowl of fruit landed in his outstretched hand.

"Er, no thank you," said Reven, and Jinx and Elfwyn shook their heads.

The Bonemaster took an apple and bit into it, then leaned back in his chair, rested one ankle on the opposite knee, and looked from Reven to Elfwyn. "So, you want these spells taken off you. You realize that may cost you something?"

"Wait a minute," said Jinx. "How can I have lost my life? What are you talking about? How can you tell?"

"I saw it when I looked into your eyes," said the Bonemaster. "Your life is gone. I assume Simon took it."

"But, well, wouldn't he have had to kill me?"

"That's a rather abrupt way of putting it, but at some point in the procedure, in order to take your life, yes. He would have had to kill you."

"Simon wouldn't do that!"

The Bonemaster smiled. "Young Simon? My good friend Simon? Oh, goodness. I don't think you know Simon as well as I do, Jinx."

Jinx tried to calm down enough to think. He was afraid of the Bonemaster in a way that he'd never been afraid of Simon. But there was no denying that spell Simon had done on him. And the glowing ball that had gone into the bottle. His life?

"He did a spell with a bottle," Jinx said.

"Yes? I'm amazed he managed it." The Bonemaster smiled. "Such a terrible, terrible thing to do. And do you find, now, that you don't feel quite whole?"

Jinx thought of his missing magic and the blank white space in his brain that still got in his way sometimes. He didn't feel whole at all.

"Simon is not a good person, Jinx." The Bonemaster sounded sad to be telling Jinx this news. "Power means too much to him. He'd do anything for new magic, for new knowledge. He'd do anything for power."

Was that true? Jinx thought of Simon staying up all night to work on new spells, of Simon driving Sophie away so he could do a spell on Jinx. So he could *kill* Jinx.

"Now that he's got your life, I suppose he thought it was safe to let you wander," said the Bonemaster. "Though as it happens, he was wrong. I once thought he meant to train you up as a magical minion to do his bidding. But perhaps he found you had no talent."

Jinx clenched his teeth to keep from retorting that he had plenty of talent. The fact was, he probably didn't. Simon certainly hadn't seemed to think so.

"I *thought* he sounded like an evil wizard," said Reven.

The Bonemaster swallowed a mouthful of apple. "Oh, he most certainly is that. He opened a way into Samara so that he could study at the university there. Magic is illegal in Samara, or so I'm told—I've never been there—but their libraries contain magical knowledge that we've never had here. Simon spent years there, learned things the rest of us don't know."

"Learning things isn't evil," said Elfwyn.

"Indeed not. But he keeps what he learned to himself. Knowledge was meant to be free to everyone."

Jinx thought of how secretive Simon was, not letting Jinx look in certain books, not letting him into his workroom at first.

"If the way into Samara was open, then everyone could go there who wanted to, and study," said the Bonemaster.

"What is this Samara?" said Reven.

"I'll let Jinx tell you," said the Bonemaster, his eyes glinting.

"Er, it's a . . . a country with no trees in it," said Jinx. He kept both eyes on the Bonemaster, but he couldn't see any harm in describing Samara. "And the houses are all close together, and people wear bright colors. And it's hot."

"Ah—so you've actually been there," said the Bonemaster.

"If there are no trees, then it seems like they would want to establish trade with the Urwald," said Reven.

"What? Why?" said Jinx.

"For trees," said Reven.

"I don't think Urwald trees would grow there."

"I don't mean live trees," said Reven. "I mean lumber."

It was like saying you wanted to sell people for meat.

"So Simon won't share the secrets of Samara with his fellow wizards, but he'll share them with you," said the Bonemaster. "Tell me, how did you fall into his power?"

Was there any harm in telling that? "I was lost in the forest," said Jinx.

"Ah." The Bonemaster tossed his apple core into the fire, where it hissed. "Just a life, lost in the forest."

Jinx felt he probably shouldn't have said so much about Samara after all. He was betraying Simon's secrets. He probably shouldn't do that. Except that he didn't owe Simon anything if Simon had—well, killed him. He didn't know who to trust. He felt miserable.

He looked across at Reven and Elfwyn, wondering what they were thinking. Elfwyn should have told Jinx that her curse required her to tell the truth. He couldn't trust her, either. Though when she looked back at him, he could see she felt bad about it.

"You know about life force magic, I take it? It uses the power in a life, which can be converted into magic," said the Bonemaster. "Most wizards have only their own lives to draw on. But when a wizard draws on another person's life, ah, then he's much more than twice as powerful."

The Bonemaster gazed into the fire, thoughtful. "Especially if the owner of the life is still alive."

"Why?" said Elfwyn.

"Because the captured life is still growing, of course. The, ah, liver is still producing power."

"Liver?" said Reven.

"The person whose life it is," said Elfwyn.

"Yes." The Bonemaster stared into the flames. "Naturally, Simon's power would be decreased if Jinx were to . . . cease to be alive."

A heavy silence followed this remark.

"What's deathforce magic?" Jinx asked. He tried to sound nonchalant. He didn't want the Bonemaster to think he was frightened.

"Ah, hasn't Simon told you about deathforce magic?"

"He says he never does it," said Jinx.

"Simon says that? *Simon?*" The Bonemaster smiled. "Well, well."

"So what is it?" Jinx demanded.

"It's magic that uses the force of a death as its power."

"Is deathforce stronger than lifeforce?" Elfwyn asked.

"That depends," said the Bonemaster. He did not elaborate.

"The Urwald has lifeforce power," said Jinx. He was just thinking it; he hadn't meant to say it aloud.

The Bonemaster chuckled. "Oh, certainly. But it's not as if any wizard could draw on it."

Jinx didn't say anything. He remembered the power from the trees coming up through his feet.

"Urwald magic is completely different from wizard's magic," said the Bonemaster. "The two can't be mixed. Well. You want these curses taken off you. But we haven't yet discussed the question of payment."

"Can you really do it?" said Elfwyn.

"I am a wizard, young lady."

Jinx untied the top of his shirt and reached into his secret pocket. He scooped out the contents in one handful. "I have five silver pennies," he said.

"You understand I can't do anything about *your* problem," said the Bonemaster. "Your life is gone."

"But, well—isn't there some way to get it back?" said Jinx, afraid of the answer.

"Not really," said the Bonemaster. "Simon has it. For the moment, it still exists and you're still alive."

The half of me that's aboveground, Jinx thought, remembering Dame Glammer's words.

He thought about all his years with Simon, when he'd thought that Simon was basically being pretty nice to him, in his cranky way. Had Simon just been waiting for Jinx to grow big enough to have a life that was worth taking?

"Do people's lives get more powerful when they get older?" he asked.

"Of course."

"So the evil wizard Simon could kill Jinx from afar simply by destroying his captive life?" said Reven.

"Yes," said the Bonemaster. He let a long pause settle over this. "It would not be to his advantage to do so, however. A captive life is a great power."

Jinx hated them talking about the life he didn't have. "Well, I'll pay for *their* curses to be taken off." He'd gladly pay anything just to get out of the Bonemaster's castle. He held out his hand.

"Five silver pennies and—what's this?" The Bonemaster reached over and plucked the tiny golden bird out of Jinx's hand. "Gold? Now why would a failed apprentice have gold? Unless you stole it?"

"I didn't steal it! Simon gave it to me."

"Gave it to you." The Bonemaster held it between his thumb and forefinger, and it glimmered in the firelight. "Now isn't that interesting."

He brought the bird a few inches from his face and smiled at it. "Hello, Simon."

The Insistent Door

J inx stared.

The Bonemaster beamed at Jinx, then went on talking to the bird talisman. "How silly of me to think you'd sent the boy into the Urwald completely free, Simon. That would be so unlike you. You're keeping an eye on him, aren't you? Well, he's here at Bonesocket. He's alive at the moment. Perhaps you'll be wanting to stop in soon for a visit."

The Bonemaster tucked the bird into a pocket in his robe and smiled at Jinx, Elfwyn, and Reven. "Come. I shall show you to your rooms."

The room Jinx had been given had purple velvet drapes. Jinx touched them—the cloth was really there but felt rough and nubbly. Not velvet, then. It seemed like a waste of magic. Simon wouldn't have approved. Simon. The thought of Simon was like a heavy weight in his stomach.

Dame Glammer had been right. The Bonemaster *had* told Jinx a few things about Simon. And Jinx didn't like any of them.

He tugged at the window. It wouldn't open. He tried levitating it, but the Urwald's power was out of reach, and he couldn't seem to find the power inside himself. Well, no wonder, if Simon had his lifeforce. And Simon had always scolded him for not being able to draw enough power! Simon. Bah.

Jinx searched for something else to draw on and immediately became aware of an enormous force. There was a massive amount of power somewhere in this castle.

Jinx didn't dare try to use it. It had to be the Bonemaster's power source, and the Bonemaster might sense him drawing on it.

There was a knock at the door. Jinx opened it. Elfwyn and Reven came in.

"Pretty strange, isn't it?" Elfwyn said when the door was safely closed.

"You could have told us you had a curse on you that made you have to tell the truth," said Jinx.

"Well, it's pretty embarrassing," said Elfwyn. "You didn't tell us that evil wizard of yours had killed you."

"I didn't know!"

"Did it hurt?"

Jinx didn't want to talk about it.

"I was trying to open the window, but I can't," he said instead. "I haven't got the power."

Reven went over to the window and pulled—he couldn't open it either. "You mean you can't do magic at all here?"

"Not really," said Jinx. "I mean, there's a lot of power here, but I can't use it without the Bonemaster noticing."

"He caused that windstorm. I'm sure of it," said Elfwyn.

"I don't think wizards can cause storms," said Jinx. He'd never read anything about wizards being able to control the weather, and Simon had never mentioned—but you couldn't trust Simon.

"We'd better leave," said Elfwyn.

"Right," said Jinx.

"What?" Reven was surprised. "But the wizard—"

"He's evil," said Jinx. "And we're getting out of here."

"But I had hoped he might—" Reven trailed off, unable to mention his spell.

"He won't," said Elfwyn. "Whatever he wants to keep us here for, it's not to take our curses off us."

"But Jinx offered to pay him," said Reven.

"Reven, look at this castle," said Elfwyn. "Look at the

velvet drapes. The Bonemaster doesn't need Jinx's money!"

"Actually the drapes are an illusion," said Jinx. "But yeah."

"He seemed quite pleased with that golden charm he took from Jinx," said Reven. "I'm sure that's worth a bit."

Elfwyn frowned. "What was it, anyway?"

"It's called an aviot." Jinx sighed. "Simon told me never to go out without it."

"Why?"

"Well, I *thought* it was for safety," said Jinx. "But I guess it was just a spell for spying on me."

"Maybe he wanted to spy on you to keep you safe," said Elfwyn.

"Elfwyn, he *killed* me," Jinx reminded her.

"But do you think he'll come here looking for you?" said Reven.

"Why would he?" said Jinx, exasperated.

"Well, because, if the good Bonemaster is telling the truth, then you give the evil wizard Simon great power." Reven frowned. "Perhaps we should at least stay here until we've had time to see whether the Bonemaster—"

"Whether he wants to turn us into more parts for his bridge?" said Jinx. "Reven, he's called the Bonemaster. He has a bridge made of bones. He's just the slightest bit creepy, or didn't you notice that?"

"Yes, all right. I noticed that. But—"

"Oh, and you drank wine out of a cup made from a skull."

Reven and Elfwyn both looked ill at that. "Are you sure?" said Reven.

"All the cups on the table were made from skulls."

"But they didn't look like skulls," said Elfwyn.

Jinx explained the technique for making a cup out of a skull.

"And I suppose you learned that from Simon the not-evil wizard," said Elfwyn.

"Of course," said Jinx. "So are we leaving?"

"Let me get my things," said Elfwyn.

Reven considered. "Very well. I had hoped he might—"

"Take your spell off you," Jinx supplied. "It's more likely he'll take your bones off you."

"Yes, I suppose you're right," said Reven.

They fetched their backpacks. Reven slipped the ax through the straps of his pack.

"It looks dark down there," said Elfwyn. "I think he's gone to bed."

Jinx crept to the top of the stairs and looked into the great hall. The fire had died down to embers, and a gray curl of smoke rose from it. He nodded to Elfwyn and Reven, and the three of them tiptoed down the stairs.

Dark shadows filled the hall. There was no sound except for the drip of water somewhere far away. They reached the great oaken door.

Reven put his hand on the latch.

"It's locked," he whispered.

Jinx tried to levitate the latch, but it wouldn't budge. "Let's look for a back door," he said.

He started back across the hall.

"Jinx!" whispered Elfwyn, just behind him.

He turned around. Reven was still standing by the door with both hands on the latch. Jinx made a come-on gesture. Reven shook his head furiously. Elfwyn went back, and Jinx followed her.

"What do you think you're doing?" Jinx whispered. "Come on!"

"I can't," said Reven. "My hands are stuck to the door."

"Just pull them away," said Elfwyn, taking hold of one of Reven's wrists. She pulled.

"Ow! Let go!" said Reven. They were all still whispering.

"I can't let go!" said Elfwyn.

This was ridiculous. Jinx reached out and grabbed Elfwyn's arm to pull her away from Reven. At least he only grabbed her with one hand—so he still had the other hand free. But the hand he put on Elfwyn's arm was stuck fast.

"I thought you said wizards couldn't do spells on people," said Elfwyn.

"He did the spell on the door, not on us. But I don't know how—"

Spells were hard to maintain if you weren't actually looking at the object you were bespelling. It depended on how complicated the spell was, of course, and how powerful the wizard was. An illusion on curtains, for example, was much easier than something like this door. Jinx knew the Bonemaster had an immense power source nearby. Still, it was most likely that—

"He's here watching us," said Jinx.

"Ah. Quite so," said the Bonemaster, stepping out of the shadows.

Evil dastard! He'd known they'd try to escape, and he'd turned it into a trap. Jinx reached with his free hand for the ax strapped to Reven's back. He had just worked it loose when it flew up out of his hand and struck the ceiling. Jinx swore.

"Tsk. Such language, and in front of a lady," said the Bonemaster.

"Let us go!" said Jinx.

The Bonemaster summoned a chair with a wave of his hand and sat down on it. "You know, manners are very important. You won't have learned this from Simon. If you don't have any manners, well, then who's going to listen to you?"

"I don't call it very good manners to stick people to

your front door." Elfwyn's voice was muffled by Reven's coat, which was about an inch from her face.

"You stuck yourselves to the door," said the Bonemaster, leaning back in his chair and looking ready to settle in for a nice long chat. "I can't think what you mean by it, but perhaps you'll explain."

Reven was frantically trying to scratch his nose by rubbing it against the door.

"Oh, it has to be a question, doesn't it?" said the Bonemaster. "Tell me, Elfwyn, what were the three of you doing?"

"Leaving," said Elfwyn.

"Now why would you want to do that?"

"Because we're afraid of you."

"Yes, yes, how tiresome of you," said the Bonemaster. "People always are. And yet they come here anyway. Don't you think that's odd?"

"Yes," said Elfwyn.

"But then they often find it quite difficult to leave," said the Bonemaster.

"The evil wizard Simon knows we're here!" said Reven.

"That's what I'm hoping," said the Bonemaster. "It will certainly be a more amusing party once he arrives."

He took the gold bird out of his pocket and spoke to it. "When you come to rescue your pet thief, Simon, be sure to bring what you stole from me. Otherwise I may not give him back."

"I'm not a thief," said Jinx. And he certainly wasn't a pet.

"No? No instructions to come here and—no, I find I don't believe that, Jinx."

The Bonemaster spoke to the bird again. "Come to think of it, Simon, bring me what you took from the boy."

He looked back at Jinx. "He does want you back, I take it."

"Yes," said Jinx, only because he figured that was the correct answer if he wanted to stay alive. "What do we have to do to get you to unstick us?"

"Ah, that's more like it." The Bonemaster smiled at Jinx. "I think—" He steepled his fingers together, leaned farther back in his chair, and looked up at the ceiling, where the ax was half buried in a beam. "I think I would like you to work for me, Jinx. As my servant. Until I find some other use for you."

"All right," said Jinx.

"Goodness, how suspiciously quickly you agree, young man. I'm afraid I'm no more trusting than you are. I wonder how I can assure myself of your loyalty? Especially when you've just attacked me with an ax."

"I wasn't attacking you. I was going to chop the door down," said Jinx.

"Ah. It's just as well you didn't. I pay a ghoul to patrol the island at night."

Jinx was getting very uncomfortable stuck to Elfwyn's arm.

"I think you'll work for me," said the Bonemaster, "because you want me to take those curses off your friends. Am I right?"

"Yes," said Jinx.

"And also because you wouldn't like your friends to be *harmed* in any way. Am I right?"

Jinx clenched his teeth. "Yes."

"Excellent," said the Bonemaster. "Tomorrow, then, you can begin working for me. Your first job will be to convince Simon that if he wants to find more left of you than bones, he'd better get here soon."

He waved a hand, and they were all unstuck. Jinx shook out his arm, which had fallen asleep and was all pins and needles.

Reven scratched his nose, stretched his arms and legs, and then charged at the Bonemaster, ready to do mayhem. He got two steps before he froze like a statue, unbalanced on one foot, and toppled. Jinx caught him and lowered him to the floor, thinking as he did that Reven probably wasn't in league with the Bonemaster after all.

"He's frozen your clothes," said Jinx. "As soon as he looks away from you, you'll be unfrozen."

"Ah, sooner than that," said the Bonemaster. He waved a hand again, and Reven was unfrozen and got to his knees, looking confused. "Let's not try that again, young Reven. I'd hate to have to damage someone important enough to have a curse like yours cast on him."

The Bonemaster's Secret

The next day Jinx and his friends explored the Bonemaster's demesnes. The Bonemaster allowed them to. In fact, he invited them to, all smiles and politeness. Jinx was suspicious.

"Do be careful out there," said the Bonemaster. "I would hate to have you fall off."

They went outside into a gray fog, moving cautiously. The fog was thick—you could see only about twenty feet ahead of you.

When they got to the place where they thought the bridge of bones should be, it wasn't.

"Maybe it's invisible," said Reven. He walked up to

the two stone posts that had anchored the bridge the night before. He felt around the edge of the cliff with his feet.

"Don't do that!" said Jinx.

"Do what?"

"Stand so close to the edge."

Reven laughed. "I'm fine—don't worry about me. See?" He stood on one foot and stuck his other foot out over the edge and waved it.

Jinx closed his eyes and felt ill.

"Stop it, Reven. That's mean," said Elfwyn. "Could he turn the bridge invisible, Jinx?"

"How should I know?" It wasn't nice, but Jinx felt unaccountably irritated with her for sticking up for him. "If Reven says the bridge isn't there, the Bonemaster probably took it away."

"Let's see if there's another way down," said Reven.

And he led the way, walking much too close to the edge of the cliff. Jinx kept far away from it, and Elfwyn walked in between.

The island was about an acre in size, and nothing grew on it except lichen and a single gnarled hemlock tree digging its roots deep into cracks in the rock and finding Jinx-couldn't-imagine-what-nourishment. There was no way down. They could hear water rushing far below.

"Is it just as far down all the way around?" said Elfwyn.

"Come and look," said Reven.

Elfwyn did, cautiously, and Jinx, hating himself for being afraid when they were not, inched forward until he could see over the edge. The canyon was filled with clouds. Nothing penetrated the fog except the black outline of a tree here and there on the cliff tops. You couldn't see the ground.

Jinx really was not a coward. It wasn't as if his brain was afraid—it was his body that was screaming at him to get away from the edge of the cliff.

They circled the island and then started around again. When they had gotten to the farthest point from the wizard's house, they stopped to talk.

"Do you think Simon will be able to get us out of here?" said Elfwyn.

"I don't think he'll even try," said Jinx.

"He must care about you. He gave you that bird so—"

"So he could spy on me!"

"—so he could make sure you were safe."

"Why are you sticking up for him?" Jinx demanded. "You *said* he was evil. You heard what he did to me!"

"I heard what the Bonemaster said he did," said Elfwyn.

"He spied on me! And he took my life!"

Elfwyn looked out at the fog. "Or anyway, that's what the Bonemaster wants you to think."

"Look, I *know* he did," said Jinx. "He did this evil spell and took away my life, and afterward I couldn't see the stuff around people's heads."

And it made sense that that talent would go away with his life, he thought—if he'd developed it to protect himself, like Dame Glammer said. There was no need to protect a life you'd already lost.

Reven cleared his throat. "What does the magic bird do, exactly?"

"Simon has this window." Jinx looked at Elfwyn and remembered how different she'd seemed in the Farseeing Window. She'd never taken Simon's side back then. But then, she'd only spoken words he'd invented for her. "Most the time it just shows you what it wants to, but he must have fixed that bird with a spell so that the Farseeing Window would follow it and he could watch me."

He wondered if Simon's spell enabled him to hear through the window as well as see.

"He won't know where you are, though, will he?" said Reven. "All he'll see is the inside of the Bonemaster's pocket."

"It'll show him Bonesocket, I think," said Jinx.

"You mean the outside of the castle?" said Elfwyn.

"Yeah." Jinx thought about how angry Simon would be if he knew where Jinx was. *Stay away from the Bonemaster.*

"So he'll be here soon," said Reven. "Once he looks in his magic window."

"I doubt it." A thought occurred to Jinx. "Besides, he's kind of sick right now."

"What's the matter with him?" Elfwyn asked.

"Somebody stuck a sword into him."

"And you left him? You didn't stay to take care of him?" Elfwyn seemed really shocked by this.

"He killed me!" Jinx said.

"Yes, but you didn't know that!"

"Anyway, his wife is taking care of him."

"I didn't know evil wizards had wives," said Reven.

"Some do. Anyway, he'll probably forget to look in the Farseeing Window. He kind of forgets about me a lot."

"He's sure to look soon," said Reven.

"I don't see why," said Jinx. "When I was little, he'd just go off places for days and leave me. He probably forgets I exist."

"So what will happen when Simon doesn't show up?" said Reven.

"The Bonemaster will kill us," said Elfwyn. "Well, me, anyway. He might not kill you because you're probably somebody very important. And he might not kill Jinx because he thinks he can use him against Simon."

"Yeah, he can use me by killing me," said Jinx. "Like he said. Because if I'm dead, Simon won't have as much power."

"I wonder how they know each other," said Elfwyn.

"I expect all the evil wizards know each other," said Reven. "How many wizards are there, anyway?"

"Not very many." Jinx had never met any others.

"Simon and the Bonemaster must've been at one time, don't you think?" said Elfwyn. "Because he said Simon stole something, and it would be hard to steal anything from Bonesocket if you weren't inside it."

"We've been inside it and we're not his friends," said Jinx.

They stood in silence for a moment, looking out at the mist.

"We'd better plan to save ourselves, then," said Reven. "The first thing we need to do is find the bridge."

"Can we find out where his power is coming from?" said Elfwyn.

"Probably not," said Jinx. "I mean, he's got a power source hidden somewhere on the island, but it doesn't matter where. He's got a lot of it; that's all we need to know. He can stick us to doors or probably turn us into toads if he wants to."

"I don't understand why you can't use his power source," said Elfwyn.

"Because he would know."

"How?"

"I don't know, he just would. Simon could always tell what I was using for power. It's just something wizards can sense."

"So shouldn't you be able to find where the power

source is, then?" Elfwyn pressed.

"No, because I am not a wizard, all right?"

"There's no need to get cranky," said Elfwyn. "I just thought if you could find his power source, maybe you could use it against him."

"Use it against him? Look, he's the *Bonemaster*. He's a really hugely powerful ferocious wizard. If I even tried to use his power, he'd know it and he'd probably kill me or something. You don't understand magic."

Elfwyn turned away, looking hurt.

"Er, perhaps we could go indoors now?" said Reven.

It was unpleasantly damp and cold out here. They went back to the castle.

"Found that there's no way down, have you?" said the Bonemaster. "Excellent. Then come along, Jinx. It's time we had a talk with Simon."

Jinx wanted no part of this. He didn't want to talk to Simon, and he didn't need Simon "rescuing" him. He was going to get away from the Bonemaster without Simon's help and without falling back into Simon's power. He glared at the tiny golden bird as it lay on the Bonemaster's open palm.

"Simon, I have your boy here, and he has something to say to you."

Jinx tried to pull away, but the Bonemaster's claws

were like iron digging into the flesh of his arm.

"Tell him to come here now if he wants to see you alive," said the Bonemaster.

Jinx said nothing.

The Bonemaster jabbed his thumb just above Jinx's elbow. Intense pain shot through Jinx's arm. He had to clench his teeth hard to keep from screaming.

"Speak," the Bonemaster commanded.

Jinx didn't say a word. The Bonemaster jabbed again, harder.

"I'm fine," Jinx said through clenched teeth.

❧ ❧ ❧

Two weeks had passed, and Simon had not shown. The Bonemaster had not tried to make Jinx speak to Simon again. But he'd kept his promise to make Jinx his servant.

Jinx was straining dragon's blood, which was a job he hated. You had to pick clots out of the strainer with your fingers. The stuff smelled like a murdered village.

Elfwyn was helping the Bonemaster make a potion. She was *always* helping him.

"There, take the phial in the clamp, dear," said the Bonemaster. "Hold it over the flame and agitate it slowly. Excellent. You would have made a much better wizard than Jinx."

Jinx tipped more blood into the strainer and watched it drizzle down into the jar below. The Bonemaster had mostly been kind to Elfwyn, polite to Reven, and domineering to Jinx. Jinx did the work that was expected of him and wished that most of it didn't involve being in the same room as the Bonemaster.

Especially not when Elfwyn was sucking up to him.

"Can girls be wizards?" said Elfwyn.

The Bonemaster beamed at her. "Oh my, yes. There have been very powerful female wizards in the past."

"Not now, though?"

"There are no truly powerful wizards at all now," said the Bonemaster. "Not like we were in the old days. Not since we lost our knowledge of Samaran magic." He clenched his fist. "We should have taken the libraries by force. We should have brought all their contents to the Urwald—take that off the flame, dear. Now just wave it gently—don't spill!—until it cools. Hurry up with that dragon's blood, Jinx."

"It won't pour any faster than it pours," said Jinx.

"Clean the strainer out!"

Jinx shook blood from the strainer and took it to the sink to rinse it out.

"Now you've spattered blood all over the floor," said the Bonemaster.

"What is Samaran magic like, Bonemaster?" Elfwyn asked.

"I don't have the good fortune to know that," said the

Bonemaster. "But it's as different from wizarding magic as wizarding magic is different from Urwald magic."

"Is this potion ready yet?" said Elfwyn.

"No, dear, we have to add half a bat wing. They're on the top shelf."

Elfwyn went for the stepladder, but the Bonemaster said, "Jinx will get them, dear."

Jinx wiped blood from his hands onto his clothes and went and got the stepladder.

"We all know about Samara, you know," said the Bonemaster, speaking to Jinx. "But the ways through were shut over a century ago, when they outlawed magic there. And when you tell me you've actually been there, Jinx, I find that very interesting. How did you get there?"

"I don't really know," said Jinx. He dragged the ladder over to the shelf. "I just sort of got lost and I was there."

"Hm. And where were you before you got lost, exactly?"

"I don't know. Around."

"And was there some sort of spell that you did in the process of getting lost?"

Knowledge Is Power. But that was Samaran magic, precisely the kind the Bonemaster didn't know about. "No, it just sort of happened," said Jinx.

"And how did you get back?"

"Simon came and got me."

"Does Simon go to Samara often?"

"I don't know." Jinx reached for the clay jar labeled BAT WINGS. Everything was neatly and carefully arranged in the Bonemaster's laboratory. It was quite different from Simon's workshop.

"Well, you must notice if he's home or not." The Bonemaster took the jar from Jinx. "There, pound half a wing in the mortar, Elfwyn, dear."

Jinx shrugged. "I never pay much attention to Simon. I just sweep up."

"Get back to that dragon's blood before it clots. You know, if I had access to the kind of secrets that you've had access to, I would have paid a lot of attention. I'm sure Elfwyn would have."

"What would you do if you could get to Samara?" she asked the Bonemaster.

"Do? With access to Samara, to the libraries? I would learn all the magic I could, of course. Knowledge is power."

Jinx started and knocked the jar of dragon's blood onto the floor.

The Bonemaster turned around and clouted Jinx on the ear, very casually. He tended to do that a lot. Jinx put his hand to his burning ear and stood staring at the spilled blood and trying to look stupid.

"Really, Jinx," said the Bonemaster. "It's hard to believe sometimes that Simon would have chosen you as an apprentice. Even if you were a free life lost in the forest."

Jinx wished the subject would stay off of Simon. The thought of Simon's betrayal still hurt. And Simon hadn't come, which meant he didn't care what happened to Jinx, which meant the Bonemaster was probably telling the truth about Jinx's life and about Simon being evil and everything else.

"I wasn't his apprentice," said Jinx. "I was just his servant."

"Whatever you were, you're a large part of his power," said the Bonemaster. "Surely he must realize that once you're dead, your captive lifeforce will be worth much less to him. Why isn't he here yet?"

"I don't know," said Jinx, doing his best not to sound as angry as he was. His ear hurt. He'd forgotten that Simon needed him to be alive—and that was the only reason Simon might come rescue him.

"Are you going to clean up that dragon's blood or not? Can't you do one single thing without being told?"

Furious, Jinx levitated the blood from the floor back into the jar.

He hardly had time to realize his mistake before the Bonemaster grabbed him, lifted him off the floor by his collar, and slammed him against the stone wall.

"That was quite a levitation spell for someone who's not even an apprentice. Using my power source, are you?"

Jinx couldn't answer—he'd had the breath knocked out

of him, and the Bonemaster was twisting his collar tightly around his throat. Things went black and fuzzy at the edge of Jinx's vision.

"Don't ever do it again," said the Bonemaster, squeezing tighter. "My power is my own."

He let go of Jinx, and Jinx slid to the floor. The Bonemaster loomed over him. Jinx struggled to his feet, raising his fists to defend himself.

"What do wizards need power for?" said Elfwyn quickly.

The Bonemaster turned away from Jinx to beam at Elfwyn. "Ah, my dear, it's what makes us wizards in the first place. Most people spend their lives being batted about by circumstances. Wizards take control of circumstances. They make things happen."

He looked at the bat wing that Elfwyn had ground into powder. "Excellent. Now we must let the potion sit for an hour, and it just happens that it's time for my nap."

"I'll go and make a hot posset for you, Bonemaster," said Elfwyn.

"Thank you, my dear. Clean up this mess, Jinx."

They left. Jinx pushed himself away from the wall, still gasping for breath. He kicked the stone wall, hard. He hurt his foot. He hated the Bonemaster, and he wasn't feeling too fond of Elfwyn, either.

He went to the window and glared out it. He couldn't

see Reven, but Reven was probably outside somewhere, exploring. Their plan wasn't going very well. Reven hadn't found the bridge, and he hadn't found a way down.

Jinx found a rag and scrubbed the remaining blood splatters from the floor. Then he put the jar of bat wings back on the shelf, making sure that it was exactly lined up with the other jars. If it wasn't, the Bonemaster would notice. He believed in everything being very regular and exact. His nap, once it began, would last exactly thirty minutes. "Nothing can be accomplished without a regular schedule," the Bonemaster always said.

The door creaked, and Elfwyn came into the room.

She hurried over to Jinx and tried to look at his throat. "Are you all right? I wish he wouldn't hurt you."

Jinx shrugged her away. "Why don't you tell him that instead of kissing up to him?"

"Because I have to make him think I'm on his side," said Elfwyn.

"He could have killed me!"

"Well, I got him to leave you alone, didn't I?"

"'I'll go make you a nice hot posset, Bonemaster!'" said Jinx.

"Oh, be quiet. I have to get him in the habit of taking a hot drink with his nap in case I decide to poison him."

Jinx stared at her. "You wouldn't do that."

"I would if I thought he was about to kill us. Listen,

did you really just use his power source?"

"Yeah," said Jinx.

"You said you couldn't do that."

"No I didn't, I said he'd know if I did."

"Well, you probably shouldn't have used it."

"Yeah, well, I kind of lost my temper. You would too if he knocked you around all the time."

"So what *is* his power source?"

"I don't know. Something underneath this room." He could feel it now. He shivered. "Something cold-feeling."

"Right down there?" Elfwyn pointed at the floor.

"Kind of off to the left. Anyway, we've looked all through the cellars and outside. There's no way to get down there."

"Yes there is. Right here," said Elfwyn. She got down on her hands and knees. "I saw it when you spilled the dragon's blood. Look, right under the sink here."

Jinx knelt down beside her. The cracks between the flagstones were filled with dust. But around one stone the crack was clean and black, as if it had been recently moved.

"What, you think that's a trapdoor?"

"Yes. It's got to be. Can you levitate it, please?"

"We don't need to look at the power source," said Jinx. "I'm absolutely sure it's down there."

"But don't you want to see what it is?"

"We don't have time—we've only got about twenty minutes."

"Oh, we have longer than that; he only just lay down. Go ahead, levitate it. Please?"

Jinx was curious too. There was plenty of power to draw on—cold, nasty power. He just hoped the Bonemaster was asleep now and wouldn't sense him doing it—Jinx had no desire to be strangled again. He easily lifted the flagstone. He pushed it aside, uncovering a dark hole beneath.

A smell of cellars and mold came up from the opening.

"Look, there are metal rungs going down," said Elfwyn. "Come on."

"Wait." Jinx got two candles from the workbench and lit them. "Here."

Elfwyn climbed down first. Jinx watched her anxiously. It seemed to be a long way down.

"I'm on the bottom. There's a sort of passage," said Elfwyn.

"We don't have much time." Jinx lowered himself into the hole.

The passage was solid stone. "I think it's carved out of the inside of the island," said Elfwyn.

"Hurry up," said Jinx.

They went along the passage, their candles a pool of light in the deep darkness. There was a smell of death and sealed tombs. Jinx could sense the power very strongly now.

The passage ended in a locked door.

"Do you know a spell that can get us through there?" said Elfwyn.

Jinx tried *knowing* the door would open. But it didn't. They were very, very close to the power source.

"Oh, wait," said Elfwyn. She held up her candle. "There are some shelves against the wall here—what are those? Bottles?"

Hundreds of bottles glinted in the candlelight.

"That's the power source," said Jinx.

But even as he said it, he wasn't sure. There was power coming from the bottles. But the power behind the door was just as strong.

Elfwyn took one of the bottles in her hand. "It looks like there's a little man inside it. No, a woman. Oh, that's awful!"

She put the bottle in front of her candle so that the light shone greenly through it. Inside the bottle Jinx could see the tiny figure of a woman dangling from a string. She looked quite dead.

"What is it?" said Elfwyn.

"I think these might be lives," said Jinx. He felt horribly sad for them.

"They don't *look* alive," said Elfwyn.

Jinx wondered if he was dangling in a bottle somewhere in Simon's house, and if the him that was in the bottle knew it.

"They look dead," said Elfwyn.

"We really need to get out of here before the Bonemaster wakes up," said Jinx.

"And leave all of them down here?" She raised her candle so that it shone on the long, neat lines of bottles, each with a dim human figure hanging motionless inside it.

"Yes. Come on." He didn't want to look at the sad bottles anymore. He didn't want to *know* about them.

"Have you ever seen anything like this before?"

"Yes," said Jinx. "I mean, no."

"Is this what Simon did when he took your life?"

"I don't know."

"Weren't you there?"

"Only kind of. There was a bottle. And he put something of mine into it."

"Why did you let him? I would never have—"

"I didn't let him!" Jinx snapped. "Look, there's some power behind this door as well."

"So Simon *is* as evil as the Bonemaster."

Jinx didn't argue. He didn't know if this was what Simon had done to him. But it looked seriously evil. And he really, really didn't want to talk about it anymore. Like, ever.

"There's just as much power behind the door as in the bottles," he said. He tugged at the door handle.

"Do you think it's more bottles?"

"It feels different."

The difference was absolute—like the difference between night and day, or living trees and cold stone.

"How can we get in there?"

"We can't. We have to go back now." He was sure it had been half an hour since the Bonemaster had begun his nap. "Put that bottle back."

"Don't you want to look at it in daylight?"

"No, I don't." He took the bottle from her hand and put it back on the shelf. The sight of all those eerily still figures hanging in their bottles made him shudder.

"You know what I think?" said Elfwyn.

"How could—I mean no, I don't. Can we—let's get out of here already." Jinx took her arm and hurried her back along the passageway.

"I think—quit shoving! I think that those are the lives of dead people."

They had reached the ladder. "Hurry up," said Jinx.

She blew out her candle, stuck it in her pocket, and started climbing toward the light. Jinx followed right behind her. He expected to see the Bonemaster standing over the hole in the floor, waiting for them. But the room was still empty.

He grabbed the trapdoor and shoved as hard as he could to get it back into place. It was too heavy. "Help me with this."

"Can't you just levitate it?"

"Not now that I've seen the power source." All those little dangling lives.

Footsteps approached in the hall outside. He and Elfwyn shoved the flagstone as hard as they could, and it grated across the floor and dropped into place. The latch on the laboratory door clicked. They both jumped to their feet. As the door opened, Elfwyn ran to the workbench and picked up the mortar full of powdered bat wing, while Jinx turned and grabbed a wet rag from the sink.

"You call this cleaning up?" said the Bonemaster. "You haven't done a thing, have you, Jinx?"

"He's been helping me," said Elfwyn.

"Has he really?" said the Bonemaster.

"Yes," said Elfwyn truthfully.

"I don't understand," Reven said. "Were they very large bottles?"

They were up in the highest tower of the Bonemaster's castle, looking out an arched window into the darkness. Jinx couldn't see the forest, and this far away, he couldn't even sense it. Reven and Elfwyn were standing sort of too close together, and Jinx had the feeling that they wished he wasn't there.

Figuring people out without seeing their thoughts wasn't always difficult.

"No, ordinary-sized," said Elfwyn. "But the people in them were tiny."

"Dolls," said Reven.

"They weren't dolls," said Jinx.

"They were real people, only they were dead," said Elfwyn.

"How could you tell?"

"Real people don't look like dolls," said Jinx. "Look, the Bonemaster did something to them, all right? That's how they got that way. He shrunk them and put them in bottles."

"And killed them?"

"Oh yes, definitely killed them. That was what made them so dead."

"But you said there were hundreds of them." Reven looked from Elfwyn to Jinx in confusion.

"About two hundred, I think," said Elfwyn.

The thought stabbed through Jinx suddenly. The Bonemaster had killed hundreds of people. And Jinx had seen them, or at least some of them. In bottles.

"And how does that give him power?" said Reven.

They both looked at Jinx.

"I'm not sure," said Jinx. "It's—well, if deathforce magic comes from a death, then I suppose he captures their deaths in the bottles. So that he can use them."

He hoped they couldn't tell he was guessing. Simon

had never told him about deathforce magic, and Jinx had never read a single book about it.

"Hm. And what's behind the door?"

"We couldn't open it," said Jinx.

"But the lady said you sensed some great power there."

"Well, ask the lady then," said Jinx, irritated.

"We have to get it open," said Elfwyn. "If we could find out what other power he has, maybe we could destroy it somehow."

"Did you try pulling really hard on the handle?" said Reven.

"No, we never thought of that," said Jinx.

"Jinx, be nice," said Elfwyn. "The door was locked."

"Magic," said Reven. As usual, he seemed to think that was an answer in itself.

Another week had passed. Jinx had just been hit by the Bonemaster for putting the dried elf livers in the jar that was meant for the dried nixie livers. Hit and called an idiot. All of this in front of Elfwyn, who at least had the grace to pretend she couldn't see or hear it. Jinx knew it was grace, but in the mood he was in, he preferred to think of it as indifference.

He stormed out of the castle and stood alone on the barren stone island in the sky. He hated it here. The sky was too big and the trees too far away. Jinx looked across the chasm to the forest on the cliff top opposite. He missed the constant living murmur of the Urwald.

Over here there was only the one lonely hemlock, and Jinx went up and leaned on it. The rough bark against his face was some comfort, but he had realized long ago that this tree couldn't talk. It had never learned how.

He thought his angry thoughts at it anyway. And he felt its lifeforce, which was so weak compared to the single pulsing flow of life that was the Urwald.

Jinx walked as close to the edge of the island as he could manage without getting dizzy. Twenty feet away. Fifteen, and he felt unsteady on his feet. Ten, and he could almost feel himself falling over. He took several giant steps away from the edge.

The trees on the shores of the river rose high on either side, so most of the day the island was in shadow, but right now, close to noon, it was bright. Looking down the river, Jinx thought he could almost see the horizon.

"Hi." Reven's head popped up over the cliff edge.

"Don't do that!"

"Sorry." Reven hoisted himself easily up to the island. He stood, looked all around, then came close to Jinx and bent down and said very quietly, "I did it. I found a way down."

"Great," said Jinx. He already didn't like the looks of Reven's way down.

"There are enough handholds and footholds if you start right here and sort of work your way around. You come out at the bottom of the cliff on the other side of the island. Or at least you do if you don't fall."

"You fell?"

"Yes, only about ten feet, going down. Coming up was all right."

"Why did you come back up, once you'd gotten down?"

Reven looked affronted. "Because you and the lady are here, of course. I think that the lady Elfwyn could make the climb," he said, looking at the cliff edge. "But you, I fear, would fall. If only I could find the bridge."

Jinx would have liked to say that he could climb better than Elfwyn could. The problem wasn't climbing, though. The problem was that there was no way he could get himself to the edge of the cliff.

"I shall simply have to keep looking," said Reven. "Never give up!"

❧ ❧ ❧

When Reven told Elfwyn about the route that he'd found down the cliff, she said, "Jinx couldn't do it."

"Of course not," said Jinx. "Jinx can't do anything." He was lying on his back on his bed with his head hanging over the side, looking at the room upside down.

"If only I could find the bridge," said Reven. "Then I could set it up at night—"

"There's a ghoul patrolling at night," Elfwyn reminded him.

"Well, I'm sure I could find a way to avoid it. Anyway, what can a ghoul do?"

"Ghouls suck all your blood out through your eyeballs," said Jinx.

"Oh," said Reven. "I thought they were like ghosts."

"No," said Jinx. "They're different."

"Ah." Reven put his hands to his eyes. "Well."

"Do you think Simon's dead?" said Elfwyn.

Jinx felt his heart give a little hiccup. "He wasn't about to die when I left. And Sophie was taking care of him."

"Sometimes injuries get infected, though," said Elfwyn.

"I know that." Jinx had thought about this already. "I think he's probably busy quarreling with Sophie and he's forgotten all about me. Which is fine. I don't care."

"Don't you?" said Elfwyn. "I mean, you know this wizard, I don't, but didn't he look after you when you were little and stuff?"

"Just till I was old enough to be worth killing," said Jinx.

"According to the *Bonemaster*. Did he treat you like the Bonemaster does?"

"Not exactly, but that doesn't mean anything." Jinx thought of those rows and rows of dangling dead lives in bottles in the dark.

But Elfwyn wouldn't shut up. "You're letting the Bonemaster do your thinking for you. Which is stupid, because he's not on your side."

"We don't want to escape one evil wizard only to be captured by another," said Reven. "I'm sure the good Bonemaster—"

"He's not the good Bonemaster!" said Elfwyn. "You haven't seen all those little people hanging in bottles. And it's going to be us hanging in bottles pretty soon."

"I know he's evil," said Reven. "'Good' is merely a figure of speech. But he does seem rather fond of you, my lady."

"I'm sure he's fonder of the power he can get by hanging me up in a bottle."

"But perhaps we'll still be alive if he kills us. Jinx is probably hanging in a bottle somewhere, and he's still alive."

Jinx sat up, and felt dizzy from hanging upside down. "Don't you remember what the bridge is made of, Reven?"

"Well, yes. Bones. I'm perfectly aware he's evil."

"They must be thigh bones, I think," said Elfwyn. "Nothing else would be long enough."

"Hundreds of them," Jinx said. "The lives are in the bottles, the thigh bones are in the bridge. I wonder what he did with the rest of 'em."

"Though they could be animal bones," said Reven.

"Stop trying to think the best of him," said Jinx. "He's completely evil and he's going to kill us."

"I know," said Reven.

"The skull cups are definitely people," said Elfwyn. "Nothing else has a skull shaped like that."

The Bonemaster had put the cups away when they'd refused to use them, and replaced them with silver goblets. Hospitality was something that magicians took very seriously.

"You must admit he's been kind to us so far," said Reven.

"No, I mustn't," said Jinx.

"He's nasty to Jinx," said Elfwyn.

"Yes, I know," said Reven.

"You're the one who found the way down! So you must want to escape!"

"Yes," said Reven. "I do. Of course I do."

"So what's your problem?" Jinx demanded.

"It's his spell," said Elfwyn. "He wants his spell taken off him."

"Oh, right. The spell that means he's somebody important." Jinx was in a rotten mood.

"You think that because I've lived at King Rufus's court," said Reven. "But my stepmother and I always ate at the lowest table, and we were very seldom permitted to attend the royal levee."

"What about your father?" said Elfwyn.

"I have—had—only a stepmother."

"Your father's dead, then?" said Elfwyn.

Reven didn't answer.

"Why—if you don't mind my asking, why did the king kill your stepmother?"

It was clear that Reven did mind her asking, but he took a deep breath and said, "Because she spoke of things he preferred not to have spoken of."

"She told people who you are?"

Reven said nothing.

"So the curse wasn't on her, then. Or she found a way around it," said Elfwyn.

"She was a very wise lady. Also good-hearted."

Jinx couldn't stand the ragged edge in Reven's voice. "Stop hassling him, Elfwyn."

Elfwyn turned on Jinx. "You still haven't figured out how to get through that door, have you?"

"What door?" Though Jinx knew perfectly well.

"The one with the rest of the Bonemaster's power behind it. Don't you know a spell to open locks?"

"No," said Jinx. "There's a spell for, you know, doors. Like, the front door of Simon's house, it knows who to let in, and that's how it knows whether to be locked or not."

"Can you make the door think you're someone it should open for?" asked Elfwyn.

"No," said Jinx.

"Why not?" asked Reven.

"Because," said Jinx. "Magic is not something I'm terribly, horribly good at, all right?"

"I thought you were a magician," said Reven.

"Yeah, so? Someone has to be the worst at things," said Jinx.

He didn't want to get through the door. The bottles had been—well, freaky. And whatever was behind the door was probably worse.

The truth was he was afraid of finding out what was behind the door.

"We'll only make the Bonemaster want to kill us," he said.

"He already wants to kill us," said Elfwyn. "I just want to see what the rest of his power looks like."

"Besides, it might help us escape," said Reven.

"How?" said Jinx.

"Well, we won't know till you look," said Reven.

"Didn't you hear me just explain that I can't—"

"What about the Bonemaster's books?" said Elfwyn. "I bet there's something in there that explains how the door spell is done. Can you read?"

"In six languages," said Jinx, feeling he had some lost ground to make up.

"Really? Six?" said Elfwyn.

"Uh-huh."

"That's very impressive," said Reven.

Jinx felt a little better.

"Some of the books the Bonemaster has are in other languages," said Elfwyn. "I've already looked through the ones in Urwish, and I haven't seen any door spells. There are some interesting potion spells, though."

"You can read?" said Jinx.

"Of course. Everyone in Butterwood Clearing can read. We're famous for it."

"I thought you were famous for cows."

"Cows and reading," said Elfwyn.

Jinx saw that he was going to have to try to find the door spell. He felt sure he wouldn't be able to do the spell, though. He didn't have the Urwald to draw on, and without it, he just wasn't much good at magic.

Among the Bones

They were at dinner. The food was cooked magically. Supplies—groceries and firewood—were delivered at the bottom of the cliff. They would be there in the morning, unattended, and the Bonemaster would levitate them to the island.

"So, how was the exploring today?" the Bonemaster asked Reven. "Have you found anything of interest?"

"No, sir," said Reven.

"Been all through the cellars and towers, have you?"

"An it please you, sir," said Reven. "Yes. Have you found a way to take my curse off me, good Bonemaster?"

"Not yet," said the Bonemaster. "But I'm studying the matter."

"And my curse too," Elfwyn put in.

"Of course, yours too, dear." He buttered a roll and turned to Jinx. "I would have expected Simon to show up by now. Don't wipe your plate with your bread like that. Where is he?"

Jinx put down the bread. "I don't know."

The Bonemaster turned to Elfwyn. "Where is Simon?"

"I don't know," said Elfwyn. "You know that potion we were working on today?"

"A moment, dear. Don't change the subject. Why hasn't Simon come here?"

"He's not well," said Elfwyn.

"Not well?" The Bonemaster leaned forward. "What's wrong with him?"

"Somebody stabbed him with a sword."

"Ha. Not before time." But the Bonemaster didn't look pleased at all. "Where did this happen?"

"In Samara."

Jinx had told her this and was silently cursing about it now. It was stupid to tell Elfwyn anything.

"Was he seriously injured? Is he dying?"

"Yes—no. I don't know."

The Bonemaster turned to Jinx. "Well?"

"Well what?" said Jinx.

Then he winced inwardly, because that was back talk. But the Bonemaster didn't seem to believe in hitting him at the dinner table. Instead he turned to Elfwyn.

"Then—is there a possibility he might be dead?" For some reason the Bonemaster looked really worried.

"I suppose so," said Elfwyn.

"And this idiot boy left him alone with no one to take care of him?" The Bonemaster's voice climbed angrily.

"His wife is taking care of him," said Elfwyn.

"His wife? Simon has a wife?"

"Yes," said Elfwyn.

"Ridiculous. Wizards don't have wives."

"Why not?" said Elfwyn, probably to stem the flow of questions.

"For many reasons, my dear. I suppose one reason is because wives and children make such lovely hostages. Is it too much to hope that there are children?"

"I don't know," said Elfwyn.

"No children," said Jinx. Revealing that was probably safe enough. Who knew what the Bonemaster would have done with Simon's children, if they'd existed? Jinx wondered why the Bonemaster looked so vexed about Simon's injury.

The Bonemaster took the bird out of his pocket. He stared at it for a moment.

"Simon," he said. "You have three days. Be here by the last day of August with what you stole from me. If you come later than that, I'm afraid you won't find Jinx at all."

There was a small stack of books waiting on Jinx's bed. Elfwyn must have brought them.

The Bonemaster didn't own nearly as many books as Simon did. Perhaps that was because he had never been to Samara. Jinx flipped through the books. None of them was in Samaran, but they were all in languages he knew.

He found the door spell in the third book. He read it over carefully, three times.

Elfwyn knocked on the door.

"Come in," said Jinx.

"Any luck?"

"Yes," said Jinx. He turned the book around so she could see it.

She frowned at it. "What language is that?"

"Old Urwish."

"It doesn't look anything like Urwish."

"It's a dead language. I never saw this spell before, but I think it's the one Simon uses. You have to tell the door who you are, and that you're in command, and then you tell it who to open for." He translated the spell into modern Urwish for her.

"So you can tell the door to open for us?"

"If I can do the spell," said Jinx. Which was a big if. He hadn't even ever been able to do the ordinary door-opening spell, which Simon said was just levitation pushed sideways.

"Oh, you'll be able to do it. We'll take Reven with us."

Wonderful. A bigger audience to see Jinx fail.

"You said half the Bonemaster's power is behind that door," said Elfwyn.

"At least half." The power behind the door had felt volatile and dangerous.

"We'll do it tonight," said Elfwyn. "After the Bonemaster goes to sleep. Oh, I can hardly wait!"

Jinx could. Utterly.

It was long past midnight when the three of them crouched in the Bonemaster's laboratory, candles beside them, and pried the flagstone up from the floor.

"Quietly!" Jinx whispered as it grated out of the opening. Everything seemed to be making too much noise. Elfwyn's and Reven's feet on the iron rungs rang like bells. Jinx followed them down, the spell book tucked under his arm.

They walked along the corridor to the iron-bound door.

"These are the bottles?" Reven picked one up and examined the swinging figure inside it thoughtfully. "Is this what happened to you, Jinx?"

Jinx ignored the question, but he couldn't help glancing at the bottles. All those dead lives. That couldn't be what Simon had done to him. It couldn't.

He studied the page of Old Urwish. "I think you both have to be standing next to me if you want to get through the door," he said.

Reven set the bottle back on the shelf—even that seemed to make too much noise—and came and stood beside Jinx. Elfwyn stood on the other side of him. Jinx looked at the book and prepared to fail. He read the Old Urwish words aloud.

Nothing happened.

Reven reached out and rattled the door handle. "Didn't work."

"Could you make any more noise?" snapped Jinx.

"Oh, he's sleeping soundly. I looked in," said Reven.

"Try again, Jinx," said Elfwyn.

Jinx started to say that there wasn't any point in trying when he knew he couldn't do it. Then Simon's voice inside his head reminded him, *Of course you can't if you think you can't.* Right. So he could. Right?

"It's not working," said Jinx. "I need more power."

"There's power all around us," said Elfwyn. "Didn't you say?"

Yes, there was. The deathly power from the bottles, and the wriggly, more alive power behind the door. Jinx tried to reach out for the power behind the door, but it was like trying to catch fish with your hands. It wouldn't hold still for him.

Besides, he had a feeling that the door spell had been cast in the first place with the power from the bottles. He drew on it. This close, it filled him with an oppressive, deathly horror. It felt half dead, half alive, and he could feel it pushing at him, telling him how to use it.

Jinx spoke the Old Urwish words again.

The lock snapped open, and the door creaked inward an inch. Elfwyn and Reven gave little murmurs of surprise. Jinx pushed the door the rest of the way open—it groaned loudly. He stepped inside.

"Wow," said Reven, beside him.

"Oh," said Elfwyn.

They were in another corridor. Its walls were lined from floor to ceiling with human skulls.

Real skulls. Jinx saw Reven reach out to touch one and check. Oh, they were real all right. Jinx knew it. Hundreds of them, glowing greenly in the candlelight.

Jinx started down the corridor, with all those empty eye sockets staring down at him.

"You think he really killed all these people?" said Reven.

"Yes," said Elfwyn. "I think they're the people in the bottles."

The skulls gave way to bones—first vertebrae, and then ribs, and then Jinx stopped looking.

"It can't go that much farther," said Reven. "We'll run out of island."

"I think we're going down a little bit," said Elfwyn.

Oh, they could go down forever.

Finally the corridor opened into a wide, vaulted chamber. In the center was a table. On the table were two bottles.

One of the bottles drew Jinx's eyes immediately. It wasn't properly a bottle at all, or not that you could see—just a bottle-shape of wraithlike ribbons of glowing blue smoke, wriggling and winding their way around and around.

The other bottle was like the ones outside—an ordinary green glass bottle.

Elfwyn and Reven hung back, but Jinx went to the table. He bent down and looked at the green bottle. As he'd expected, there was a person inside it.

The person was sitting on the bottom of the bottle, its arms wrapped around its knees. When Jinx approached, it raised its head and opened its eyes.

Slowly, carefully, Jinx reached out and picked the bottle up. It was hard to lift—there seemed to be some force attaching it to the weird smoky bottle-shape on the table, and Jinx had to tug at it.

The person in the green bottle stood and looked at Jinx, but didn't seem to see him.

Elfwyn and Reven drew closer, peering at the bottle in Jinx's hand.

"This one is alive," said Reven.

"It's wearing robes, like a wizard," said Elfwyn.

"Yes, well," said Jinx. "This is Simon."

The other two crowded closer at that, trying to shine their candles on the man in the bottle. The heat didn't seem to bother Simon. He didn't seem to know they were there.

"I thought wizards were old," said Reven.

"It's alive," said Elfwyn. "Do you think that's because *he's* alive, and those people in the bottles out there are all dead?"

"I don't know," said Jinx, still staring at Simon. How had this happened, and when?

"What I mean is that that's what *I* think," said Elfwyn.

"That's why he hasn't come to find you, I swan," said Reven. "He's down here in a bottle."

"I don't know if he is," said Elfwyn. "This might just be his life. Like Jinx."

"So is that what you look like, then?" said Reven. "Standing around in a bottle like that? Not hanging like those people out there?"

"How should I know?" said Jinx.

"Perhaps he's down here because he's in league with the Bonemaster," said Reven.

"Or because he's already come to look for Jinx, and battled the Bonemaster, and lost," said Elfwyn.

"This is like a picture in a book that Simon has," said Jinx. "It's in a language I don't know—"

"There's a language you don't know?" said Reven.

"—and it shows a man trapped in a bottle. Not hanging like those people out there. Alive, like this."

"That sounds like a book only an evil wizard would have," said Reven.

Elfwyn nodded at the bottle. "You're going to take it, aren't you? You can't leave it here."

"The Bonemaster will notice it's missing," said Reven.

"Maybe not before we escape," said Elfwyn. "Anyway, we can't leave it here."

"Maybe Jinx doesn't want to take it," said Reven. "After all, Simon's keeping *him* trapped in a bottle."

"But that's Simon," said Jinx. "It's not like down here."

Wasn't it really, though? How did he know Simon didn't have a dungeon under his house lined with skulls and bones and full of lives in bottles?

An image of Simon in his kitchen, surrounded by cats and cooking smells, came into Jinx's head. It was a world away from this charnel house.

Jinx remembered Simon saying, *Anyone could have power the way he gets it. If they were willing to do the things he's willing to do.* Was this what Simon wasn't willing to do? He'd certainly done *something* to Jinx, and it had involved a bottle, and it had been pretty bad.

But somehow—when? Jinx wondered—Simon's life had been captured by the Bonemaster, and put down here in this dungeon, and used as a power source for the Bonemaster's evil magic—things like turning people into bone bridges and skull cups, sucking out their souls and stacking their bones crisscross. For things Jinx suddenly *knew* Simon wouldn't do. Dame Glammer could cackle and the Bonemaster could make arch hints, but Jinx knew Simon.

"You don't think he'd leave you down here?" said Reven. "If he found you like this?"

"It doesn't *matter* what Simon would do," said Elfwyn. "What matters is what Jinx would do."

Elfwyn was right. And whatever Simon had done to him and to his life, Jinx wasn't going to leave him here among the bones. He stuck the bottle in his pocket.

"Very well. At least you'll be able to keep an eye on him," said Reven.

What about the other bottle, though? It had power too. Jinx reached out his hand toward it.

Blue sparks shot from the bottle, snapping and cracking.

Jinx drew his hand back, and the sparks subsided. The ghostly ribbons kept winding and diving around it. Jinx reached out again. More sparks, louder. They spattered at him. He reached through the sparks. Elfwyn grabbed his arm.

"Jinx, I don't think you should touch that one," she said.

"I just want to see what's in it." Suddenly he felt he

had to see what was in it. He reached out his other hand, and Reven grabbed it.

"She's right," said Reven. "Leave that one alone."

"There's power coming from it," said Jinx.

"Dangerous power, I swan," said Reven.

"I don't like the look of those sparks," said Elfwyn.

Jinx made another try at reaching for the bottle, but Reven and Elfwyn wouldn't let him get at it.

As they left the dungeon, Jinx felt the force that attached Simon's bottle to the one on the table stretch thinner and thinner, and then break.

It was the twenty-ninth of August. The day after tomorrow was Simon's deadline—the day the Bonemaster had said he'd find some other use for Jinx. Jinx had been trying all day not to imagine what other uses the Bonemaster might be thinking of.

"He'll kill all of us, I'm sure," said Elfwyn.

"There's no good reason for him to kill you or Reven," said Jinx.

"You think he needs a good reason to kill anybody?"

Jinx did not.

The three of them were gathered in Jinx's room. Simon was on the bedside table, pacing round and round in tiny circles on the bottom of his bottle.

Elfwyn was watching in fascination. "Isn't it kind of

creepy, having him in here?"

"Yes," said Jinx.

"Has he been going round like that for long?"

"On and off. Sometimes he sits down."

"I'd think it would keep you awake at night."

"I just throw a sock over him and stick him under the bed."

"What do you think would happen if you opened the bottle?"

"I think that would be a really bad idea," said Jinx.

"That's what I think too," said Elfwyn. "It was closed with magic, and it has to be opened with magic. And the right kind of magic."

Jinx thought of the spell Simon had done on him. What had really made it hard to sleep was thinking about himself, stuck in a bottle somewhere, pacing around in little circles like Simon was. When he thought about that, it almost made him want to take Simon's bottle and drop it off the edge of the island and watch it smash on the rocks below.

The other thing that kept him awake was watching the Bonemaster's deadline creep closer.

"It's just lucky the Bonemaster hasn't gone down to check on it," said Elfwyn.

"Maybe he doesn't go down there much," said Reven. He'd been sitting and listening to them with a small smile, like someone who has a secret. Jinx was trying not to be irritated by it.

"I think I might have told the door that I'm its boss now, and he isn't," said Jinx.

"Won't he be able to fix that pretty easily?" said Elfwyn.

"Yeah, probably. And he'll know we've been down there."

"Anyway, we only have two days left," said Reven, still with that annoying smile.

"Tomorrow and the next day. One day, really. He might just kill us on the morning of the thirty-first, you know." Elfwyn sighed. "Although he still talks as if he expects Simon to show up. Do you think he will, Jinx?"

"Doesn't look like it, does it?" said Jinx. "Look, you guys are just going to have to climb down that cliff and leave me."

"I'm sure you can do it too," said Elfwyn, not sounding sure at all. "Well, you have to at least try, Jinx."

Reven's smile broke into a grin. "Indeed, he needn't, my lady."

He took a small silver box from his pocket and placed it on the bed with a flourish.

Elfwyn lifted the lid. "Oh."

Jinx leaned forward and saw, folded up on the box's black velvet lining, what looked like a tiny model of the

Bone Bridge. It could have been made of mouse bones, tied together with thread.

Elfwyn picked up a bone between her thumb and forefinger and lifted the bridge by it. As soon as it came out of the box it began to expand. Reven put out a hand to stop her.

"It's quite difficult to get it back into the box if you let it grow."

"Where did you find it?" said Elfwyn.

"In a secret compartment in the back of a drawer in the kitchen," said Reven. "I'll put it back there tonight, in case he looks. But you can see, it looks as if the bridge is actually made of the bones of something quite small."

"No," said Jinx.

"No?" Reven raised an eyebrow.

"You can shrink big things to hide them," said Jinx. "But there isn't any kind of magic to make small things big. It's not possible. Small things just fall apart when you make them bigger. Anyway, we've seen that he has no shortage of bones."

"So now we can get away," said Elfwyn. "We just have to fix the bridge to the posts—oh. I suppose it has to be attached at the bottom, too."

"That's no problem," said Reven. "I'll just attach it at the top, and climb down the cliff, and fix it to the anchors at the bottom. There are two more posts down there."

"Then all we need is for the Bonemaster to be out of the way for a while." Elfwyn sounded thoughtful.

"He takes a nap every day," said Reven.

"For thirty minutes," said Elfwyn. "That's not long enough to set up the bridge."

"And get the bottles," said Jinx.

They both looked at him. "I think if we take the bottles with us," he said, "then the Bonemaster won't be able to use their power anymore. At least if we get them far enough away from him."

"Good. So the Bonemaster can't send any more windstorms after us," said Reven.

"I don't think he can have caused the windstorm," said Jinx. "But at least he won't have his power."

"Besides, it's *people* in the bottles," said Elfwyn. "Even if they're dead."

"Yeah," said Jinx. He remembered the feeling of the power he had drawn on when he opened the door. There was something—not alive, exactly, but *real* about that power, and it didn't deserve to be locked up in the dark, serving the Bonemaster.

"Good," said Reven. "When the Bonemaster lies down for his nap, I'll fix the bridge to the top of the cliff, climb down, and fix it to the bottom, while you two fetch the bottles."

"That will take more than half an hour," said Jinx.

They thought for a minute.

"You can climb down the cliff before he takes his nap," said Jinx. "He won't notice, because you're always off exploring. Then when he lies down for his nap, I'll take the bridge out of the box, fix it to the top posts, and throw the rest of the bridge down the cliff—" He had to stop because he felt ill.

"Perhaps it would be best if the lady fixed the bridge to the top of the cliff."

"And you can be stealing the bottles at the same time, Jinx," said Elfwyn.

"It still seems like it will take more than half an hour," said Jinx.

"That won't matter," said Elfwyn. "Because of the posset that I'll give him before his nap."

"You're going to poison him?" Jinx felt a little uncomfortable about this in spite of the skulls and all the times the Bonemaster had hit him.

"No, I'm going to make a sleeping potion."

"You know how to make a sleeping potion?"

"Not exactly. But I found a recipe for one in one of the Bonemaster's books. And I'm sure you can help me figure it out."

"We'll have to do it tonight," said Jinx.

There wasn't much time left.

They made the potion at midnight. The castle was silent when they snuck downstairs.

Reven stayed in the great hall, hidden in the shadows, keeping watch. At the first sign of the Bonemaster, he would cough to warn them, and they would do what, exactly? They weren't sure. Besides the door, there was no way out of the Bonemaster's laboratory.

"We could hide down in the dungeon with the bottles," said Elfwyn.

But neither of them liked the idea.

"We start out with dragon's blood the size of a hen's egg," said Elfwyn, looking at the book. "Mixed in with nixie's eyeballs—oh, that's not very nice!"

"They don't sell the eyeballs till the nixies are already dead," said Jinx, climbing up the stepladder to get the jar. "From natural causes. Or anyway, you know—other causes."

Dying of natural causes wasn't common in the Urwald.

"The dragons too?" said Elfwyn.

"The dragons aren't dead. They just make a little slit in their underbellies and—"

"Who does?"

"I don't know. I think the dragons do it themselves."

"They sell their own blood?" said Elfwyn.

"Why not? It's their blood." Jinx fetched down the other jars, one by one: grated gryphon claw, bat wings, werebear hair, and dried leaves of night-blooming bindweed.

Elfwyn had already started the dragon's blood heating in a retort over a lighted candle and was pounding the nixie's eyes and bindweed leaves together in a mortar. Jinx leaned against the workbench and watched. It didn't seem fair that she was so much better at this stuff when he'd spent half his life in a wizard's house. Still, he had to admire how neatly and skillfully she did it.

"Are you listening for Reven?" said Elfwyn.

"Yeah," said Jinx, who had forgotten all about it.

"Good," said Elfwyn. "I keep forgetting to."

Smack! Something hit the window, hard. Jinx whirled around and saw a white-green, rubbery creature clinging to the outside of the window, its skinny limbs splayed against the glass.

It stared at them with yellow bubble eyes. Its mouth was a tube protruding from its face, with pale white lips working back and forth, as if they couldn't wait to start sucking someone's blood out through their eyeballs. It emitted a long, groaning howl.

"What *is* that?" Reven was in the doorway.

"The ghoul," said Jinx.

"Come on, into the kitchen," said Reven. "The Bonemaster will hear that."

Elfwyn blew out the candle and they hurried out into the hall and into the kitchen, where they crawled under the table and waited, listening. The ghoul howled again.

It sounded like the wind on a stormy night. In fact, Jinx realized, he'd heard it before and had thought that was what it was. They waited for the sound of the Bonemaster's footsteps on the stairs, in the hall.

Time crept past.

"He's not coming," said Elfwyn at last.

"I'll go look," said Reven.

He left the kitchen, moving so quietly that Jinx almost couldn't hear him. Several minutes passed. Finally he came back.

"He's snoring," he reported.

Jinx and Elfwyn went back to the laboratory, and Reven went back to standing guard.

The ghoul came twice more while they were working. It stared at them with its big yellow eyes and worked its mouth hungrily, and Jinx wondered how strong the glass in the window was.

"Hold this over the candle and agitate it, please," said Elfwyn, handing him a glass phial in a clamp.

Jinx shook the potion over the flame, gently, just enough to stir it. "It would be easier to just poison him," he muttered.

"You said we couldn't do that."

"Oh, no, we can't," said Jinx.

"It would make us as bad as him," said Elfwyn. She was cleaning up the workbench.

"I know," said Jinx. "I just said it would be easier, that's all."

"Well, we can't, because he asks me if it's poisoned."

"He what?"

"When I give him the posset, he sometimes asks me if it's poison."

"Oh." Jinx thought about this. "Won't you have to tell him about the sleeping potion if he asks you, then?"

"No, because a sleeping potion isn't poison," said Elfwyn. "And he's never asked me if it's a sleeping potion. I think it's done."

Jinx took the potion off the flame. It smelled like rotting slime. "You think he'll actually drink something that stinks this much?"

"Oh, yes. The posset will hide the smell and the taste—I've been making it extra strong on purpose."

She held out a bottle, and Jinx carefully tipped the contents of the phial into it. The ghoul smacked against the window again, but they were used to it now. They didn't even jump.

⌐ ◢ ◢

Jinx was in the laboratory alone. He had his backpack, and Elfwyn's and Reven's backpacks, and an empty gunny-sack from the kitchen. It was time to steal the bottles. Reven had climbed down the cliff already. Elfwyn had given the Bonemaster the potion and gone outside with the Bone Bridge in her pocket.

Jinx had to draw on the power in the bottles beneath him to lift the stone trapdoor. He hated doing it.

He took Simon out of his pocket and set him on the floor—he didn't want him falling out of his pocket when he climbed. He threw the backpacks and sack into the hole and then clambered down after them. In the cold silence of the passage, he felt completely alone in the world.

In the yellow flickering candlelight the tiny people were just shadows of themselves through the curved glass. Jinx tried not to look at them as he put them into the bags, one by one. He could feel the power reaching for him. Trying to use him, maybe.

The bottles rang when they touched each other. Jinx worked as quickly and quietly as he could. He knew he had more time because of Elfwyn's potion, but he couldn't quite make himself believe it.

At last all the bottles were in the bags. Jinx picked up his own pack and put it on his back. He put his arms through Reven's pack and wore it on his chest. Then he picked up Elfwyn's pack in his left hand and the sack in his right—*clank*. He took a step. *Clank, clank.* Another step, carefully. The bottles rattled and clunked. Jinx stopped and set the bags down.

He looked at the beam of light from the trapdoor. It wasn't just the noise—how was he going to climb back up the ladder laden like this?

Then he heard footsteps in the laboratory overhead.

He froze. The trapdoor was open, plain to see. And Simon in his bottle beside it.

The footsteps came up to the trapdoor, and the light beam was broken by something moving across it. Someone was coming down the ladder.

"What's taking you so long?" It was Elfwyn.

"The bags make too much noise," he said.

"So levitate them."

"I can't. I can't use the power, it's all evil-filling. I'll end up like him."

"No you won't. Not from a levitation spell. It's just till we get down from the island."

Jinx didn't like it, but he didn't see any way around it. He drew on the power in the bottles—the cold from it seemed to fill his bones. But evil wasn't the right word for it, he realized. It was more like the power had been . . . wronged. Twisted. He levitated the bottles.

"Now just float them up through the trapdoor," said Elfwyn.

"I know what to do," said Jinx. "You don't have to tell me."

The bags were weightless now, and he pushed them along the passageway on a cushion of air, making very little noise. When he reached the light beam, he sent them up it to the trapdoor. He sent them up higher still, out of sight—he'd never done magic out of sight before. He had to draw more of the cold, dead-alive power to do it.

Elfwyn came behind him, carrying the candle. They climbed up the iron rungs. The four bags were waiting for them, floating three feet above the floor. Jinx picked up the bottle of Simon he'd left by the trapdoor.

"The Bonemaster's not here yet," said Jinx, speaking in a whisper.

"Of course not. That potion will put him out for hours."

They pushed the bags through the air. Now and then there was a *clank* from a bottle sliding against another, and each time Jinx froze and listened. Elfwyn had more confidence in their sleeping potion than he did.

The front door creaked too loudly. Outside, Jinx saw that the Bone Bridge had been neatly reattached to the stone posts. By Elfwyn, who had never done it before. Previously, it had been set up by the Bonemaster, who presumably knew just how to do it.

"You'll be fine, Jinx. Don't be afraid."

"I'm not afraid."

"You're trembling."

"I am not!"

They stood at the top of the bridge, and the four bags floated beside them. Simon was clenched tight in Jinx's fist.

"I'm not afraid of heights," said Jinx. "It's only this cliff that makes me sort of nervous."

"I'll go first," said Elfwyn. She reached for two of the bags.

"No, I'll take them," said Jinx.

"You can't handle all of them."

"Yeah I can. It's not like they weigh anything."

"Well, I'll at least take Simon, then." She took the green bottle out of Jinx's hand. Then she turned around, gripped the ropes, and stepped backward onto the Bone Bridge. It swayed sickeningly from her movements as she started down.

It was Jinx's turn to follow. He put one backpack on his back and strapped another to his chest. The levitating bags floated him slightly. He looped the remaining backpack over one arm and slung the gunnysack over his back.

Elfwyn was a quarter of the way down already, moving over nothing but bones and empty space. Jinx felt ill and looked away. Right. He could do this. He put a hand on one of the stone posts at the top of the bridge.

The front door of the castle creaked open.

At the same moment, Jinx felt the sudden weight of the bags—they were no longer floating. He turned around. The Bonemaster was coming down the castle steps.

"So." The Bonemaster strode toward him. "Leaving without saying farewell?"

Jinx threw his arms out across the front of the bridge, barring the Bonemaster's way. Jinx was far too close to the edge, and now he had his back to it. He could hear the clatter of bones as Elfwyn worked her way down, unaware of the danger.

"Out of my way, brat." The Bonemaster seized Jinx by the shoulders and heaved him aside.

Jinx landed on his back and heard glass crunch under him. Waves of filmy smoke rose from his backpack and floated away in the air. The Bonemaster headed for the bridge. Jinx scrambled to his feet. He stumbled forward and grabbed the Bonemaster's arm. The Bonemaster spun around and punched Jinx in the face. Jinx didn't let go. He dragged the Bonemaster away from the bridge. They both fell to the ground.

Jinx dug his fingers in and held on to the Bonemaster as tightly as he could—the Bonemaster was still hitting him. Then Jinx couldn't move—his clothes were frozen. He still didn't let go of the Bonemaster. Then the Bonemaster grabbed Jinx's hands and squeezed them till Jinx felt the bones crunch together. He yelled in pain and had to let go.

"Jinx! What's wrong?" Elfwyn's voice came from over the edge of the cliff.

"Run, Elfwyn!" Jinx yelled.

The Bonemaster scrambled up and made for the bridge. Jinx's clothes stayed frozen even when the wizard looked away—he was able to do this spell better than Simon. Jinx heard the rattle of bones as Elfwyn climbed back up the bridge—could she see the Bonemaster yet? Did she know she was climbing right into his arms?

Jinx felt the Bonemaster drawing on the cold power in the bottles for whatever he was going to do to Elfwyn—kill her, probably. Bottle her life and take her bones.

Don't let him do it. The power in the bottles was telling him that. It reached out to Jinx, as it had before. Jinx grabbed the alive part of the dead-alive power and wrenched it away from the Bonemaster.

The power was less than it had been, because of the broken bottles. Jinx unfroze his clothes—the power showed him how—and got to his feet. He picked up the bag of bottles he'd dropped, and he swung it at the Bonemaster's head.

The Bonemaster ducked, raised a hand toward Jinx, and drew on the power in the bottles again. Jinx drew it back, as hard as he could.

"You can't take my power!" the Bonemaster cried.

"Can too." But Jinx felt it slipping away as the Bonemaster pulled back.

Jinx fought for control of the power. The alive part tried to stay with him, but it was too closely bound to the dead part, and that part belonged to the Bonemaster. The power was slipping away from Jinx—he didn't know enough, curse it. He didn't have the Bonemaster's experience, and he hadn't even known a power struggle like this was possible. He pulled and pulled at the power, but it was like trying to get a firm grip on a slippery rope. The Bonemaster would have control in a minute, would use it against him, would get Elfwyn—

"Bonemaster!" Elfwyn had reached the top of the cliff. She came at him, her right fist swinging, her left hand clenched around bottled Simon.

The Bonemaster was distracted for a second, and the magic slid into Jinx's control. Jinx scrambled to think what to do with the magic, quick, he had enough power to—what? He didn't know, so he set the Bonemaster's clothes on fire.

Except it was more fire than that. The air caught fire. The whole island was a roar of orange flame. Jinx heard the sizzling terror of the single gnarled hemlock that had never learned to talk. He couldn't kill the tree. Or Elfwyn. He stopped the fire. It had lasted less than a second. At the same instant he felt a slithering jerk as the Bonemaster seized the cold power away from Jinx.

The wizard's clothes were blackened, soot-stinking rags, and his hair and beard were frizzled. Behind him, Elfwyn looked singed and stunned.

Jinx could read his own death in the wizard's eyes. The Bonemaster took a step toward Jinx, his hands raised to cast a spell. Jinx took a step backward.

"I don't think that Simon is coming for you," said the Bonemaster. "And with your life gone, you're really not worth anything to me."

"I'm useful cleaning up," said Jinx.

"I think I'm tired of you." The Bonemaster took another step forward, and Jinx took another step back.

Jinx still had one bag of bottles in his hand and one on his chest. The one on his back jingled with broken glass. He would swing the bag in his hands at the Bonemaster. In a second. It wouldn't do much good, but he had to do it, because the Bonemaster was about to kill him.

He tried to draw on the power in the bottles but he couldn't. The Bonemaster had a firm grip on it now. The only thing for Jinx to do was go down fighting. He clutched the bag tightly and took a big step backward so he could swing it freely.

A big step backward onto nothing.

Things Seen from Above

Jinx plummeted. Wind rushed in his ears, and there was screaming—maybe Elfwyn's, possibly his own.

He had the sensation of being punched very hard, all over his body at the same time.

It only hurt for a second, and then he was high in the air, not frightened at all. Hah, he wasn't afraid of heights! Just of that cliff, and with good reason. Around him wisps of smoke streamed upward, one by one—lives escaping from the smashed bottles.

The Bone Bridge rattled—Elfwyn scrambled down it, followed much more slowly by the Bonemaster. Why didn't he immobilize her? Jinx wondered. Then the dead lives drifting upward answered.

He can't. We're free.

The Bonemaster's power had escaped with the lives. Except for the part of his power that was in Simon, in the bottle in Elfwyn's hand.

Reven was running toward the bridge—he must have wandered away, exploring. It probably hadn't been a minute since the Bonemaster had first appeared at the castle door.

Elfwyn tripped and fell forward. She grabbed desperately at the bones of the bridge and dropped Simon's bottle.

The bottle fell.

Elfwyn slid a few feet down the bridge and nearly went over the edge before she succeeded in stopping herself. She looked back—the Bonemaster was still coming. She got to her feet fast and kept climbing down. Jinx flew down and got in front of the Bonemaster, trying to stop him. The Bonemaster passed through him as if fighting his way through deep water. It gave Jinx a sick, ripply feeling.

Simon's bottle was still falling. Jinx flew toward it, made a grab, and caught it. It tumbled slowly through his hands.

Reven, still running, put himself under the falling bottle of Simon and caught it. He stuck it in his pocket without looking at it. Elfwyn reached the bottom of the bridge, and Reven hurried over to her.

Jinx watched Elfwyn and Reven splash back across the

stream and run to Jinx's body—that was his body, wasn't it? It was harder to see than it had been the time that Simon had killed him. It wasn't shaped right.

Elfwyn was crying, and Reven was white in the face. Jinx felt bad about that. He wanted to tell them not to worry, he was right up here and he was fine, but when he tried to call out, he found he couldn't make any noise. He sailed up higher and saw the river rushing between its stone banks. Two figures were running toward the Bonemaster's island—one was running, rather, and the other hopping along in giant leaps.

Jinx drifted back down to warn Elfwyn and Reven that someone else was coming. Reven was just pulling his hands away from touching Jinx's body. The Bonemaster was creeping down the Bone Bridge—slowly, backward, careful not to slide on the slippery rungs. Elfwyn and Reven needed to get out of there. And so did Jinx, but he didn't see how he could when he was separated from his body like this.

"Run!" Jinx shouted—or tried to, but he didn't make any noise.

Reven straightened up, putting his hands on his knees and leaving two crimson handprints on his breeches. He looked up at the Bonemaster, his eyes diamond cold.

"I'll kill you, you evil scum," he said, very calmly. He stood up and started toward the end of the bridge.

Was Reven going to climb the Bone Bridge and fight the Bonemaster in midair? That was certain to end badly. Jinx swooped down and spread his arms out to stop Reven. Reven walked through him. Jinx felt a ripply sensation, as if he were water turning into waves, forming a wake behind Reven.

"Reven, stop!" yelled Elfwyn.

Jinx tried to stop her too, though he knew now he could only slow her down. Elfwyn stepped into Jinx, then stopped exactly inside him. Jinx fluttered and burbled around her and couldn't get himself organized. Everything that happened next came through as blurred, wavy images and voices speaking underwater.

Reven took the ax that was strapped to his back, swung it four times, and chopped through the ropes that held the Bone Bridge in place. The bridge came free, like a ghastly ribbon floating in the air, then smacked against the cliff. The Bonemaster hit the cliff hard but did not let go of the bridge.

Two people came charging up the shore, yelling.

"Jinx!" It was Simon. He sloshed across the shallow stream to where Jinx's body lay on the stones.

With a mighty thump, Dame Glammer landed her butter churn and reached through the blurry waves of Jinx to grab Elfwyn. Dragging Elfwyn along beside her, she hopped over to where Simon knelt.

Now Jinx could see and hear clearly again. He drifted over to where everyone was gathered around his body, which, now that he saw it up close, was quite a mess.

Simon's face was the color of parchment—probably he was still sick from his injury, Jinx thought.

"Not much to be done, I'm afraid," said Dame Glammer.

Simon rounded on her. "You shut up! If you hadn't sent him here—"

"Manners, Simon. Manners." It was the Bonemaster who spoke. "Haven't I always told you the importance of manners?"

He was clinging to the bridge, thirty feet over their heads. His arms were tightly wrapped around a thighbone. The bridge hung straight down the side of the cliff like a rope ladder.

"Shut up," said Simon. "I'll deal with you later."

"I don't know what you're crying about," said the Bonemaster. "You have the life bottled, don't you? Though I must say I never thought you'd manage such an advanced spell, Simon."

"Shut up."

Simon didn't look at the Bonemaster; he didn't take his eyes off Jinx, which Jinx found embarrassing, as he wasn't exactly looking his best. Jinx preferred to look at anybody but himself—Dame Glammer standing up in her butter churn, the Bonemaster hanging from his bridge, Elfwyn gazing at Simon as if she was trying to decide whether he was as evil as the Bonemaster, Reven with the ax in his hands, standing directly behind Simon—

Jinx tried to cry out as Reven raised the ax. No one heard him—except Dame Glammer, who looked up sharply.

Jinx flew forward and tried to knock Simon out of the way, but he ended up inside Simon, all wobbly and blurred. Looking out from the back of Simon's head, Jinx watched helplessly as the glinting sharp ax blade descended.

Dame Glammer's stick come down hard on Reven's arms. The ax flew through the air and landed several yards away.

Simon spun around and froze Reven's clothes. He stepped forward, out of Jinx, and grabbed Reven by the collar.

"Who are you?"

"He can't tell you that," said Elfwyn.

"Of course I can. I'm Reven. Unhand me, evil wizard."

"Oh, for pity's sake, even if he *is* evil, he's only Simon," said Dame Glammer. "You've no call to be chopping him up."

"*Are* you evil, Simon?" said Elfwyn.

"Of course not," Simon snapped. "Look, see those blankets over there, girl?"

"Yes."

"Go get them."

Elfwyn gave Simon a look but went and got them. "Are they to bury Jinx in?"

"Of course not! Fold them in half and lay them out flat."

"What for?" said Elfwyn.

"Don't you ever do as you're told?" said Simon.

"Sometimes," said Elfwyn. "Aren't you going to unfreeze Reven?"

"No, because he might try to kill me again."

Dame Glammer watched this exchange with great amusement. "Perhaps if you tried explaining things to the dear little chickabiddy, he wouldn't be so eager to fillet you."

Simon spared her a disgusted glance. "Look, boy—"

"Reven," said Reven, through clenched teeth.

"Reven, then. I'm not here to hurt anybody. And I'm not *going* to hurt anybody, provided they keep their flippin' axes to themselves. Good enough for you?"

"You killed Jinx," said Reven.

"I most certainly did not."

"Trust Simon, ducks," said Dame Glammer. She chucked Reven under the chin, which Reven was unable to avoid. "Not long term, mind. But right now, just for the moment, he means no harm."

Just then Simon noticed the bottle half sticking out of Reven's frozen pocket. Simon wrenched it free, stared at his tiny self for an instant, and then stuck the bottle into his own pocket. He went over and picked up the ax. Jinx watched Reven discover he could move again.

"Hurry up, lay those blankets out flat," said Simon. "Make a pallet out of them."

"Don't you ever say please?" said Elfwyn.

No, he never does, Jinx realized. But that isn't evil, that's just rude.

With the ax tucked safely under his arm, Simon knelt down and helped her arrange the blankets to make a pallet just about Jinx-sized. Reven helped too—but he kept darting angry looks at Simon all the same. Dame Glammer just stood in her butter churn and watched.

"Now we need to slide this under him while disturbing him as little as possible," said Simon.

"Hey, you made the blankets stiff," said Elfwyn. "Is that the same spell as the clothes?"

"Yes," said Simon. "Now, I'm going to levitate . . . Jinx, and when I do, you two slide the blankets under as quickly as you can, without touching him."

Jinx hovered closer to watch. Simon frowned with concentration. This was magic on a living person, wasn't it? The hardest kind to do. Except, Jinx thought, looking at himself, it *wasn't* magic on a living person, was it?

For a moment, nothing happened. Jinx could feel Simon trying to draw on power that wasn't there. Then

Simon took the bottle containing himself out of his pocket. He scowled at his captive life—power and concentration, thought Jinx. He's drawing on his own bottled lifeforce for power. Can you do that?

Jinx realized for the first time that he had learned to sense what power a wizard was using.

Simon was struggling with the bottled power—it was floppy and unwieldy—so Jinx supplied a little power of his own. Some of it came from his own, well, death. And some came from the freed dead lives, a few of which were still drifting upward. They were happy to come to Jinx's assistance. It was sort of like drawing on the Urwald's power, only a little more slippery.

Simon looked startled. He stared right at where Jinx was floating, and for a second Jinx thought the wizard could see him. Then Simon shook his head, gathered up the power Jinx was feeding him, and directed it at the body on the rocks.

Jinx's body rippled a little, like cloth floating on the surface of water, and rose a few inches into the air. Elfwyn slid the pallet underneath, and Jinx's body settled gently down onto it.

Simon levitated the pallet. Then he stood up, the ax still in his hand. "There seems to be a power vacuum in this vicinity, Bonemaster."

"Is there? I hadn't noticed."

"Something's destroyed nearly all your power. Care to tell me what it was?"

"Nonsense. I've simply found a way to conceal and guard my power," said the Bonemaster. "If you had any skill at magic, you'd be able to do the same."

"Is that so?" said Simon. "There's a lot of broken glass around here. It looks like bottles." His hand closed over the bottle in his pocket. He turned to Elfwyn. "Take . . . Jinx and start back down the canyon. I'll catch up with you."

"Are you just going to leave the Bonemaster dangling there?" Elfwyn demanded. "He killed Jinx!"

"Never mind what I'm going to do, girl. Take Jinx, and be extremely careful with him. You too, boy. Go."

Reven scowled but gave a curt nod, like a bow. Elfwyn and Reven each put a hand on the floating pallet, and it glided easily beside them as they splashed across the creek. Dame Glammer thrust at the ground with her stick and crossed the creek in a single bound.

Jinx himself stayed behind, floating between Simon on the ground and the Bonemaster clinging to the broken bridge. *Was* Simon going to kill the Bonemaster?

Simon took a piece of chalk out of his pocket and began drawing symbols on the rocks. He took out some dried leaves and scattered them on the ground.

"Are you using the boy's lifeforce too?" asked the

Bonemaster, peering down at the drawings and sounding as if the whole thing was only mildly interesting to him.

"Shut up."

Simon walked along the rocky shore, away from the Bonemaster, circling the island. Jinx followed, feeding him power from the lives that were still hanging around and from his own death.

Every fifty paces Simon stopped, drew symbols again, and then scattered more leaves. He kept his bottled life-force clenched tightly in his fist the whole time. Jinx could feel the power that came from the drawings and the leaves, and he suspected that Simon could feel the power Jinx was feeding him—the wizard looked at Jinx several more times, but still didn't seem to see him.

When they got back around to the bridge, the Bonemaster was still standing on a bone rung, with his arms folded around another rung. He reached out one hand and poked at the air. He frowned, then put his palm out and pushed. Jinx watched the Bonemaster's palm and fingers flatten as though he were pressing against glass.

"Think that'll hold me?" said the Bonemaster.

Simon glared up at the Bonemaster. "Have you done anything to him? Other than push him off a cliff? Anything I'll need to know about the life? You'd better tell me now."

"Or what?"

You had to be impressed with a wizard who could

ask "or what?" when he was hanging from a broken rope bridge and trapped inside an invisible wall, Jinx thought.

"Or I'll leave you in there to starve," said Simon.

"Nice try, Simon," said the Bonemaster. "But you simply cannot afford to do that."

"Don't bet on it."

"Think about what's in that bottle. You're not still counting on the boy, are you? I only ask because I've spent some time with him. He wasn't a very talented magician, was he?"

"Just tell me if you've done anything to him."

Considering the condition he'd been in the last time he saw himself, Jinx thought that sounded odd.

"I'm afraid you'll have to figure that out for yourself," said the Bonemaster.

"Right," said Simon. "Either way, I'll be back."

"Bring the girl with you when you come," said the Bonemaster. "She'll be welcome anytime."

Jinx had never flown over the Urwald before.

He saw the Urwald as an endless expanse of green cloud-shaped treetops, stretching on and on in all directions to the horizon. He soared higher, and the horizon grew farther away, but he never saw any place that wasn't trees, any place where kings might live.

He felt wonderfully free.

He glided back to the river and saw the Bonemaster slowly, painfully, making his way up the cliff face. Jinx flew on to find his friends. They were marching along, sad and silent, and he got bored with them and drifted up above the Urwald again.

When night fell, the plain of treetops grew dark and shadowed, outlined with silver from the starlight. Some bond seemed to be connecting him to the trees, and he realized that through it he could listen to the root networks far below.

The Terror was there. Following Reven, of course—him with his talk of chopping down trees and trading lumber to Samara. But it reached in from the unseeable borders of the Urwald, too. Somebody was cutting down trees, out there at the edge of the Urwald. And Jinx saw that this was connected to Reven in the mind of the Urwald—that Reven had the power to make the cutting grow and spread until there was no Urwald left.

The trees mourned this, and they mourned Jinx too. The Listener was dead—this news susurrated through the branches, crept along the root networks.

But I'm not dead, Jinx thought. I'm still here. If he was dead, wouldn't he have, well, gone somewhere? Wouldn't he see his mother, who'd been carried off by elves, and his father, done in by werewolves?

Or was this where people went when they died? He

saw no one else floating over the top of the Urwald. But then—looking down—he didn't see himself, either. Was he nothing but eyes? Then shouldn't there be other eyeballs floating around up here?

The last of the Bonemaster's captive lives had floated away. Jinx didn't know where they'd gone, and he didn't feel any urge to follow them anyway.

He flew far, looking for more dead people. From up here, the troubles of the Urwald were invisible. Trolls and ogres and werewolves lurked under those trees, but you couldn't tell it from here. You could hardly even see the clearings.

Everyone and everything was part of the Urwald. Jinx didn't feel alone, because he was connected to all of it.

And then a sudden surge of panic disconnected him—he had no idea where he was. He didn't even know if he'd gone east or west, north or south from where his body was—or how far he'd floated, or for how long.

Maybe it didn't matter anymore, but he felt as if it did. He wanted to know where his body was, and where it was going, and where he belonged.

The sunrise caught him by surprise. The sky went purple and golden-pink. A red sliver appeared on the horizon, growing into a great fireball, and the birds twittered and screamed in celebration. Jinx had never seen this before, and he understood why Reven missed it.

The sunrise had interrupted his panic, and now that he was calm, he heard the trees again. He followed the thread of their thoughts, and it guided him back to the path where the four people accompanying his body were walking.

～ ♪ ✔

It was midday when they reached Simon's house. They had walked all night. Elfwyn and Reven stopped at the edge of Simon's clearing and stared, dismayed. Jinx could guess what they were thinking. Simon's stone house looked too much like the Bonemaster's castle. The two of them looked at each other and then back at the forest. But they followed Simon and Dame Glammer (who left her churn at the door) and Jinx's floating body into the house.

"Eat something," Simon ordered. "All of you. Dame, get them some food."

"Can't we help you—" Elfwyn began.

"No! Do as you're told." Simon shoved Jinx's body along ahead of him toward the south wing.

Elfwyn moved to follow him. Simon turned around and gave her such a look that Jinx was surprised she didn't turn into a toad on the spot. Simon went into the south wing, and the door slammed behind him.

The door was no barrier to Jinx—he floated right through it. He watched as Simon cleaned the workroom out with a few quick spells, sweeping the floor with a sudden wind that gathered all the dust into a ball and carried it out the window.

Simon laid Jinx's body in the center of the floor. He dug out the book bound in red leather. He mixed herbs in a mortar. Jinx recognized the roots that smelled of betrayal. Then Simon dug a piece of chalk from a jar and began sketching symbols around Jinx's body. Sometimes he checked a symbol two or three times, looking worried. It was clear that Simon had never done whatever he was doing before and didn't really know if he could.

This went on for a long time. Jinx got bored. He sailed to the window and then out it, into the summer daylight. He soared high over the treetops and saw green stretching to the horizon in every direction.

He felt at peace up here . . . except for the Terror. Except for the tree cutting that would spread until there was nothing left. No trees and therefore no people or creatures that lived beneath them.

Jinx flew back down into the clearing. He flew through the window and into the workroom again.

A cat came and sniffed at Jinx's body.

Simon scooped it up. "Jinx is not a cat person," he said, and dropped it in the hallway.

Widdershins

Simon knelt on the staircase up to his tower and touched the thirteenth step from the bottom. He said a word that Jinx didn't recognize. There was a click and whirr of things unlocking, and the stone lifted upward. He reached into a hollow underneath and pulled out a green glass bottle that Jinx just had time to recognize before Simon stuck it in his pocket.

He's been walking on my life, Jinx thought angrily, as Simon put his own bottled life under the step and locked it in.

Simon went down to the kitchen. "Right. I need you all to come help me."

"Are you going to put Jinx's life back in him?" said Elfwyn.

"The one you've got in a bottle," said Reven.

"Aren't they clever?" said Dame Glammer. "Goodness, do you keep the little chipmunk's life in a bottle, Simon? That's dark magic, that is."

"It is not," said Simon. "It's wizard's magic."

"What I said," said Dame Glammer. "Dark magic. Wizard stuff."

"I can't do any magic," said Reven.

"You'll do magic if I say you will," said Simon. "Wash your hands and come on." He turned and stalked off to the south wing, leaving the door open.

When they got to the workroom, Elfwyn and Reven froze and stared at Jinx's body. It did look a bit mystical, in the middle of all those chalked symbols.

Dame Glammer entered the room, skirted around the sides, and went to stand by one of the braziers. "Come in, little chickabiddies."

"Watch where you're walking!" Simon snapped, as soon as Elfwyn and Reven moved.

"Now, Simon, the chickabiddies won't want to help if you yell at them," said Dame Glammer, grinning. She found the whole thing wonderfully amusing, Jinx could tell.

"Right. Stand next to a brazier, chickabiddies. *Don't*

step on the symbols!" Simon was as tense and cranky as Jinx had ever seen him, and Jinx suspected that this was because Simon was really nervous about the spell. Which was not exactly reassuring.

Jinx ducked through the window and flew up over the Urwald again. He wasn't sure he wanted to be alive again. He was free up here, and he could see sunrises and sunsets forever.

On the other hand, Jinx was the only person who knew about the danger to the Urwald. And if he stayed floating up here, he probably wouldn't be able to do anything about it.

And there were Elfwyn and Reven, who had looked pretty upset about Jinx being, well, dead—and there was Simon.

He drifted through the stone wall into Simon's workroom.

Simon was handing a torch to Elfwyn. She took it and stepped gingerly over to the brazier Simon indicated. She set it smoking. Meanwhile Simon summoned Reven and, very slightly more politely, Dame Glammer and gave them torches. He took a torch himself and lit the fourth brazier.

"Now you stand in a circle around Jinx—no, not that close! I said a circle, not an isosceles triangle." Simon walked around, pushing and jostling them into place. "And face inward."

When he had Elfwyn, Reven, and Dame Glammer arranged to his liking, Simon stepped forward toward Jinx's body.

"Well, what are you waiting for? Move!"

"You mean us?" said Reven.

"Yes, you, who did you think I meant, Jinx?"

"Well, you might have meant Jinx," said Elfwyn, as she and the others walked forward toward Jinx's body.

"Now walk around him! No, no, widdershins!"

"Widdershins means this way, chickabiddies," said Dame Glammer, giving Reven a little shove. "To reverse the spell."

"I knew what widdershins meant," Elfwyn muttered.

Seen from above, the flames streaming behind the torches formed a ring over the four people's heads. Jinx watched the ring of flame rotate slowly around his body, which almost looked alive with flickers of yellow and orange light rippling across it.

Simon began to chant in a language Jinx didn't know.

"Are we supposed to chant that stuff too?" said Reven.

"Shut up. No." Simon went back to chanting.

Smoke drifted upward from the torches and braziers and swirled around Jinx like the lives from the Bonemaster's bottles. Jinx began to feel confused, as if what was happening below was a dream and not real. The ring of flame and the rhythmic chanting rocked him out of reality, into a place where he wasn't sure anymore why he was up here on the ceiling instead of down on the floor with the rest of himself.

Simon stopped and knelt. Reven walked into him.

"Kneel down, all of you. Put your hands on him."

Now there were four people kneeling around Jinx and six hands on him—everyone's but Simon's.

Simon looked up at the ceiling, directly at where Jinx was no longer sure if he was really floating. "Jinx, if this works, you're probably going to feel as if you've just fallen off a hundred-foot cliff. Sorry."

He took the green bottle out of his pocket. He leaned over Jinx, uncorked the bottle, and quickly put it to Jinx's lips.

Jinx felt himself sliding back toward his body. He didn't have to go. He had a choice. He could go on floating around the Urwald instead. He stopped for a moment, drifting just above himself, and then made his choice.

The last part of the slide was the hardest. Instinctively, he struggled.

"Don't move, boy!" Simon's hands were on Jinx's shoulders.

And then Jinx didn't feel even slightly like moving. His whole body was a universe stretching to an endless horizon of pain. There was nothing but pain. As far as Jinx knew he was alone in the room with pain, if there was even a room. Then the pain organized itself into bones fitting themselves back together, muscle reconstituting itself, marrow producing massive amounts of blood to replace what he'd lost—Simon had told him about all these things that bodies contained, but now he could feel his own body containing them for all it was worth.

"Go get him something to drink." Simon's voice cut through the pain at last, echoing and repeating itself ringingly on the inside of Jinx's skull. "Something to drink thing to drink thing to dri dri dri . . ."

He wanted to get out of this aching body again. It had been a mistake to return.

"You're all right," said Simon. "Jinx, you're all right." It sounded pleading, not reassuring.

"Yeah," said Jinx, at last, with great difficulty. He was all right. The pain was gone, just a horrible memory that he decided to do his best to forget.

"There, bring that drink here, put it—no, don't spill it on him, you fool. Go get him another one."

"Sorry," came Elfwyn's voice. "But would it kill you to say please once in a while?"

"Please. Jinx, don't move. Just lie still until your bones have finished knitting."

"Think they've finished," said Jinx.

He was aware of claws pinching and prodding at him, an invasion that infuriated him but that he didn't have the strength to avoid. "Yes, the little chipmunk is all fixed up," said Dame Glammer. "See? Bones as good as new." A hand slipped underneath him. "Even the backbone."

He couldn't see her thoughts. He never had been able to. But even with his eyes closed, he could see that Reven was astounded, in a great orange blob of surprise. Elfwyn radiated relief and shimmered bright blue happiness that Jinx was back, just like Simon did.

He could hear Elfwyn crying. Which didn't go with the feelings she was having at all. People were funny.

"Get out of here and let him rest," said Simon.

Jinx heard their footsteps on the floor as they left, all but Simon. Slowly Jinx opened his eyes. Simon was looking down at him, but as soon as he saw Jinx's eyes open, he made a *hmph* sound and stood up and started putting things away. Simon normally never put things away. He waited for Jinx to do it.

Jinx followed Simon with his eyes. Simon certainly didn't look happy or relieved. His expression seemed to say that Jinx was a nuisance, which showed that the expressions and words people chose weren't always like what was going on inside their heads. Underneath it all, a warm blue cloud surrounded Simon and reached out and included Jinx, and Jinx realized for the first time that it had always been there.

"But it's not enough," said Jinx.

Simon turned around from shaking ashes out the

window. "What's not enough?"

"The blue stuff."

A ripple of pink worry rustled past but didn't show up on Simon's face. "Supposing you let me in on the part of this conversation that is only happening in your head."

"You didn't have any right to take my magic away," said Jinx. "Or my life. Can I have another drink? Please," he added, hoping to set a good example for Simon.

Simon knelt down and gave him a drink of water.

"Thanks," said Jinx. "Why didn't you come before?"

"What, to rescue you? You go off to the one exact place that I specifically told you to stay away from—"

"No, you didn't."

"Yes, I did. I told you to stay away from the Bonemaster. Do you ever listen?"

"Yes. All the time," said Jinx. He felt tired. "But you were watching me through the Farseeing Window, with that gold bird thing. Why didn't you come sooner? Were you really watching me?"

Simon looked away. "I was busy."

"You forgot. You *always* forget about me."

"Nonsense. I give you room to grow, that's all."

"You were too busy fighting with Sophie to remember me," said Jinx. Oh, right—"Are you feeling better, then?"

"Much better, thanks so much for asking," said Simon sarcastically. "I watched the first few days you were gone but then, yes, it did slip my mind. I didn't realize what had happened until Dame Glammer came to visit and merrily told me how she had sent you off to Bonesocket, and that the Bonemaster intended to kill you on August thirty-first—which happened to be the very next day."

"How did she know that?" said Jinx.

"I suppose the Bonemaster sent her a message."

"He sends messages to her? You mean she's in league with him?"

"Dame Glammer's not in league with anyone but herself."

"But she—"

"People have their friends," said Simon shortly.

"How can she be friends with—"

"I did tell you to stay away from her. Now, since you're all wide awake and chattery, supposing you tell me about your visit with the Bonemaster."

So Jinx did. It seemed strange that he'd thought he couldn't trust Simon. But that was life when you were missing your magic. Now that he could see clearly, he knew that he could trust Simon—to be Simon, at any rate. Which was its own problem.

At least he seemed like the old Simon again—the one before the bottle spell.

"He said you'd killed me," said Jinx when he was finished.

"Did he? Well, he was wrong."

"You did, though. You put my life in a bottle—"

"And then I gave it back. You have it back now, correct?"

"Yes, but the Bonemaster said—"

"And suddenly the Bonemaster is the arbiter of truth, is he? Not killing you was the whole point. That's what makes it such a difficult spell."

"He did the same spell on you that you did on me."

Simon said nothing.

"He put your life in a bottle."

"Yes." The thought that went with this was cold, green, and angry.

"He thought you'd sent me to steal it back," said Jinx.

"I would never have done that," said Simon. "However—" There was a long, difficult pause. "Thank you."

"You're welcome. Why did he have your life? I mean, he took it to use your lifeforce power, all right, but why did you let him? Did he trick you?" *Like you tricked me?*

Simon got up, went to his workbench, and began fiddling around. Jinx heard boxes being opened and jars sliding about. He thought Simon wasn't going to answer him. Different layers of thoughts and feelings were kicking each other angrily across the surface of Simon's mind.

"It's the usual price," said Simon at last. "The apprentice

permits the wizard to use his lifeforce for the length of the apprenticeship."

"You were his apprentice?" Jinx had not been expecting that.

"Yes. Don't look at me like that."

"But why?"

"Because I wanted to learn to be a wizard, of course." Simon began grinding something in the mortar.

"But—didn't you realize he was evil?"

"No." Simon sighed. "That is, yes. At first I didn't think about it, because I was only interested in finding someone to teach me. And then I didn't think about it because it wasn't . . . convenient."

"Wasn't convenient," Jinx repeated.

"Well, if *you* never in your life find yourself making excuses for things you know are wrong, wonderful," said Simon. "But in the end, I couldn't pretend any longer that I didn't know what he was, and I told him I was quitting. And he claimed that because I hadn't completed my apprenticeship, he didn't have to give my life back."

This all came out of Simon's mouth freely enough, but his thoughts were struggling with one another—some of the thoughts didn't want Jinx or *anyone* to know these things, and others were insisting it was for the best that they be spoken. Jinx wondered if this was what made Simon so cranky: having a brain like a dogfight.

"Why didn't you take your life when you left? And the other bottles?"

"I didn't know about the other bottles," said Simon.

"How could you not know—"

"They were hidden. I never found that underground passage, never knew to look for it. I knew he'd killed people."

"Did you see him kill people?"

A door slammed shut across Simon's thoughts, so hard that Jinx flinched. "Enough talk. You need to rest."

"What's the difference between the dead people in the bottles and—us?"

"The difference between being dead and being alive."

"Are the dead people in the bottles really completely dead?"

"They are now," said Simon. His thoughts were making a cage around his words. "It wasn't their lives that were bottled, it was their interrupted deaths. There's power in that. He stole the moments of their deaths, and bottled them. He stopped them from going on."

If you know that, Jinx thought, you must have known the bottles existed. "So when the bottles smashed, when I fell—"

"You set the deaths free."

"So will they come back to life, those people who were in the bottles?"

"No," said Simon. "But they will be free."

"What's that mean?"

"I don't know," said Simon. "You think I know everything?"

He lit a candle and held a glass phial over it in a clamp, turning it slowly. Jinx saw him reach for the powder in the mortar, and for things on the shelf that Jinx couldn't see, and add them to the phial.

"You destroyed most of the Bonemaster's power," Simon said after a while. "It was well done."

Praise from Simon was so rare that it took Jinx a minute to realize that that was what it was. "Well, I mostly had a lot of help," Jinx said. "But why didn't he bottle them alive?"

"Because it's a much more complicated spell."

"It requires a human sacrifice," said Jinx.

Simon turned around fast. "Who told you that?"

"Isn't that what deathforce magic is? And you did that spell on me!"

"Don't be ridiculous," said Simon. "You were here. Did you see me sacrifice anybody?"

"Didn't you sacrifice me?"

"Of course not. I told you." Simon went back to fussing with his phial. "There's a way around most things in magic, if you know how to look. That's what Dame Glammer's roots were for."

And Jinx could see he was telling the truth.

"What do you think that other bottle was?" Jinx asked. "The one with all the ribbony smoke around it?"

"I have no idea," said Simon. "But you were right not to touch it."

Then you do have some idea. So did Jinx. "I think it's the Bonemaster's life."

"Perhaps," said Simon.

"He'll kill more people now, won't he? To get his power back?"

"I intend to prevent that."

But you didn't prevent it before, Jinx thought. He remembered the green, bottle-shaped fear that everyone had of the Bonemaster. Usually different people had different-looking feelings, but this one was the same for everyone, as if—oh.

"Did you cast a spell, before, to make people afraid of the Bonemaster?" said Jinx.

"Of course not," said Simon. "I simply told them about him."

"You made up stories. Like that he could suck out your soul with a straw."

"It's more or less the truth. And it kept people away from him."

"Then where did all those dead people come from?"

"Mostly they happened before," said Simon.

The word *before* lay smack across the wall around Simon's thoughts.

"Before you left?"

"Yes."

"And after people heard your stories, it wasn't so easy for him to catch people," Jinx guessed. "What did you steal from him?"

Simon rapped a knuckle against the red-bound book that lay open on the workbench.

"But that's the book you used to—"

"It's the book he used to kill people with," said Simon.

"The book *you* used to take my life."

"And to put it back."

"Can he still do the bottle spell now that he doesn't have the book?"

"How should I know? It depends how good his memory is."

"Why didn't you kill him?" Jinx asked.

"You think I go around killing people?"

Jinx looked up at Calvin the Skull, resting near Simon's elbow on the workbench. "Well, but if killing him could save a lot of people's lives—"

"Or cost them. I don't know whose death he's tied to his own. Mine, naturally, that goes with the bottling—"

"You mean if you killed him, you'd die?"

"Probably. Along with I-don't-know-who-else." Simon

dribbled something from a jar into the phial he was heating.

"Are you going to take your life out of the bottle now?" Jinx asked.

"Can't. I need another wizard to give it back to me. The spell's quite complicated."

"The spell you just did on me."

"Yes. I can't do it on myself."

"But there are other wizards in the Urwald."

"Not any that I'd trust with my life."

Jinx was beginning to see the shape of this. "Why can't you teach Sophie to do the spell? She likes magic really."

At the mention of Sophie, Simon's thoughts turned all orangeish gray, like a log about to fall apart in the fire. "Because Sophie does not know my life is in a bottle, and I do not wish her to find out."

"You don't trust her?" Jinx was surprised.

Annoyance crackled around Simon's head. "Of course I do. It's just not the sort of thing you tell your wife."

"Where *is* Sophie?"

"She left."

"Did she go back to Samara?"

"Yes."

"Is she coming back?"

"How should I know? Now if you—"

"Well, did she *say* she was coming back?"

"She said she has to think about things. Now if you're quite finished interrogating me—"

"What kind of things?"

"Things. Sometimes women need to think about things. You'll see—when you're older, they'll do it at you."

"Things like whether she wants to stay married?"

"Jinx, this is not something I care to discuss."

Jinx could tell from the shape of Simon's thoughts that he'd guessed right, and that it would be best to drop the subject for now.

"So you want me to learn to do that spell," said Jinx. "I'm not very good at magic."

"You'll get better. Age helps. Sometimes." Simon took the phial off the flame and poured steaming liquid into a cup.

Maybe Jinx *was* getting better at magic. Like the way he'd been able to draw on the Urwald's power, just recently. Except that after that—

"I couldn't do magic in Dame Glammer's house."

"Wizards' magic does not work in witches' cottages."

"Why not?"

"How should I know? Ask a witch."

Jinx thought of something else. "The Bonemaster was really worried when he heard you'd been injured. Was that because if you die, your bottled life won't be as powerful?"

"You told him I was injured?" Angry little lightning bolts.

Elfwyn had actually told, because of her curse. Jinx decided not to say this. "Not intentionally."

"That was a foolish thing to do."

"Sorry," said Jinx, since it was less trouble than arguing.

He didn't think it would be tactful to add that he'd thought Simon was evil at the time.

"Is my life tied to yours, then? Would I die if you died?" he asked.

"In the first place, no. Because your life is no longer in the bottle. And in the second place, no. Because I happen to understand the bottle spell a great deal better than the Bonemaster does. And in the third place, no. Because the curse is only triggered if the apprentice kills the master."

"I would never have—"

"I know that, of course." Simon even managed to sound irritated at Jinx for not wanting to kill him. "But a great many apprentices have tried to kill a great many wizards. That's why the spell was originally constructed as it was."

So Simon had changed the spell, Jinx thought. And used roots, and made it not involve a human sacrifice. And now Jinx had to learn to do it in reverse—to put Simon's life back inside him, so that there would be no chance of the Bonemaster ever getting his hands on it again. Jinx had trouble even with easy spells. He really doubted he would ever be able to do this one. And do it right, without killing Simon. The thought was both frightening and exhausting. Why did it have to be him?

"Because I was just a life lost in the forest," Jinx answered himself.

"What, you think I would have just left you to the trolls if I didn't have a use for you?" Simon jiggled the liquid in the cup, cooling it.

"But you didn't even teach me to read, at first."

"Well." Embarrassment, of all things, in a little lavender cloud. "I never really thought of making a wizard of you, but then *she* kept saying you were clever."

So I was meant for something else, Jinx thought. To do work that you could easily do yourself with a few spells? To be better company than the cats? Or just to be a living life trapped in a bottle? Jinx didn't know.

Simon came over to Jinx and knelt down, the cup in his hand. "Drink this."

The potion was bright green. "What is it?"

"A sleeping potion," said Simon. "It's not that easy to get over being dead. You need to rest and give yourself time to heal."

"It doesn't look anything like the sleeping potion we made for the Bonemaster." It didn't smell like it either. It smelled quite pleasant, like autumn leaves.

"Mine is a vegetarian recipe. No bat wings."

"Ours didn't work," said Jinx, remembering how the Bonemaster had caught them at the top of the cliff.

"I'm sure he didn't take it," said Simon.

"But Elfwyn hid it in the drink she always gave him every day."

"Which he certainly never drank. He wouldn't. The Bonemaster's not an easy wizard to fool."

Jinx tried to take the cup, but his hand didn't want to do what he told it to. It flopped around and wouldn't close. That scared him.

"You'll be fine when you wake up," said Simon.

He held the cup to Jinx's lips.

It could be anything, really. Simon wouldn't poison him, not if he was telling the truth about what he wanted Jinx to do. But the potion could be something to put Jinx under Simon's control, take away his power to choose— there were potions that could do that.

Would Simon do that? Even now that Jinx had his magic back and could (sort of) read minds, he didn't know. But on the whole he thought not—not right now, not when Simon was so relieved to see Jinx alive. Jinx examined all the clouds around Simon's head. There was no guilt now. There was that warm blue cloud. And there was the wall, and everything that lay behind it.

Jinx drank the potion. It didn't taste bad at all.

He burrowed into the warm blue cloud and fell asleep.

Reven's Curse

Jinx awoke in the first gray light of dawn. He went out to the kitchen. Elfwyn was sitting by the fire, surrounded by cats. When she saw Jinx, she jumped up and hugged him.

"Where is everyone?" said Jinx.

"Reven's asleep, up in your tower. And Simon's back there somewhere." Elfwyn gestured toward the south wing. "He just got home last night."

"What do you mean? We all got back yesterday." Jinx went to get some cider.

"Simon and my grandmother left again, after we did the spell on you. They went to strengthen the wards Simon

346

put around the Bonemaster's island. They spent a couple
days doing that. And then I guess my grandmother went
home."

"A couple days? But—"

"You were asleep for three days."

"That's ridiculous. Nobody can be asleep for three
days."

"You were."

Jinx didn't believe her. "Was I really?"

"Yes." And since it was a question, it must be true.

That explained why his mouth was so dry. He drank the
cider down in one long gulp. "I thought your grandmother
was friends with the Bonemaster."

"Of course she isn't. Who could be?"

Jinx didn't argue the point. "So you didn't go home
with your grandmother?"

"No, well, I'd already been to visit her," said Elfwyn.
She sat down at the table and scooped a cat up into her lap.

"Yes, but—"

"I told you, I don't want to live with her. I like it here.
It's such a lovely clearing. And I milked the goats!"

"Don't you have goats in your clearing?"

"No, we have stupid cows. And Simon's really nice
when you get used to him—"

This was so patently untrue that Jinx had to laugh.
"When I act like Simon, you say I'm not nice."

"I never said you weren't nice."

Jinx decided to let that go. "So are you going to go back to Butterwood Clearing, then?"

"I don't know. There are things I need to think about." She did not elaborate.

Jinx poured some more cider and got a piece of pumpkin pie from the cupboard. He ate it and then went outside to tell the trees that he was alive.

Jinx wormed his feet into the warm soil of the Urwald. He had a feeling that since his death, he no longer needed to do this to listen. He was connected to the trees in a way he hadn't been before his flight over the Urwald. But it was comforting to feel the dirt between his toes. The forest spoke of late summer and the way it made your leaves feel, of the pain at the edges of the Urwald, of the Terror lodged in Simon's house.

The Listener is alive, said the forest, after a while. *He's sprouted fresh greenery.*

Jinx had never heard the Urwald's voice so clearly before. It wasn't one tree speaking—things went from root to root, and the forest spoke. The Urwald couldn't read Jinx's mind, but he found that now, as he stood rooted into the soil, he could send messages. He told about his bottled life being restored to him.

Wizard's magic, said the forest.

Wizard's magic is different from Urwald magic, said Jinx.

Wizard's magic, witch's magic, it's all magic. It's all of the Urwald.

Then I can do wizard's magic and still do Urwald magic? Jinx asked. *I mean, the Urwald magic that is not wizard's magic.*

You can, Listener. We don't suppose anyone else can. But you, yes, probably, perhaps, maybe. There was some disagreement about this along the crisscrossing lines of roots.

You've let me use your power.

It's your power.

The power that comes from the trees, I mean, said Jinx. *That comes from the Urwald.*

The trees thought this was funny. *The trees aren't the Urwald. Yes, the trees. No, not the trees. Not only the trees. The creatures that live in the Urwald. All the restless ones. Even the scheming humans. Even the wizards are the Urwald.*

Jinx had felt that when he flew over the Urwald.

But the other wizards don't use your power, he said. *They can't, can they?*

Can't. Don't listen. They'd misuse it, of course. You will too.

No, I won't.

You will.

Jinx decided not to argue this point. They'd see in time that he didn't. Instead he said, *About the Terror . . .*

Fear rippled through the roots.

I'm going to take him out of the Urwald, Jinx said. *I'll travel with him to the edge of the forest and not let him hurt any trees on the way. But can you promise not to harm him while I do it? Don't drop anything on him, don't send any ogres, and let him get safely out? I will tell him never to come back.*

We will try. But we have no control over the Restless. The ogres, the werewolves, and vampires. The humans. Yes, we do. No, we don't. We shall see what can be done.

Thank you, said Jinx.

Then he asked the trees if they knew who Reven was. But they didn't, or not in the way Jinx meant—he was just the Terror.

Reven was outside chopping firewood. Simon was in the kitchen kneading bread dough.

"Can I help?" Elfwyn asked.

"I do the cooking," Simon snapped.

"You could scrub the potatoes," said Jinx. "He lets people do that."

"It can't be messed up too badly," said Simon.

Jinx brought some potatoes from the bin and dumped them into a tub of water that Elfwyn pumped.

"Did you decide about going back to Butterwood Clearing, then?" Jinx asked her.

Elfwyn scrubbed hard at a potato. "Yes. I'd better not go back. They kind of got tired of me there. Because of my curse."

"You could stay here," said Jinx.

"Don't mind me, I'm just the cook," said Simon.

Elfwyn looked at him. "About my curse—"

"I can't take your curse off you," said Simon. "It's not wizards' magic."

"Because it was put on me by an evil fairy?" said Elfwyn.

Simon frowned. "Who told you that?"

"My mother."

"There's no such thing as fairies," said Simon. "Except in fairy tales."

Elfwyn pursed her lips and nodded. "I see. Then who put the curse on me?"

"I have no way of knowing that," said Simon. "But I doubt it was a wizard. It takes a huge amount of power to put a spell on a living person, and it's hard to see the point of wasting that much power on you."

Elfwyn nodded again. "So there are no fairies, and a wizard wouldn't bother. How about a witch?"

"A witch can cast a spell on a person much more easily than a wizard can," said Jinx, remembering this.

"I don't see why a witch would bother casting that spell on you either," said Simon.

"Because she didn't like little girls to tell lies," said Elfwyn. "She came to visit us in Butterwood Clearing when I was two years old. I *thought* I remembered it, but my mother said I was wrong. And she told me that little girls shouldn't tell lies, and then she put the curse on me."

"This would be your grandmother, I take it," said Simon.

Elfwyn nodded. "That's probably why she never came to visit again. I think my mother was very angry at her. There was yelling."

"What was the lie you told?" said Jinx.

Elfwyn looked embarrassed. "I ate all the strawberries we picked, and then when she asked, I told her I hadn't."

"Don't ask questions of a person who has to answer them, Jinx. It's not polite," said Simon.

"You're telling me what's polite?"

"Yes. Go get some more firewood."

Jinx went, in a huff. The idea of Simon telling anyone how to be polite was ludicrous.

Reven was still out by the woodpile, splitting logs. Reven dearly loved splitting logs. The logs had all been as split as they could be and still be firewood. Now he was splitting them up into kindling.

"Are you ready to go where you were going when I met you?" Jinx asked.

A yellow line appeared fuzzily around Reven's thoughts, and Reven turned away. Jinx thought the line might be Reven's curse. He wondered if he could do anything with that yellow line now that he knew it was there.

Elfwyn was coming toward them across the clearing.

"I want you to leave the Urwald," said Jinx. "Is that what you were planning to do anyway?"

Reven smiled. "*You* want me to leave? I thought the Urwald had no king."

"It doesn't," said Jinx. "But, well, the trees want you to leave."

"You can't tell me trees are like people."

"I know I can't. That's the problem."

"Maybe if he stayed longer, he'd understand," said Elfwyn, coming to stand beside them.

"The trees don't want him to stay longer." Jinx hated doing this. "You want to leave anyway, don't you? It's not like you belong here."

"'Tis a fascinating place to visit," said Reven.

"You were on your way somewhere when I met you," said Jinx. "You were crossing the Urwald. You were going east."

The yellow line around Reven's thoughts turned orange. This was getting closer to his curse.

"Toward Butterwood Clearing," said Elfwyn. "Toward King Bluetooth's country."

"Orange," said Jinx. Oops. He didn't intend to tell anyone that he'd regained the power to see thoughts. Elfwyn had been right; it was the kind of thing that could make people want to kill Jinx. "Keyland, right? Were you going to Keyland?"

"*They* want to cut down the trees," said Elfwyn.

"I guess they're doing it," said Jinx. "The trees say someone is."

"King Bluetooth is evil," said Elfwyn. She was watching Reven carefully.

"Aye, you speak sooth, lady." Reven didn't seem to have any trouble saying this, but the lines around his thoughts went orange again.

"He killed your father," said Elfwyn.

Bright orange. Reven said nothing.

"How do you know that?" said Jinx.

"I suspected it ever since the Bonemaster said Reven was important. He's just the right age to be the boy that King Bluetooth said he'd killed. And it fits in with all the things he can't say."

Jinx didn't understand. "What boy he killed?"

"His nephew. King Bluetooth killed his own brother, who was the real king of Keyland, and he killed the boy and the stepmother. I *told* you that."

Reven looked embarrassed. He tossed the ax into the air and caught it left-handed.

"But I guess what really happened was that your stepmother, the dead king's new wife, took you and ran away to Bragwood," said Elfwyn. "Or, no, that can't be quite right, because you were a prisoner of King Rufus of

Bragwood, weren't you?"

"No," said Reven. "We were guests of a sort."

"But he killed your stepmother because she said who you were," said Elfwyn.

"Alas, my lady." The lines were orange-red, and Jinx could see that Reven was feeling carefully for things his curse would let him say.

"Why would he have done that?" Elfwyn wondered aloud. "Perhaps King Bluetooth was paying him to keep you there and keep your identity secret."

The lines around Reven's curse went bright red. "I think that's true," said Jinx.

"Once he found out that that was where you had taken refuge," said Elfwyn, "he just told everyone that you'd been killed. He must have been paying an awful lot for King Rufus to be that desperate to guard the secret. To do what he did to your stepmother, I mean."

"King Rufus was ever ruthless, my lady. He enjoys that sort of thing."

"Yech," said Elfwyn. "I'm glad we don't have kings. But now you're a king, I suppose."

Bright red again, Jinx saw. "It's going to be hard to claim your throne when you can't even tell people who you are."

"Many things in life are difficult," said Reven, choosing his words carefully. "But to those who persevere, all things are possible."

"Sometimes people are happier if they don't persevere," said Elfwyn.

"That may be true, my lady."

Jinx thought what lay ahead for Reven—trying to seize the throne of Keyland from evil King Bluetooth when Reven couldn't even say that he was the rightful heir. It gave Jinx a headache. He was glad the Urwald didn't have kings. But it could still be threatened by them.

"Would you cut down the Urwald too, if you were king? Like King Bluetooth is doing?" he asked.

Reven smiled. "How is it possible to cut down the Urwald? You see how vast it is."

Uh-huh. "I'm going to go with you to the edge of the Urwald," Jinx told him. "I promised the forest I would."

Maybe, Jinx thought, he would even go on to Keyland. He remembered Tolliver the Wanderer saying that they killed magicians there, and since Jinx could do magic, they would certainly consider Jinx a magician. But then, Tolliver had also said that if you never went anywhere you'd always be stupid.

"I shall be glad of your company, friend Jinx."

"I'll come along," said Elfwyn.

She smiled at Reven, her thoughts pink and fluffy. If she'd liked Reven as a thief and a banished courtier, she didn't like him any less as a deposed king. Jinx realized with a start that Reven wasn't thinking any pink fluffy thoughts back at her. His thoughts were square and calculating.

Jinx picked up an armload of the much-split logs and walked back to the house. He thought Elfwyn would stay with Reven, thinking her pink fluffy thoughts at him, but she ran to catch up with Jinx.

"You got your mind-reading power back, didn't you?" she whispered.

Jinx started to lie and say no. But it didn't seem fair, lying to Elfwyn when she couldn't lie back. "Don't tell anyone, please."

She gave him a look—of course, it was stupid asking Elfwyn to keep a secret. Jinx sighed.

"I'll really, really, try not to," she said.

❧ ❧ ❧

"You're going *where?*"

"To take Reven to Keyland," Jinx said. "I have to. I promised the trees that I would."

"Is this that nonsense about talking to the trees that you used to spout when you were little?"

"You don't think it's nonsense," said Jinx. "You never did." He should have realized that before. But being deprived of his magic, and having to figure people out from the outside, made it much easier to understand their thinking now.

"Were you going to ask my permission at all, or were

you planning to dispense with that?"

"You said I could go. You said I should get out and explore the world."

"Before. When I knew you had some protection, and that I could probably save you as long as you hadn't actually been eaten. Now you haven't got a bottled life anymore." Simon frowned. "I suppose I could bottle it again before you go, but—"

"No," said Jinx.

"You're right. It's too soon—the life hasn't had time to recover its strength."

"I mean no, never," said Jinx. "You're not getting my life back. It was never just lost in the forest; it was mine."

Simon wasn't surprised by this, Jinx could tell, but he acted surprised and looked at Jinx through narrowed eyes. "Lending your life to a wizard is the usual price of apprenticeship. Besides, it's why you're alive right now."

Jinx wasn't going to lose his magic again. If only he'd been able to see the Bonemaster's thoughts, he'd have known the wizard wasn't going to take Elfwyn's sleeping potion and Jinx probably wouldn't have fallen off the cliff.

"I brought your life back, and I'm going to put it back in you someday," said Jinx. "And that's the price of my apprenticeship. And I'll work for you like I always have, clean up and stuff. That's the price. Not my life."

"You make the rules around here, do you?"

"It's my life."

"And what if you end up not being able to do the spell at all? Or what if you run off on me?"

"I won't run off," said Jinx. As for doing the spell—well, yes. Jinx was worried about that. He remembered how nervous Simon had been about doing it on Jinx—there were probably a lot of ways it could go wrong, all of them disastrous. At least Jinx had a lot of power to draw on. He had the Urwald.

He wasn't about to tell Simon that. Because the trees were right—other wizards *would* misuse the Urwald's power, and Simon was "other wizards" with a capital OW.

"You can't stay away long," said Simon. "You have to come back. There's a lot to learn." He thought for a moment. "I suppose I'll have to send you to Samara to study."

Samara—Jinx definitely wanted to go back there. Then a dismal thought struck him. "I promised Sophie I wouldn't."

"Wouldn't what?"

"Go back to Samara."

"Was this a real promise, or was this one of those Sophie promises, where you didn't actually have a choice?" said Simon.

Jinx could see where this was going. "I guess it was that kind, yeah."

"Doesn't count," said Simon.

Jinx felt his mood lighten. He wasn't sure Simon was right. In fact, quite likely Simon was wrong. But he would work it all out with Sophie when he got to Samara.

Jinx was ready to see the world.